Hounding the Pavement

Center Point Large Print

**This Large Print Book carries the
Seal of Approval of N.A.V.H.**

Hounding the Pavement

A DOG WALKER MYSTERY

JUDI McCOY

CENTER POINT PUBLISHING
THORNDIKE, MAINE

This Center Point Large Print edition
is published in the year 2009 by arrangement with
Obsidian, an imprint of New American Library,
a division of Penguin Group (USA) Inc.

The text of this Large Print edition is unabridged.
In other aspects, this book may vary
from the original edition.
Printed in the United States of America.
Set in 16-point Times New Roman type.

ISBN: 978-1-60285-474-1

Library of Congress Cataloging-in-Publication Data

McCoy, Judi.
  Hounding the pavement : a dog walker mystery / Judi McCoy.
     p. cm.
  ISBN 978-1-60285-474-1 (library binding : alk. paper)
  1. Dog walking--Fiction. 2. Large type books. I. Title.

PS3613.C385H68 2009b
813'.6--dc22

2009001195

To Rudy, the best dog in the whole world. We've been together thirteen years, little buddy. If God is willing, we'll be together many more.

To my sister, Nancy, for selecting a title for this first book and hashing over plots for a dozen others.

To Helen Breitwieser, agent extraordinaire. Helen, do you realize we've been together for eleven years? Thank you for accepting a total newbie as a client, and a bigger thank-you for believing in Rudy and Ellie as much as I do.

Acknowledgments

This book is a labor of love, written to support Best Friends Animal Society, the country's largest sanctuary for abused and abandoned animals. To become a member of Best Friends, go to www.bestfriends.org, or write them at 5001 Angel Canyon Road, Kanab, Utah 84741. All donations of twenty-five dollars or more will entitle you to a copy of their monthly magazine, plus bulletins and updates on their latest rescue ventures.

Thank you to Jordan Kaplan, owner of the ultimate dog-walking business in Manhattan: Petaholics, 1375 Broadway, New York, New York 10018 (www.petaholics.com/866-910-5430) for his advice, quips, and fascinating stories about dog lovers and the things they do for their canine pals.

As a writer, I used my imagination for many of the scenarios depicted throughout this story, so please don't blame the two very patient and informative detectives from the Central Park precinct (They said I can't use their names . . . Hmm, I wonder why.) who spent several hours answering my questions and giving me details on how a murder/robbery might be investigated in the Big Apple. Any mistakes on proper police procedure are mine and mine alone, but hey, the book is a great read, so who cares?

Hounding the Pavement

Prologue

"Psst. Down here."

Ellie jumped at the almost childlike voice dancing in her brain. Standing alone in the holding area of her local ASPCA on Manhattan's Upper East Side, where she'd come to celebrate her first day of real freedom in ten years, she gazed at the kennel housing orphaned dogs of all shapes and sizes. Did the elation of signing her divorce papers cause her to hear voices when no one was there?

"You're lookin' in the wrong direction, Ellie. I'm about five feet lower."

She glanced down, but all she saw was an adorable gray-and-white bundle of fur, its head cocked, its big brown eyes staring at her as if she was a king-sized Milk-Bone. Smiling at the pooch, she squatted and read the information card attached to his pen.

Breed: Yorkshire terrier/poodle mix
Age: Approx. one year
Name: Unknown. Found in alley behind building
Temperament: People friendly, intelligent, non-
    aggressive

Standing, she scoured the room, noting the cameras she'd originally thought kept an eye on the dogs. With all the reality shows on the air these days, the possibility that one might be filming here was feasible. They might even be taping scenes for Animal Planet's *Funniest Video* series or some other inane happening, and she'd just become the show's latest star.

"You're still not getting it, Ellie. I'm down here."

She gave the room another careful scan. It had been tough giving up her dog when she'd married her ex-husband ten years ago, but at the time the dickhead had insisted he was allergic and couldn't live with canines, even those that didn't shed. She'd left her pup with her mother and gone on her honeymoon, and Georgette had greeted them on their return holding a sealed wooden box. Rudy had run from her mother's brownstone and into traffic, where he'd been plowed down by a speeding taxi. Ellie hadn't been able to live with another furry friend since.

Until today.

After a third inspection of the room, she again focused on the dog in front of her. She'd never had a psychic experience before, so she had no idea if that was what was happening now, but lots of people conversed with animals, though most didn't expect an answer. Neither did she, not really, but she did want to take a better look at the dog in the pen.

"Are you talking to me?" she asked jokingly.

"Do you see anybody else in this prison?"

With a hand on her heart, she dropped to her knees on the cement floor. Staring at the dog, she shook her head. "This is not possible," she muttered, "unless I'm going crazy."

The terrier mix rose on its hind legs and licked the fingers anchoring her to the cage door. *"If you ask me, you were crazy when you married Larry Lipschitz and left me with your dingbat of a mother."*

He knew about Georgette? "What . . . how?" Could getting a divorce be so liberating that it allowed her to open her inner self to animals? Or was she really losing her mind?

"Come on, Triple E. It's me—Rudy," the pooch continued, his eyes bright and attentive. *"Don't you recognize me?"*

Okay, this was too weird. The dog's muzzle was creased upward in a grin. "Rudy?" She opened and closed her mouth. "But—but you're . . . dead."

"Er . . . not really. I mean, the old body's been gone for a decade now, but somebody must have known it was time for us to get back together and sent me here to wait for you. I have to admit, there were a couple of close calls where I was almost adopted, but a few snarls kept that from happening. I had a feeling you'd be here soon, so I just kept hangin' on."

"And I can hear you . . . understand you? And you can understand me?"

13

"Don't ask me to explain it. Besides, as long as it works, who cares?"

Inhaling a breath, she pressed her forehead to the mesh. "Oh, Lord, this is absurd. I'm talking to my dead dog."

He gave her fingers another sloppy lick. *"So, you gonna bring me home or what?"*

She read the information card again, then rose to her feet. She'd come here to find a companion that would treat her with respect . . . compassion . . . kindness. A friend that would be more trusting and truthful than her ex. The gray-and-white mix was the perfect size and age, and seemed to have the right temperament. Who gave a damn whether he talked to her or not? She was looking for a pal, and this guy was ready, willing, and able to fill the bill.

Ellie checked the room a final time, in case she'd missed the video cameras, tape recorders, and reality-show spies. Or the men in white coats. Positive she was alone with only dogs to witness her folly, she nodded. "I'll be right back."

Chapter 1

She scooped poop for a living.

If Ellie didn't know it to be true, she would never have believed it. A few months ago she'd marched into the ASPCA on Ninety-second Street looking for a pet, and the search had led her to a dream job as a professional dog walker on the

Upper East Side of Manhattan. And not only that. Her *pet* had become somebody she could talk to: a best friend who cared about her as much as she cared about him.

She put her hands on her hips and gazed at the dog nuggets, a by-product of her best friend Vivian McCready's Jack Russell. This was the downside of the job, she thought, picking up the leavings with a sandwich-sized plastic bag. But the profession made perfect sense. She loved dogs. She walked Rudy and Twink several times a day. How difficult could walking a couple more canines be?

She'd already devised a few rules for her business, the most important of which was: dogs of fifteen pounds or less, only. Small pups meant small poops, and if she was going to do this right, small was the key to her success. Of course, Rudy had to approve of the each pooch she agreed to walk, but he liked playmates, which make her work all the easier.

Ellie deposited the bag in a plastic grocery sack and slid the larger receptacle into the side pocket of her coat. "You fellows need to keep your paws crossed that I'll earn enough to pay the mortgage so we can continue this profession," she reminded her companions out loud. "It's an added plus that, according to everyone but my mother, I'm providing an important service—to both man and dog."

*"Hey! Hey! Hey! Stop the chatter. Mr. T is dyin'
down here,"* said the hyperactive Twink.

She grinned at the Jack Russell, now doing a trampoline act at the end of his leash. It had taken a while, but she'd learned to live with the amazing phenomenon. No one, not even Georgette or Vivian, knew it, because she still had a difficult time believing it herself, but she could hold honest-to-God lengthy and somewhat intelligent conversations with dogs.

Not that she was a true-to-life Dr. Dolittle or anything. As far as she knew, her mental gymnastics worked with canines alone, and only those with which she shared an intimate bond. And not all the time, either, except for her own pooch, who was the first she'd actually heard in her head.

She gave a sideways glance at the pedestrians going about their morning routines, and noted that, as usual, no one paid a bit of attention to her banter with Rudy and Twink. This was the Big Apple, after all: a perfectly normal city for a woman to converse with herself, a squirrel, a tree, or a trash basket, even on the corner of Eighty-eighth and Third. Hearing a dog speak in her head and talking to him out loud was downright acceptable compared to some of the things people did in this town.

Gazing at the terrier, she said aloud, "You're watching too much TV Land, so drop the Mr. T jargon. And why aren't you through with business?"

16

Twink lunged on his leash. *"Mr. T's gotta get to that tree over there. It's just beggin' to be sniffed . . . fool."*

"Hey, easy on the insults," Ellie ordered. Just what she needed. A dog who thought he was the canine version of a character from the *A Team.* "What do you say, Rudy? Think Buddy and the others will mind if we're a few minutes late?"

The twelve-pound Yorkiepoo peered at her with a knowing grin. *"Time is relative, a dimension not a reality."*

Before she could respond to his outlandish remark, Twink shot her a snotty look, gave a jerk, and, with Rudy at his side, dragged her across the street like a torn kite on a balmy day.

Ellie led her canine pals to the Davenport, an upscale Fifth Avenue complex housing all her pooches, including Buddy, an adorable Bichon owned by Professor Albright. She'd befriended the professor a few weeks earlier when she and Rudy were sitting on a park bench near Sixty-sixth. Buddy had hit it off with Rudy, and his master, realizing she had a way with dogs, had encouraged her to try dog walking.

So the Bichon had become her second customer after Twink, even though Vivian, her best human friend who lived in Ellie's own building, didn't pay for the walks. Through them and the Davenport's doorman, she'd picked up a few more customers and now looked forward to a bright and rosy future.

"Hey, Randall," she said when the elderly doorman escorted her into the building. She gave a nod to the red carnation in his lapel. "You're looking spiffy this morning. Anything new on the dog walking front?"

"I sang your praises to the new tenant in 3-G. Hazel Blackberg moved in over the weekend with the cutest little fellow. I believe she called it a Maltipoo."

"That's a Maltese/poodle mix, the perfect size for me. Did you know Jessica Simpson has one? It's made the Maltipoo a very popular, and very expensive, designer dog."

"I'm sure Ms. Blackberg had no hardship purchasing the pup, and neither Eugene nor Bibi have gotten to her yet. I told her you'd stop by today, around six. She's usually home by then."

Ellie considered it a good-luck omen that Randall was the doorman here when she and her mother had lived in this very building with her father fifteen years ago. As soon as Randall spotted her coming in to walk the professor's dog, they'd held a reunion of sorts, and he was now one of her allies. It helped that he didn't much care for Eugene and Bibi, the two dog walkers who took care of the rest of the building's clients, either.

"Thanks. You're a peach. Has everyone left for the day?"

"All but the professor," he answered. "Do you want me to keep the boys?"

"Not today. I think it's better if we're together when Sweetie Pie is introduced to Twink, but thanks for the offer." She went to the elevator with her hand in her pocket, on a hunt for her key ring. The keys were her lifeline to success, and she guarded the bits of metal as carefully as she would her wallet. Pinpoint organization, coupled with the keys entrusted to her by her clients, would keep her business ticking like a Swiss watch.

Exiting on the correct floor, she strode down the hall to the apartment of Barbara Jaglinski, CEO of a major advertising firm, and one of Vivian's referrals. Ms. Jaglinski's devotion to her Westie, a snow-white terrier with unbridled energy and a happy disposition, never wavered. She so loved the animal, she paid twenty dollars a walk, the same exorbitant price all New York City dog walkers charged, to see that her pup was taken out twice a day, which made her a potential prized client.

"Sweetie Pie," Ellie called after unlocking the door, "you ready to go?"

Holding the leash in its mouth, her charge trotted to the foyer and waited to be hooked to the lead.

"First day together and I certainly hope you like us more than Bibi," she said, mentioning the dog's last walker. "You've already met Rudy, and this is Twink."

Twink pushed Rudy aside to give the first butt sniff while Sweetie Pie stood submissively.

"Mr. T says she's a little too girlie, but we'll get along. Now let's get moving."

"Hang on and let Rudy say hello."

Rudy did his thing; then he and the Westie touched noses and licked. Ellie said, "So, Sweetie, tell the boys a little about yourself."

The dog held her nose in the air. *"I'm a pure-bred, of course, though I've never been on the pageant circuit. My main job is protecting my owner from unscrupulous men."*

"Keeps you busy, does it?" Ellie asked, grinning. Her favorite time with a new client was the first few days, when the canines were so happy she understood them that they seemed to blab anything and everything about their life and their owners.

"I'll say. Just last night, Babs had a gentleman caller, so I had to sleep in my own bed," Sweetie responded in a sour tone. *"Fortunately, I have an easy way to take care of those uncomfortable situations."*

"I'm almost afraid to ask—what did you do?"

"Left a present in one of his shiny Italian loafers, just like I do to every interloper. I heard them arguing about it before they left for work." The Westie gave a tiny yip. *"He won't last the week."*

"How very . . . um . . . creative of you," Ellie said, not sure she wanted to know that much about

20

Ms. Jaglinski's personal life. "I only hope Rudy wouldn't do that to me."

The new pup did a four-legged shuffle, reminding her of their objective. *"I gotta pee—really bad."*

"Cross your legs," ordered Ellie. "We still have to get the rest of the crew." They rode the elevator down while she pondered the bond she and Rudy had formed. If and when the time came, she sincerely hoped the little guy wouldn't resent a new man in her life, but with no prospects in sight, it didn't pay to worry.

They picked up their other customers, the usually cheerful Stinker, a smallish beagle with a perky gait, and Jett, an adorable Scottie, and waited while the dogs got acquainted with the new lady of the group in their usual sniff-and-growl manner. Then they headed to Professor Albright's to collect his pride and joy, a registered AKC champion and Westminster Best in Show Bichon better know as Buddy.

Now at the professor's apartment, Rudy hung back while the rest of the gang grew strangely silent. *"Uh, Ellie,"* he began, *"something's not right. I don't think we should go inside."*

"We're not going inside, silly. Buddy will be waiting at the door, as usual."

"If you say so . . ."

Because Randall hadn't seen the professor leave, she knocked before using her key.

Receiving no answer, she slid the key in the lock, and the door automatically opened. Worried about the easy access, she called the professor's name. Met with silence, she forged ahead but didn't get the door open more than a couple of inches when something on the other side blocked her way.

Raising a brow in Rudy's direction, she looped the leashes over the knob and used her body weight and a couple of shoulder slams to muscle past whatever was holding the door in place. After squeezing her five-foot-eight-inch frame into the apartment, she stumbled over the object barricading the door.

Glancing down as she righted herself, Ellie let out a shriek. The professor's body, pasty-faced and lifeless, lay at her feet. Steeling herself, she sucked in air and called his name. When he didn't answer or twitch or bat an eyelash, she dropped to her knees and touched his neck to check for a pulse. Then she placed her ear on his chest. With ice-cold skin, no sound of a heartbeat, and no trace of a breath, she knew he was beyond her help.

Standing, she inhaled another gulp of air, collected her wits, and used the intercom to rouse the doorman. "Randall, call nine-one-one. I think Professor Albright is dead."

Ellie stood in the hallway, breathing deeply—in, out, in, out—while she waited for Randall to arrive. She'd peeked inside the apartment and called Buddy's name a half dozen times, waiting for him to show, but that hadn't happened. With Rudy and her charges lying quietly at her feet, she accepted that the worst had happened—the professor was dead. But it was Buddy, Professor Albright's baby, who had her most concerned. She owed it to the professor to do the job he'd hired her for and see to the Bichon's welfare.

The elevator opened and Randall rushed toward her. "I've called the police. Are you sure about the professor? Is he really dead?"

"I'm sure. And I need a favor. I haven't seen Buddy, and I'm worried he's cowering under the bed or something. Can you bring the dogs downstairs and keep them occupied? When I find him, I'll come to the lobby and take the crew for their walk."

"If I must." Randall gathered the leads. "But don't be long. I'm not supposed to leave my post, and if these dogs decide they can't . . . you know . . ."

"Take them outside and let them inspect a tree. I swear I'll clean up after them. Please?"

Tight-lipped, the doorman nodded and headed toward the elevator with the five dogs in tow. When the door closed, Ellie returned to the apartment, tip-toed past the professor, and began her search for the bichon. She checked beneath the bed, inside the closets, under the sofa, even looked in a few of the cupboards, but the dog was nowhere to be found.

Back in the foyer, she gazed at her deceased client, a nice man she'd liked and respected. His facial features, so animated in life, were set in a scowl that made it look as if he'd been in pain. When his wide-open eyes started giving her the creeps, she returned to the hall and rested her bottom against a wall.

What had happened to him? How long had he lain there? Did he have a heart attack? And where was Buddy?

The apartment intercom buzzed, drawing her inside the foyer again. "Ellie, the police and EMTs are on their way and these animals need to go out. You'll have to come down." Randall sounded as if crying would be his next order of business.

The moment she returned to the hall, the elevator slid open. Two uniformed officers and three men in navy jackets and pants hurried toward her, the men in jackets steering a gurney loaded with equipment. She waited while the policemen entered the apartment and, a few seconds later, came out.

Giving her a pointed look, the taller of the two said, "I'm Officer Martin, this is Officer Burroughs. We need your name, address, and identification if you have it on you."

She searched the leather pouch hanging from her shoulder, found the requested item, and passed it to Martin, who handed it to Burroughs. "Was it a heart attack?"

The officer raised a brow. "Won't know until after the circus arrives. In any case, we're not at liberty to say." Officer Martin held up his clipboard and continued his inquiry. "You want to tell us how you found him?"

"I walk his dog every morning, usually after he goes to the university."

"Columbia?"

"Yes. He's a professor of animal behavior, I think. And a very—I mean, he was a very sweet man."

"How did you know he was dead?"

"I wasn't sure at first, so I checked for a pulse, a breath, signs of a heartbeat. When I couldn't find anything positive, I used the intercom to inform Randall."

"Did you know him well?"

"Just to have a few friendly words and walk Buddy."

"Buddy? One of the dogs the doorman's holding downstairs?"

"No. Buddy is the professor's dog. Randall came up and took the others so I could search the apartment, but there was no sign of him."

"You inspected the scene?" the officer asked, his voice almost a snarl.

"Walking Buddy is my job, and he's used to going out every morning at this time. When I realized I couldn't help the professor, what else was I supposed to do?"

"Haven't you ever watched a cop show on television?"

"No, and I don't intend to start," she shot back. She wasn't into murder, mayhem, or anything that might make her head hurt. She'd had enough unhappiness of her own over the past ten years, and didn't want to witness anyone else's.

"If you had, you'd know you never contaminate a crime scene by tromping through the premises. Tampering with evidence is a serious offense."

"But you just said you weren't sure a crime had been committed. How was I supposed to know, if you don't?"

"Look, Ms.—"

"Engleman. Ellen Elizabeth, but I go by Ellie. And for the record, I didn't touch anything. I just looked for Buddy."

"Uh-huh." Martin continued to frown. "How, exactly, did you enter the premises?"

"With my key, of course, like I do every morning."

"You have a key to his apartment?"

She fished the color-coded ring from her bag. "I have a key to each of my clients' homes. All dog walkers do. It's the only way they can get the job done."

"I see," he answered blandly, but the words reeked of suspicion. "How long have you been walking dogs?"

"A little over three weeks."

He raised a brow. "I assume you're bonded and insured?"

Oh, Lord. Getting the proper paperwork was on her to-do list, not the one she should have completed before she began accepting clients. And she'd be darned if she'd waste a thousand dollars on the proper licensing fees on the off chance the job wouldn't work out.

"Um . . . everything is in the pipeline. I'm waiting to get my paperwork," she said, crossing mental fingers.

"Stand over there." Martin pointed to the wall across the hall. "And don't move."

"Is someone going to hunt for Buddy? Give the apartment a more thorough search?"

"We have a dead body on our hands, Ms. Engleman. We don't have time to look for some mutt—"

"Buddy is not a mutt," she interrupted, taking the insult personally. "He won at Madison Square Garden, so he's a champion, and he's sweet and adorable and—it was an accident, right? I mean, the professor did die of natural causes?"

"The ME will make that decision. Until then, we treat all deaths of this type as suspicious."

"Then you'll search for Buddy?"

"Detective Ryder will decide."

"Who's Ryder?"

"He's the lead on this one, along with his partner Fugazzo. We do the preliminary, and they'll assume command when they arrive on-scene. You'll have to talk to them."

The intercom sounded and the officer answered.

"Ms. Engleman needs to get down here right away. There's a crowd gathering outside and these dogs—" Crazed yapping echoed in the background. "Tell her they have to go out."

"Hang on a second." Officer Martin glanced at Ellie. "You aren't supposed to leave the scene."

The canine racket grew louder.

"Ellie, I need you," Randall shouted over the din.

"Please? The doorman knows me personally. You can even keep my ID until I return," she pleaded. "I'll be back in thirty minutes, honest."

"Sorry, but—"

"Surely I can go on one trip while you're doing . . . whatever it is you do? I have to finish, or there'll be a mess downstairs."

Martin gazed at Burroughs, who shrugged. "I don't know—"

"I'll be back as soon as I can. I give you my word."

Sighing, the officer said, "All right, but make it quick. Ryder doesn't like to be kept waiting."

Chapter 2

Ellie scurried to the elevator and rode down to the main level, where a small crowd had formed. Rushing past the doorman and another cop, she grabbed the leashes and raced to the sidewalk before anyone could ask questions.

She imagined Randall and the officer would have their hands full in a few minutes. Sometimes, being invisible was a good thing. People who performed daily service jobs, like window washers, bicycle messengers, trash collectors, and dog walkers, were often overlooked by the self-absorbed residents of Manhattan's Upper East Side. Though she'd only been at her job a short while, she realized this *non*existence made it easy to overhear conversations or slip into and out of places that might be off-limits to the rest of society.

Crossing Fifth Avenue, heading toward Central Park, she spotted an ice-cream vendor hawking the ideal antidote to her rising stress level. After paying for the dark chocolate confection, usually the best pick-me-up of her day, she unwrapped it and moaned when the cold creamy filling and thick, rich coating melted in her mouth.

Thanks to the difficult time her overbearing ex had given her when they'd split, her single-digit dress size was a thing of the past. Also gone were her strenuous morning workouts at the health club, ditto her lunchtime salads and grilled chicken dinners. Once she'd hit a plateau of sorts, she'd sold her most extravagant clothes, donated the rest to a women's shelter, and spent the last of her savings on a new wardrobe, sans panty hose, tight skirts, and heels. These days, she ate real-people food and exercised by climbing stairs and walking her charges—a much more interesting and fulfilling way to stay fit.

While the dogs groused, sniffed, and took care of business, she scarfed down the ice cream and swiped a hand over her mouth. Then she removed a couple of plastic bags from her pocket, collected the droppings, and deposited the bags in the nearest trash bin. It was time to return to the Davenport.

"Come on, fellas. Let's go."

"Hey, what's the big idea . . . fool?"

"But I'm not through."

"This is a rip-off!"

The impatient voices, surprisingly human in her mind, made her smile. Canines had opinions, just as their caretakers did. Rudy was sensitive to her every thought, much as Sweetie Pie was to Barbara Jaglinski's. Unfortunately, the new man in the CEO's life would probably screw up their relationship by refusing to accept the Westie. Rudy was her best friend; she couldn't imagine anyone taking his place, even Mr. Perfect, the man she'd conjured over the past year.

Mr. Perfect stood right at six feet, with wavy blond hair, a square jaw, wide shoulders, and eyes that saw straight into her soul. He enjoyed chick flicks, walking in the rain, breakfast in bed, and Chinese takeout. He didn't chew with his mouth open, leave the seat up on the toilet, or belch and pass gas in front of her, at least not on purpose. And he was a considerate yet commanding lover who always made sure she had an orgasm before he crossed the finish line.

Most important, he liked dogs, which made him so far removed from her semibald, potbellied ex that the two men couldn't even share the same planet. And probably didn't, because Ellie doubted she'd find Mr. Perfect anywhere on Earth.

She'd take a dog over a man any day. Dogs let you know exactly what they wanted in a relationship, and it wasn't much. Regular food, an occasional tummy rub, a few treats and playtime, and they loved you for life.

Embarrassed by such personal thoughts in the midst of a crisis, she rounded the herd toward home. She had to think of Professor Albright and poor Buddy. Where the heck was he?

"Mr. T's gotta have one more leg lift or he's gonna burst."

"Sorry, but no." She tugged on the leashes. "Let's go."

"What's the hurry?"

31

*"Can't you figure it out? Buddy's missin',
sucka,"* Twink informed the pack before Ellie
could respond.

The statement caused a near riot. Interspersed
between frantic barks and worried yips came
questions, too many for Ellie to answer as she
walked down the block. And while she did, her
mind continued to assess what had happened. The
idea that someone might actually harm a man as
nice as Professor Albright seemed bizarre. She
hadn't known him well, but he lived alone, he
acted pleasant enough, and he was a dog lover.
Though not ancient, he was in his sixties, so a
heart attack was the most logical reason for his
death. But if that were the case, why did the police
need to conduct an investigation?

Nearing the Davenport, she slowed, and her
charges began to circle, wrapping themselves
around her calves and ankles until she arrived in
front of the building in a tangle of yapping dogs,
intertwined leashes, and frustration.

Sam Ryder's day had started out like a brick on
the head and skidded downhill from there. First,
his younger sister, a psychology major at NYU
and a self-proclaimed expert on the world in gen-
eral, had called at just past six a.m. After
reminding him that tomorrow night was his
standing date to have dinner at their mother's, she
threw in a comment about how he'd missed the

family gathering the last three weeks in a row and hung up before he could tell her he'd been too busy to eat a regular meal for at least a month.

He figured their mother's girdle was too tight, and she'd nagged Sherry into conveying her displeasure. Which meant he'd have a hell of a lot of explaining to do if—and it was a very big if—he made it to dinner.

After that, he'd indulged in his usual morning workout and pulled a muscle, creating an ache in his shoulder that definitely didn't sit well. He'd eaten a quick breakfast with the hope of taking a hot shower to ease the shoulder and, thanks to the lousy plumbing in his apartment, had about frozen his gonads off in the ice-cold spray.

On his way out the door, he'd taken his second phone call of the day, a possible homicide on the Upper East Side, and then, as an additional insult, he'd stepped in a pile of dog shit as he walked from his building to his car.

"People have no respect for the law," he grumbled, as he climbed into his beat-up Chevy. With Fugazzo out on family leave, it was going to be a long couple of months.

After fighting crosstown traffic, he turned onto Fifth and spotted his destination, noting the flashing lights of patrol cars and an ambulance, as well as the crowd assembled in front of the building. Though it was early in the season for the ghouls to be out full force, spring had arrived just last week, which always seemed to lure the weirdos from their lairs.

Parking behind the patrol car, he set his dome light on the sedan roof, dodged the mound of dirty slush melting in the gutter, and strode to the main entrance, prepared to push his way through the throng. At the complex door, he collided with a dog walker. Bent at the waist, the person was attempting to wrestle a gaggle of noisy mutts into the building.

"Hey, that's enough. Quiet now."

Considering the walker was dressed in army fatigues, the distinctly feminine voice surprised him. Too bad he didn't have time to take a step back and get a better view.

"Oh, jeez, excuse us," the woman muttered when she danced backward and bumped into him.

Not thrilled about the distraction, he leaned down, grabbed her wrist, and pulled the knot from her fingers. "Here, let me." He guided the unruly ankle biters around her legs until they were free and returned the leads. Expecting gratitude, he instead found himself staring into twin pools of icy blue.

"Thanks, but I could have handled it."

"Sure you could," he answered, his tone sarcastic. He gazed at her flushed face and bit his lip to keep from laughing. He'd never met a woman who used dog crap for skin cream before. "And while you're *handling* it, you might want to—uh—"

"Want to what?" she bit out.

He nodded toward her left cheek. "Take a gander in the mirror."

Color heightened her already-pink complexion, and she smacked her smudged face with her free hand. Grinning, he strode into the lobby.

Riding skyward, Ellie checked herself in the mirrored wall on the back of the elevator. Just like the guy she'd met downstairs had indicated, a dark smear marred her left cheek. She pulled a tissue from her bag, spit on it, rubbed, and brought the tissue to her nose.

Chocolate?

She inhaled again. It was chocolate, all right. She must have enjoyed that Dove bar a lot more than she realized, and if she saw that guy again, she would tell him so. He had some nerve, automatically assuming her foundation of choice was puppy poop just because she was in to dogs.

She delivered her charges to their homes; then she, Rudy, and Twink beat feet to Buddy's floor, positive that, by now, someone had found him. Until they located one of Professor Albright's relatives, she intended to bring the little guy home and give him a place to hang his leash, so to speak. The city pound would house the champion over her dead body.

When she arrived, a half dozen people crowded the hallway in front of the professor's apartment, some knocking on doors, some talking into cell phones. Prepared to apologize for being late, she zeroed in on Officer Martin. She had zilch to add to what she'd already explained. If Buddy was still missing, she planned to search for him outside on the off chance he'd somehow gotten out of the apartment or evaded the boys in blue and found his way to the street.

"Sorry I took so long," she said, approaching the officer. "I decided to bring the dogs home so I could talk to that detective without interruption. Is he here yet?"

"He's here," said a surly voice from behind the partially open door.

Officer Martin shrugged and returned her ID. "I'll leave the two of you alone. And don't say I didn't warn you."

The door swung inward, revealing a tan trench coat covering a broad chest and a set of line-backer-sized shoulders. Raising her head, her gaze met that of the man she'd tangled with in the entryway: Mr. Dog Doo.

"It's about time—" he began. Arching dark brows, he stared at her face. "Nice to see you were able to clean up before you showed. Smart move, Ms."—he consulted his notebook—"Engleman."

"You," Ellie huffed, trying to ignore his coffee-colored eyes, rumpled blond curls, and amazingly square jaw. Had he appeared this . . . this impressive downstairs? Probably, but she'd been too flustered to notice.

He held out a case with his ID and shield, then flipped it closed before she read a word. "Detective Sam Ryder, NYPD. Tell me how you found the body."

Determined not to drool, she stepped to the side and peered into the foyer, where three or four more people were huddled. "Lying right there, like it is now."

"Officer Martin said you had a key?"

"I have a key to all my clients' homes, as do most dog walkers."

"And how many clients might that be?"

"Right now, five. I've just started my business."

"I take it you're bonded, with the usual licenses required to run a dog-walking service?" His smug smile made the question sound as if she were guilty of a crime. Which she very well might be, if she didn't get her tail in gear and apply for the necessary documents.

"I'm . . . um . . . in the process," she lied. "I'll be legal as soon as the paperwork is finished."

"Do your clients know you tromp through their homes if the dog isn't immediately there waiting for you?"

Leaning against the doorjamb, she took note of his imposing height and vowed not to sigh *or* drool. "As a professional, I hardly ever go farther than the foyer. My charges learn to expect me at a certain time, and they're usually standing at the ready when I arrive."

"But not today."

"No. Randall told me he hadn't seen Professor Albright leave the building, so I knocked. When he didn't answer, I used my key, but the door was already unlocked. It took a couple of good shoves before I could get it open enough to—" Realizing she'd just confessed to assaulting a dead body forced her to fumble. "I . . . um . . . I didn't know it was him, of course."

"And that was the first time you saw Albright today?"

"First time all week, really. He usually leaves for school before I get here." She ran trembling fingers through her hair. "He was a nice man. It was a shock to find him like that."

"I imagine so. Anyone else lurking in the hall, maybe waiting for the elevator or collecting their newspaper?"

"Didn't Officer Martin already give you this information?"

"He did, but I want to hear it from your perspective, if you don't mind." He glanced at the floor, where Twink and Rudy watched with interest. "I take it neither of those dogs belongs to the professor?"

"Not too bright, is he, Triple E?"

She cast Rudy a glare of disapproval. "The Yorkiepoo is mine. The Jack Russell belongs to a friend."

Ryder's full lips twitched. "Yorkie what?"

Her temper simmered, causing heat to rise to her cheeks. Great. Leave it to him to find a way to slide dog poop into the conversation. "Rudy is a Yorkshire terrier–poodle mix," she said, proud to have circumvented the distasteful word. "Twink is a Jack Russell. Buddy is a bichon frise and an AKC champion."

"You're sure the dog wasn't here when you found the body?"

"No, and I thought it was odd. I called the doorman and asked him to phone nine-one-one. Then I waited until Randall came up. He took my charges downstairs so I could inspect the apartment. If Buddy were here, he would have told—" *Oops.* "He would have showed himself. When he didn't, I spoke to the officers."

"Martin and Burroughs?"

"Right. Then Randall called to tell me the dogs were restless. If I didn't get downstairs to do my job there'd be—" She glanced at Rudy and Twink. "A.C.C.I.D.E.N.T.S."

"Accidents?"

"*Shh.* And yes."

A corner of his mouth lifted, and she huffed out a breath. "It was nice of Officer Martin to let me go."

"Hey, Martin," he shouted down the hall.

The patrolman raised his head from his paperwork and trudged over. "Yes, sir?"

"Take these two dogs to the lobby and ask the doorman to hold them for Ms. Engleman."

"Hey," Ellie said, inching forward.

Ryder speared her with a brown-eyed glare. "You've probably done a job on the crime scene. And I have more questions." Taking the leashes from her hand, he passed them to Martin, who quickly disappeared with Rudy and Twink in tow.

"Detective?" someone said from the other side of the door. "Take a look at this."

Unable to watch the officer striding away with her pals and pay attention to Ryder at the same time, she followed the detective into the crowded foyer.

"Any idea what did the damage?" Ryder asked, studying the back of the apartment door.

A thin balding man wearing latex gloves used tweezers to pluck a chunk of wood from around the knob, then dropped the bits into a plastic bag and sealed it. "Nope, but I'm fairly certain it's fresh. We'll know more after the lab runs a scan. And there's something else." He moved to the body, squatted, and held up the professor's left hand. "Look at his fingers."

She couldn't get down on their level without being obvious, so it was difficult to see. From this distance, the professor's fingertips appeared red, almost as if they'd been burned.

"The marks are fresh," Ryder observed. "How do you suppose they got there?"

"I'd say that's another question for the ME."

Both men stood. "She should be here any minute, by the way."

At that moment, a woman in her midfifties with neatly tied gray hair and wise blue eyes stepped through the door.

"Dr. Bridges," said the detective. " 'Bout time you showed."

"A girl needs her beauty sleep," the ME answered, her face a blank. She glanced around the hall. "Did Fugazzo's wife have the baby?"

"Last night," Ryder answered.

Nodding, she stared at the professor. "This our guy?"

"That's him. We need to get a handle on what we're dealing with." Raising an arm, he pinned Ellie to the foyer wall, gave her a look of warning, and took a step toward the body.

The doctor spoke quietly to the EMTs, then squatted and spread open the professor's shirt. Ryder dropped beside her, and she shook her head.

"What?" he asked.

Ellie strained to hear her response.

"Best guess, that's an incision for heart surgery, maybe a pacemaker."

"And that means . . . ?"

"Can't say until I open him up." She checked the reddened fingertips. "Any idea where this came from?"

"Not sure, but it might be connected to the charred area around the doorknob."

"Care to show me?"

She and the detective stood, and Ryder let her inspect the area in question. "Hmm. Okay. For now, let's call the death suspicious," Bridges said. "Have your crew handle it like a homicide in case it's for real."

"Fuck."

Ellie bristled at the unpleasant word, though everyone else seemed to take it in stride.

"You ready to let us have him?" asked one of the techs.

The ME nodded. "I'll meet you over there."

"Send me the report ASAP," Ryder said as she walked into the outer hallway. Turning, he shuffled to Ellie's side and rested a shoulder against the wall to face her. "Did the professor ever mention a heart condition?"

"Not to me."

"Did you smell anything unusual when you checked his pulse? Like burned flesh or maybe wood smoke?"

"Nope. Then again, it wasn't something I'd think to notice. By the way, that stuff on my face before—"

"Yes," he said, a distinct smirk on his lips.

"It was chocolate."

The smirk morphed into a grin. "If you say so."

"Yes, I say so, and never mind. Who's going to search for Buddy? I'm really worried about him."

They lifted the professor, and Ryder held out his

arm to keep her in place. "We have a body, Ms. Engleman. That's our only priority."

"Are you telling me no one is going to hunt for Buddy?"

He heaved a sigh. "I'll see what I can do."

"You'll order a patrolman to start a search?"

The detective met her glare. "Maybe after we're through at the station. If I have time, I'll see if somebody in stolen property can take a look."

Stolen property? "You think someone took Buddy?"

"At this point, I don't think anything. I'll know more after I get the ME's report and the evidence is processed."

"Would it be against the rules if I ran my own search?"

"Knock yourself out," he countered. "But you'll have to call me immediately if you locate the dog, and you can't start until I'm through with you."

"Through with me?"

"I have to give a few orders. Then you'll be joining me at the Nineteenth."

"But . . . but I can't. What will I do with the boys?"

"The dogs?" He ran a hand over his jaw. "Burroughs!"

The patrolman arrived so quickly Ellie figured he'd been outside waiting for the summons.

"Yes, sir?"

"Take Ms. Engleman and her dogs home. Then

escort her to the precinct. Put her in a room and show her some of the NYPD's finest hospitality."

Burroughs grabbed her elbow, but Ellie stood her ground. "Hey, can he do that?" she asked the officer.

"He can do anything he wants."

Before she knew it, she, Rudy, and Twink were in a squad car riding home.

Chapter 3

Ellie swiped at her still-smudged fingertips. She couldn't decide what was worse: standing in the hallway of the Davenport while a forensics expert rolled a lint brush over her entire body or having her prints on record with the NYPD. Though Ryder had assured her the defuzzing was for her benefit—to help them rule her out as a suspect—she doubted the explanation. Especially since he'd acted as if she was guilty from the moment she walked into the professor's apartment.

She leaned back in the molded plastic chair and glanced at her watch, then shifted her gaze across the drab, functional gray table. "Are we finished? Because I have to leave."

"Got a hot date?" Ryder asked, his handsome face set in stony disapproval.

The comment was his most recent in a string of personal questions with which he'd hounded her since he'd begun the interrogation. During that time, he'd made it clear she was his most *suspect* suspect, even though she'd done her best to profess her innocence.

"I have an appointment, and as of about thirty seconds ago, it's doubtful I'll make it on time."

"An appointment with who?"

Seething inside, she shrugged as if the query meant nothing. "A potential client."

"Someone in the Davenport?"

"Yes," she responded, trying to hold to the single syllable answers she had learned kept her out of trouble.

"On the same floor as the professor?"

"No."

He raised a brow and she sighed. "Several flights down. Why?"

"I'm the one who needs to know, Ms. Engleman."

Another glance at her watch told her she had to wrap this up, whether or not the disagreeable man approved. "I've given a sensible answer to every question you've asked. By now, you must realize I had nothing to do with the professor's death."

"I don't realize anything. All I know is, I have a dead body on my hands and you had motive and opportunity. The situation speaks for itself."

The comment niggled at her brain. She hadn't spoken to her lawyer, Fred Hutchins, since her divorce was final, but she was fairly certain he didn't practice criminal law. Until Ryder's last comment, she was certain she'd be let go. Now she wasn't so sure. "Motive? What kind of motive?"

"A dog you claim is valuable is missing."

"And you think I killed the professor and stole it?" The man was a cretin. "Does the city know what kind of idiot they pay to investigate their murders?"

"We have yet to determine if the death was a homicide, Ms. Engleman, unless you know something I don't," he stated, rolling past her insult.

Ellie shifted in the chair, her lips matching his frown. "You can't be serious."

"I'm good at my job, Ms. Engleman. Have no fear of that. And right now, you're the only one who had the opportunity to do the deed."

She scooted her seat back and stood. "In that case, I want to call my lawyer." She'd phone Stanley, the retired judge her mother was dating, and ask him to recommend someone. "But if I'm not being charged, let me go."

He muttered something unintelligible under his breath, then said, "There's no need to lawyer up. You're free—for now. But don't leave town. I'll be in touch."

"I'm going to search for Buddy, you know, with or without your permission."

"I'd expect nothing less," he answered in a dead-pan tone.

"Can I keep him if I find him?"

"That could be a problem. He's Albright's property—"

"But the professor won't care."

"That's true, but one of his relatives might." He flipped a page in his notebook and scribbled a line. "Just let me know if you remember something—or your story changes."

"I have no reason to change one word of my story, and you know how to reach me."

He pulled her card from his shirt pocket and eyed her printed information. "'Paws In Motion,'" he read aloud. "'Dog walking for small breeds only.'" Tucking it back in his shirt, he said, "You got something against normal-sized canines?"

"I've already told you, I'm a fan of all breeds, but I can walk more of the tiny ones at a time, plus small dogs make small messes, an advantage in my business."

Detective Ryder narrowed his eyes, stood, and ambled to her side of the room, where he propped a hip on the table. "I see."

"Is that it?" she asked, ready to bolt. The detention room suddenly felt downright claustrophobic, as if the hunky pain in the butt was sucking up all the air for himself.

"Unless Albright's death is natural, you'll hear from me in a day or so. Remember, I expect you to call if you think of anything that might help the investigation."

"And if I find Buddy?"

He studied the ceiling, then focused on her face. "Let me know if you locate the mutt."

Annoyed that he still insisted on calling the bichon a crude name, she squared her shoulders. "As I've already explained, Buddy is not a mutt. He's a champion. And I've been thinking"— *unlike you,* she almost added—"have you ever considered that finding him might lead you to the killer . . . if there is one?"

She regretted the words the moment they left her mouth, because it gave credence to his idea that she knew more than she'd admitted to. "I've already given you permission to search my condo, though common sense would tell you I didn't have time to murder the professor, hide Buddy, and come back to the building, where I then pretended to find the body."

"People have accomplices."

Ellie's lips thinned. Not only did Ryder have a low opinion of canines, he had a low opinion of her, which meant he wasn't worth a second more of her worry. Contrary to his Mr. Perfect looks, the guy was a jerk, and she'd interacted with enough of them to last a lifetime.

"Can I go now?" she asked in a forced tone.

He folded his arms and nodded.

Instead of shaking his hand or spewing insincere words of farewell, she raised her nose and strode out the door with all the chutzpah she could muster.

On the street, she headed for the corner. Since the precinct was a long way from the Davenport, she'd have to run at lightening speed or catch a cab, a near impossibility at this hour. Not only was she exhausted—she hadn't eaten a thing since that chocolate ice-cream bar and a tuna sandwich on cracker-dry whole wheat that the detective had tossed her way around two.

After ten minutes of frantic waving, she spotted a free taxi. Racing toward it, she reached the door at the same moment a blue-haired grandmotherly type elbowed past pedestrians and arrived at her side. When the woman grabbed the cab door, Ellie arm wrestled her to a standstill, slid into the back-seat, and shouted, "Sorry. It's an emergency," as she slammed the door.

The furious granny whacked her umbrella on the taxi trunk, and the driver steered into traffic, asking, "Where to?" without a backward glance.

Ellie gave him the Davenport address and leaned back. With only twenty minutes left to cover the blocks between here and her destination, there was a good possibility she'd be late. And if she was late, Eugene or Bibi might get to Hazel Blackberg before she did and secure a client she had a right to, which would give her two main competitors a reason to do the happy dance for scamming her out of a client.

The taxi pulled in front of the complex at six-o-five. Ellie tossed the fare into the front seat, raced to the sidewalk, and frowned when the evening doorman, a glowering giant named Kronkovitz, welcomed her into the building.

"Hey, Kronk," she called, hoping to pass without a hassle.

Kronk stepped in front of her, blocking her way. "*El-ee*. I hear we have great tragedy this morning," he said in heavily accented English. "Professor Albright, a very nice man, is no longer with us."

"Sad but true," she agreed, trying to edge around him. "Did Randall tell you to watch for his dog?"

"I look, but see nothing," he confessed. "You *theenk* there is *ree-ward* for person who finds *lee-til* white dog?"

She imagined the giant's salivary glands working exactly like Rudy's did when he smelled a burger sizzling on the grill. "I don't know for certain, but probably. It depends on the professor's relatives."

"You can *feex*, no? Tell them I am hero when I rescue *lee-til* pup."

She'd heard that the Russian mafia had infiltrated the doorman's union but, until now, hadn't taken the rumor seriously. Kronk's greedy leer was an eye opener.

"Provided it happens, yes. I'm hoping that tonight, after things quiet down, Buddy will come out from wherever he's been hiding and find his way here." She spotted a man and two women entering the building and followed them to the elevator with Kronk on her heels. "Most of the tenants get home about now. Can you ask them to be on the lookout for him?" It was possible someone had seen something this morning, and the police had yet to reach them.

"I ask," said the doorman. Throwing out his barrel chest, he raised a bushy gray eyebrow. "But I collect *ree-ward*, no matter what. Yes?"

"Um, sure, *if* you find him, and *if* they offer one," she said, waiting for another man to enter the car. "I'll do my best to see you get what you deserve." Which amounted to a kick in the head, if she had anything to say about it. "Of course, it'll be up to whoever inherits Buddy to hand over the cash."

With his mud brown eyes narrowed to slits, Kronk folded his arms. "Is good."

Standing in front of 3-G, Ellie inhaled a calming breath, plastered a smile on her face, and pressed the buzzer. Her day wasn't over yet. She still had to charm her way into Ms. Blackberg's heart and sign her on as a customer; then she owed Sweetie Pie her second walk of the day. Only afterward could she head home to Rudy and a decent dinner.

The door opened almost immediately, and a short, rotund woman dressed in a full-length, boldly patterned gown that could have doubled as wallpaper stood before her.

"Hazel Blackberg?"

"That's me," said the portly prospective client.

It was then Ellie noticed the small black dog tucked against the woman's massive bosom. "Randall said you might be interested in my services—for your dog."

The woman took a drag on the cigarette in her other hand. "You're late."

"I know, and I'm sorry. It won't happen again."

Like a scientist examining culture in a Petri dish, Ms. Blackberg's eyes roamed over Ellie. "Come on in," she said, taking a step back.

Ellie walked into a foyer much like the professor's, cluttered floor to ceiling with furniture, boxes, and towers of books. The woman waved her down the hall. "Excuse the mess. We'll be right with you."

Dodging the collection of cartons and mismatched tables, Ellie entered the living room and admired the view from the sliding plate-glass door that led to a narrow terrace.

"I take it you're bonded and insured?" Ms. Blackberg asked when she toddled in from the kitchen at the opposite end of the sitting area.

Well, crap. "Of course." She pulled a business card from her bag and passed it over. "Here's my information."

Ms. Blackberg gave the card a mad-scientist

inspection. "There aren't any license numbers on here."

"What? No." Ellie brought out another card and stared with wide-eyed innocence. "Oh, gee. I guess I have to go to the printer and complain, then demand a new batch for free." Demanding anything in this city always seemed to garner respect for the *demandee*.

"I'd ask for a double order." Her potential client stuffed the card in her pocket. "It's Hazel, by the way."

"I assume that's Buckley?"

"My baby," Hazel replied. Her stern gaze softening, she nuzzled the pup with her chin. "Does Buckley-wuckly want to meet the nice way-dee?"

Ellie bit the inside of her cheek to keep from laughing. "I talk to my dog, too," she confessed.

"How could I not? Look at that little face."

Nearing the dog, Ellie held out her hand and let Buckley sniff her fingers, then moved to gather him in her arms. When the pooch growled, she backed away in surprise.

"Oh, hush," Hazel ordered the pup. After taking another drag on her cigarette, she blew the smoke cloud toward the ceiling. "He does that all the time. Madam Orzo says it's a self-defense mechanism. He's small, and the growl is all he has for protection."

"Madam Orzo?"

"Jeanette is a wonderful woman. Her specialty

is communing with our four-legged loved ones, no matter if they're alive or have passed to that big doggie park in the sky."

A pet psychic? Thinking it might be a good career move if this profession failed, Ellie raised a brow. "Does Buckley bite?"

"Goodness no, but he is a bit of a grump. Here." She thrust the Maltipoo at Ellie, and the dog settled comfortably in the crook of her arm. "See what I mean? He likes you."

"Uh-huh," she answered, a tad unsure of the petite canine. "When did you visit a psychic?"

"We go every month, just to stay connected. Take him on the terrace if you like, and see if you get along."

Ellie walked onto the terrace and sat in one of the two wicker chairs arranged around a matching table. When the dog gazed up at her as if she were a Godzilla-sized flea, she said, "So, Buckley, hello. I'm Ellie, and I want to be your new caregiver, if you'll let me."

The dog opened his tiny mouth and yawned, showing a pink tongue and a row of small but sharp teeth. She set him on the table, where he continued to eye her with suspicion.

"What do you think?"

"I think," the words echoed clearly in her brain, *"you're a whole lot better at communicating than that nosy psychic who has no idea what's on my mind."*

She grinned at his enthusiasm. "Then you can hear me?"

"Of course."

"And it doesn't frighten you?"

"There's not a human born who scares me. But I'll tell you what does crank my chain," he responded, his voice sounding very much like a grousing Pee Wee Herman.

"What?"

"The fact that I'm gettin' freakin' lung cancer from the secondhand smoke I suck down shacking up with Hazel. It really frosts my buns."

"And that's why you growl?"

"Yep. Convince her to stop, and I'll be your pal for life."

"I'm not promising anything, but—"

The sliding door opened, and Hazel stuck out her head. "You're talking to him." She smiled. "That is so wonderful."

"I speak to all my charges. You never can tell what they do and don't understand." She carried Buckley inside and passed him over. "Ms. Blackberg—"

"Hazel, please," the woman cooed. "When can you start walking my baby?"

"Tomorrow morning? I usually get here around nine."

"Perfect. Randall said you charge twenty dollars for a half hour walk, and I want my darling to have two a day."

After working out the details, including a price break for the second walk, Ellie accepted a check for the balance of the month. At the door, she turned and shook her new client's bejeweled hand. "There's just one more thing."

"Oh, and what might that be?"

"Do you realize that cigarette smoke is as bad for dogs as it is for humans? It might be causing Buckley harm."

Tears filled Hazel's eyes as her hand fluttered to her bosom. "I've tried to quit so many times but . . . you're sure dogs react identically to smoke?"

"I've read articles and done a bit of research, and trust me, it's a fact."

"I had no idea," the woman said with a moan.

"Think about it. And don't worry. I'll take good care of Buckley when he's in my charge."

She raced to Sweetie Pie's apartment, hooked her to the lead, and headed downstairs, where she dodged a group of people surrounding Kronk, and headed for the park. After the Westie did her business and she and the dog exchanged a few words, Ellie escorted her home and stopped in the lobby, where she hoped to question Kronk further. But the doorman was occupied with apartment dwellers, so she took off for her brownstone.

Earlier, Officer Burroughs had allowed her to take Twink to his apartment before she'd dropped Rudy at home, and Vivian had more than likely already given the Jack Russell a walk. But her best friend knew nothing of her dilemma, so Viv wouldn't have thought to take Rudy out with Twink.

Arriving at her building, she collected her mail, ran the two flights to her apartment, and opened the door. Before she hung her coat, Rudy was dancing around her feet.

"Outside, outside, outside," he commanded. *"Then it's dinnertime."*

"Okay, let's go," she agreed as she snapped his leash to his leather collar. They skipped down the steps and onto the street, where Rudy watered the side of the building, a sure sign he'd been in need of relief.

After two more leg lifts, he dragged her to the complex's front door, his chant of *Dinner, dinner, dinner* ringing in her brain. "You sound like a food-aholic. Don't you ever think of anything else?" she teased, stooping to give him a pat.

"You mean there's more to life than a decent dinner?"

"You know there is," she told him as they took the staircase up to their floor. When they arrived in the kitchen, she filled his bowl and added a few extra kibble. "Sorry I had to leave you today, but we'll go for a nice long walk before bed, okay? We have to search for Buddy."

Rudy buried his nose in his dish, and she hoped he'd talk to her about the missing bichon after he ate. He was as spoiled as all the dogs she walked, most of which ate gourmet meals, got regular exercise, and spent time in a variety of shops in business to pamper pets. There were at least six on this side of town including Canine Styles Uptown on Lexington, Finishing Touches on Seventy-fourth, and Dogs, Cats & Company on Eighty-second. Well-to-do owners cared for their four-legged pals like children, and made sure they had every advantage. And since her surprise mental connection, she realized that once they had experienced it, most dogs looked forward to the special treatment.

She threw a Lean Cuisine in the microwave, walked to her bedroom, and changed into a more comfortable oversized T-shirt and leggings. As she glanced around the recently redecorated room, a wave of contentment filled her. She'd hand-painted a border of pink flowers over the serene green walls, and added several photos of herself and her father, plus one of her with Georgette and a few paintings she'd kept after she'd sold the pieces the D hadn't wanted. With the simple yet elegant furniture, the room was completely devoid of her ex's ratty presence. With her business off to a good start, she'd repay her mother for the new furniture and borrowed mortgage payments well within their agreed-upon time frame.

Back in the kitchen, she removed the heated dinner from the nuker and wolfed it down, then took a pint of Häagen-Dazs from the freezer. Still thinking about the professor, she dug out a spoonful and let the creamy blend of caramel, chocolate, and vanilla slide down her throat.

Finished with his own dinner, Rudy gazed at her from his empty dish. *"Caramel Cone, my favorite,"* he said with longing.

"Please don't let's have this conversation again. You know chocolate isn't good for dogs."

"A little of the caramel wouldn't hurt."

Careful to avoid the chocolate swirls, she scraped up a bit of the ice cream, squatted, and gave him a taste.

"That's my girl," Rudy said after licking the spoon clean. *"Now what was that you mentioned earlier? Something about a long walk?"*

"I think we should go back to the Davenport. It wouldn't hurt to check the alley and a few of the side streets or, much as I don't want to, speak to Kronk again. He might have learned something from a resident or found Buddy in the building."

"How about we stop at Bread and Bones on the way?"

The gourmet bakery was one of Rudy's favorites, especially since they made a batch of tasty dog treats every day. "If they're open, sure. I'll even buy an extra biscuit as a lure. Maybe Buddy will come out if he smells it."

The Yorkiepoo's ears twitched, and he headed for the door. *"So what are you waiting for? Let's go."*

• • •

Outside Bread and Bones, Ellie broke the home-made carob-filled cookie in two and tossed Rudy a piece. After she stuffed the other half into her fanny pack, along with the biscuit for Buddy, they continued walking toward the Davenport while she kept her eyes peeled for any sign of the bichon.

Turning north on Fifth, she stopped to speak to the doormen she'd met when she'd dropped off Paws in Motion business cards. Sadly, not one of them had seen a lone fluffy white dog on the streets. When she arrived at the Davenport, she prepared herself to go another round with Kronk.

The giant doorman, hunched over a newspaper spread out on the registration desk, raised his shaggy gray head as she and Rudy approached.

"*El-ee.* This is surprise. Since when you are walking clients at night?"

"I'm here to check on the hunt for Buddy, Kronk. Any sign of him?"

Kronk heaved a sigh. "No."

Not used to getting such a terse answer from him, she raised a brow. "Have you spoken to any of the tenants?"

The Russian shrugged. "A couple."

Weird alert. "How many is a couple, and who were they?"

"I only remember faces, not names." Dismissing her, he returned his gaze to the paper.

Ellie smacked a palm on the countertop. "Kronk, what aren't you telling me?"

"Leave the man be, Engleman," said a voice she recognized.

She turned and Rudy lunged on the lead, growling as if he'd cornered a rat. "Eugene. What are you doing here?"

"Hey! Hey! Hey! Control your mutt, or I'll use my Taser on him." With that, he knocked on the counter as a good-bye to the doorman and headed outside.

It was then she realized that Kronk hadn't told her what he knew because one of her prime competitors, a gay dog walker who apparently had no last name, was in the vicinity. Taking control of Rudy, she followed Eugene onto the sidewalk, practically jogging to catch him.

Eugene was the undisputed king of dog walkers, at least in the Davenport and a few of the surrounding buildings, and when she'd traded words with him the first morning she'd taken Buddy out, the man had been over-the-top rude. That was the moment she came to grips with the rumors she'd heard of cutthroat dog walkers and the lengths they took to keep the clients they had and corral new ones.

Until Eugene, she hadn't conversed with anyone who matched the D in nasty banter. She could only imagine the oily sneer on his thin lips when he'd heard about the professor's demise.

Catching up to him, she worked her way to his front and walked backward as she spoke. "Eugene, stop for a second. I want to talk to you."

Frowning, he shuttled past her, but she pressed her position, finally touching his sleeve. She'd need a shower when she got home, but the contamination was worth it if it helped find Buddy. "Please, give me five minutes."

He skittered to a stop and glared. "It's late, and I've got a client down the street. And don't try to follow me and steal the job, either. Bibi and I are on to you."

Bibi Stormstein, a woman of indeterminate age and indiscriminate fashion sense, was the feminine version of Eugene, though Ellie had no idea of her sexual orientation. But Ellie felt certain Bibi was equally disreputable and discourteous, and hated her just as much as Eugene did.

"I'm not out to steal your clients," she explained, and it was almost the truth. "This is about a different matter."

"Oh, yeah. Kronk mentioned Buddy was missing, but it doesn't have anything to do with me." He propped a shoulder against the building. "Too bad about the professor, ain't it?"

"It's terrible. But I'm worried about his dog."

"That spoiled mutt? I hope he got run over by a bus."

Rudy snarled while Ellie blinked, too shocked to speak.

"Don't play little Miss Innocent with me. You're in this profession for the money, just like I am." He glanced at the terrier. "And keep your dog away from me."

"Yes, I walk canines for the money, but I love dogs. How can you do this job and not care about them?"

"Easy. I put on my pants every morning and go to work. It'd be the same as if I was a waiter or a street cleaner, that's all. Besides, dogs are animals. What do they know?"

"Please let me bite him," Rudy begged with a snarl. *"Just a nip on the ankle or maybe the knee. I've had my shots, so it'll be okay."*

"No, you may not," Ellie answered, then realized what she'd done. "I mean, they know a lot. Dogs have personalities, feelings. They love, hate, understand. I can't believe you don't see that."

"Blah, blah, blah," he said with a grimace. "So now that we're talking, what did you want?"

"You go to a lot of buildings, walk a lot of dogs. Have you seen Buddy wandering the streets or Central Park? Did any of your customers mention him?"

"No and no. Now move. I'm late for my next appointment." Brushing past her, he charged up the sidewalk without a "so long" or a backward glance.

"What a creep."

"I know, but shots or no shots, you still aren't

63

allowed to bite him. He'd sue us, and then where would we be?"

"Sue us? If I caught something from him, I'd be the one who needed time at the vet. We could sue him."

"He has a Taser, you dope. If he uses it, you could be killed." She heaved a sigh. "And we'd be separated again. Do you want that?"

Rudy plopped his butt on the cement and gave her a sincere grin. *"I'd come back."*

She dropped to a squat and pulled him near. "I'd go crazy if I lost you a second time, and there's no guarantee we'd ever find each other again." Hugging him, she whispered in his ear, "You mean everything to me, little man."

"Aw, I love it when you get all weepy." He gave her cheek a sloppy lick. *"Okay, I'll be good. But he'd better not lay a finger on you, or all bets are off."*

Sniffing, Ellie stood. "It's getting dark, so I guess we should walk home a different way. If I hold out that extra biscuit and call Buddy's name, we might find him."

"You do that while I put my nose in gear. But first, how about the other half of my treat?"

She complied, then walked to the back of the Davenport, but aside from a neatly stacked Dumpster, there were no signs of an animal—not even a rat. Dejected, they headed home.

Chapter 4

Sam stared at the mound of paperwork that had piled on his desk over the past week. Completing the forms required in this job was the bane of his existence. The city had everything programmed online, but the system was down more often than it was up. Not a computer kind of guy, he did most of his work in erasable pen and ate the nasty comments his sergeant tossed out on a daily basis. Truth be told, aside from fiddling with e-mail, he couldn't do a damn thing on a computer.

Pulling out a file, he opened it and checked the spiral notebook he kept for each case. After finishing the first round of forms, he moved to the second, which belonged to a case that had wrapped this morning.

Then he calculated the number of hours that had passed since the ME had taken control of the professor's body. Until he had a preliminary report, his hands were tied, even though he had a gut feeling it was a homicide. And according to police protocol, he couldn't even do anything about the missing dog until he knew for sure that a murder had been committed. Not that he cared about Billy—or was it Bobby?

Removing the dog walker's business card from his shield case, he took a second look. The cartoon image of a fuzzy mutt was imprinted in one corner, and her phone number in the opposite, while professional info was crammed in the middle:

Paws in Motion
Dog walking for small breeds only
Pet and apartment sitting available
Ellie Engleman

Ms. Engleman had curly gold-tinted hair, a heart-shaped face, and pouting lips. But what stood out in his memory were her dark-lashed blue eyes gazing at him in frank disapproval whenever he asked a question or made a comment.

She had some nerve, acting as if he was a criminal for not loving dogs. So what if he wasn't fond of ankle biters? He'd been raised in a row house in Queens, with a small backyard and even less front. He, his parents, and two sisters had shared a single bath and three bedrooms, and they'd barely had room for themselves, never mind a dog.

Pet sitters marched up, down, and across Central Park every day, and all their clients had money to burn. Besides paying high rents, the inhabitants of the swanky apartments and condos gave dog walkers about the same amount they paid the nannies of their children. He'd heard it was a cutthroat business, with many of the walkers pulling down six figures, which gave him another angle to consider.

Had the killer, if there was one, murdered the

professor for a dog? Had someone been out to steal the mutt, and Albright got in the way? It was hard to fathom anyone taking a life for the mere privilege of walking a dog, but in this city, people had been murdered for less. Still, who would snuff someone over a pet? And why?

His desk phone rang and he answered, "Ryder."

"Sam. It's May Bridges."

He opened the spiral notebook he'd begun on Albright's case. "What do you have?"

"Your body from the Davenport—definitely a homicide. I'm still running tests, but he did wear a pacemaker, and from the look of it, someone or something screwed it up big-time."

"What the hell does that mean?"

"I sent the pacemaker to a lab for testing, but best guess is something scrambled the signal and the system shorted out."

"And that was evident because . . ."

"Once I got him on the table, I found a burn line running from his left fingers straight to his chest. When I opened him up, the pacemaker was out of commission. It makes sense."

"No shit?"

"No shit."

"When can you give me more?"

"Once someone from the manufacturer gets back to me. Then there's the toxicology screening. I should have a better picture in a couple of days, but for right now you've got yourself a murder."

Sam disconnected the call. A burn line, a pace-maker with a short, and seared fingers. Couple those facts with a charred door, and it was unlike anything he'd ever run across. All the more reason to track down witnesses.

His gaze focused on the card for Paws in Motion, and he realized he'd have to speak to the Engleman woman again. Always willing to play it for laughs, he admitted it had been a stitch yanking her chain about the chocolate on her face.

"Ryder!" The captain's voice echoed across the bullpen. "In here. On the double."

Figuring the summons was about the Monetti case, Sam grabbed the file and sauntered to his boss's office. At the door, he leaned against the frame. "You want to see me?"

Captain Mitchell Carmody, a bear of a man with huge hands and a ruddy complexion, sat hunched over his desk, his gray eyes narrow, his mouth grim. "Come in and shut the door."

Sam did as requested.

"Have a seat. What's that in your hand?"

"The Monetti file."

"And?"

"Babcock and DeNunzio made the collar earlier in the day. Suspect's in jail, and the arraignment's set for tomorrow."

"Good." Carmody tapped the eraser end of a pencil on his blotter. "I heard they found a body in the Davenport today."

"Yes, sir."

"Crime or happenstance?"

"I just got off the phone with Bridges. She's fairly certain it's a homicide."

"How'd it happen?"

"Something funky with the guy's pacemaker caused his heart to stop."

"Last I heard, a heart attack's not murder. And death by faulty pacemaker isn't a crime, either."

"Bridges didn't think it was a malfunction. There were burn marks on the vic's fingers and a red line running up his arm straight to his chest. She's on it."

"That's a new one. Any leads?"

"No, sir."

"Suspects? Witnesses?"

"The body was discovered by the victim's dog walker. I had her in for questioning most of the afternoon, but my gut tells me she isn't the guilty party."

The captain's eyes crinkled at the corners. "Dog walker, huh? So the guy had a pet?"

"It appears so. But the mutt's missing."

"Missing? What the hell happened to it?"

"We don't know. The dog walker is on the lookout but—"

"'The dog walker is on the lookout'?" his boss repeated in an exaggerated tone. "Who is she?"

"Ellen Elizabeth Engleman. She handles several dogs in the building. Opened the door to pick up Albright's and stumbled on the body."

"I like dogs," said the captain. Staring into space, he appeared lost in thought. "Louise and I owned one of our own a couple years back. Hit us hard when he died."

"So you got another dog?"

Carmody's expression turned mutinous. "Hell, no. There's not a canine around that could replace our little bichon."

At the name of the breed, Sam swallowed. If he wasn't careful, he was going to be holding his ass in his hands.

"Jocko was one of a kind. It about killed the wife when we had to say good-bye." Clearing his throat, he rearranged a stack of files. "What kind of dog was it?"

"Uh, I believe the woman called it the same as Jocko, sir. A bichon."

"A bichon frise?"

"Maybe."

"Hell in a handbasket." Carmody's face turned brick red. "And it's missing?"

"Yes, sir. At least, that's what Ms. Engleman said."

The captain heaved a breath. "Listen up. Stay in touch with the dog walker and keep tabs on her progress. Report the dog to animal control, and talk it over with stolen property." He ran a hand over his face. "Was it a purebred?"

"She mentioned that the dog had won at Westminster a couple of years back."

"Goddamn." Carmody shook his leonine head. "I remember the year that bichon won. The wife and I were sitting on the sofa with Jocko, watching the competition on the tube when he took Best in Show." He twirled the pencil between his fingers. "Keep on top of it, and stay in touch with the city pound, too. Maybe they picked him up or someone turned him in."

"Yes, sir. Is that all?"

"A bichon. Son of a bitch."

The captain's phone rang, and Sam let himself out. Just his luck he had a dog lover for a boss. He dropped the Monetti file on his desk and headed for the door. Time to make rounds at the Davenport. After that, he'd call on Ellie Engleman.

"I'm telling you, something's not right." Ellie spoke to Vivian as she paced her living room after returning from the Davenport. Viv had walked her own dog, deposited Twink in her apartment, and climbed the stairs for a chat. "It doesn't make sense that Buddy would just disappear."

Vivian blew a huge bubble and let it pop. "If Buddy's out there, I'm sure he'll find his way back." She ran her fingers through her stick-straight dark brown hair, then smoothed hot pink spandex workout pants over legs a runway model would kill for and headed for the kitchen. "Got any ice cream?"

"Caramel Cone," Ellie answered, heading for the kitchen. She'd given up being jealous of her best friend's high-fashion figure months ago. "And what do you mean if he's out there?"

Viv plopped into a chair while Ellie opened the freezer. "He has to be somewhere, doesn't he?"

"He's somewhere, all right, but it makes more sense that someone stole him. Rudy and I did a lot of walking tonight, and there was no sign of him." Taking a seat, she passed over a spoon and a fresh container of Häagen-Dazs, then opened the pint she'd snacked on earlier. "Unfortunately, the police don't care that he's gone."

Viv peeled the protective seal from the carton and dug in. "What's the cop's name in charge of the case?"

"Detective Ryder, and he's a moron."

"Another D?"

Ellie almost wished Ryder was another dick-head, because it would make him forgettable. Sadly, that wasn't the case. "I have no idea what type of private life he leads. I just know he's surly and suspicious and—"

"What on earth did he do to you?"

"Do? Absolutely nothing . . . much."

"Doesn't sound like 'nothing much' to me." She swallowed a scoop of ice cream. "Come on, tell me."

Mortified, Ellie confessed. "He brought me in for questioning."

"Questioning! You mean like they do on CSI? Did he make you sit under a bright light and threaten you with a rubber hose? Or play good cop–bad cop with another guy?"

"No lights, no hoses, and the beating was strictly mental. Just the two of us arguing while a gaggle of officers and other public servants tromped in and out of the room, continually interrupting us. And it was embarrassing. According to Ryder, I'm his prime suspect."

"You're kidding."

"Unbelievable, isn't it? And it didn't matter how many times I told him Buddy's disappearance was the key to solving the crime."

"Is he sure it was murder?"

"Not one hundred percent. Apparently there's evidence to gather, tests to run, people to hassle. They're waiting on the medical examiner's decision, forensics, too." She sighed. "The main thing is, Buddy is gone." She scanned the kitchen for Rudy, then remembered he was asleep on the living room sofa. "And it only makes sense that someone stole him," she whispered. Then she frowned. "Or maybe he's dead, just like Albright. Either way, it's a tragedy."

Viv waved a spoonful of ice cream. "If he sneaked out of the building, there's a good chance he is. Traffic in this city is a bitch."

"I know," Ellie said, her own spoon poised over her near-empty container. "Poor little guy."

"Hah!" Viv responded after swallowing. "To hear you tell it, that pup was more than spoiled. Slept on a bed bigger than mine, wore a diamond-encrusted collar, and wasn't the professor the client who demanded you take his dog out in bright yellow rain gear if the sky was cloudy?"

"Yes, but that's understandable. Buddy's worth thousands, and his stud fees are astronomical."

"Just like a man, expecting a woman to pay him for giving pleasure," Viv said with a snort. "Both my exes thought they were God's gift, too." She rolled her expertly made-up eyes. "I'll take ice cream and BOB over Walter and Steve any day."

Ellie ignored the reference to a battery-operated boyfriend and gave her opinion on the only husband of Viv's she'd met. "Steve was a prick. Is he still a client rep at your firm?"

Vivian shook her head. "Left for the Chicago office a week ago. Said the sight of me made him so miserable he couldn't concentrate." She capped her ice-cream container, set down her spoon, and deposited the carton in the freezer. "Save this for me. I have a feeling I'll be needing it. I've just about given up on men."

"I thought things were okay with Jason," offered Ellie.

"Too okay. Which means the ceiling's about to fall down around me." She shrugged. "It never fails. As soon as I connect with a guy, something comes along to ruin it. At this rate, I'll never get married again."

"Why would you want to?" asked Ellie, recalling her four-times-divorced mother. Georgette was a firm believer in the institution of matrimony. After Ellie's father had died and left them a less than decent nest egg, her mom had married an attorney, then a banker, an aspiring artist, and a stockbroker, and received huge settlements from three of them. Currently, she was dating a retired judge who was well into his eighties.

"Not for the money, that's for sure. I was thinking more along the lines of great sex and someone to rub my feet when I have a hard day."

"Oh, right, as if Walter and Steve ever did that."

"Okay, they didn't. But that doesn't mean I can't look for a guy who will."

"Not even a great foot rub would get me to marry again."

"Of course not. Because you'd actually have to share a conversation, maybe even have a date or two with a man before you refused to tie the knot."

"I'm happy with things the way they are. I have Rudy—"

"Rudy is a dog. A woman has needs."

"That's what BOB is for," Ellie reminded her with a giggle.

"And a big supply of batteries." Her cell phone

rang, and she jumped. "Who the heck can that be? It's almost eleven." Digging in her bag, she flipped the unit open. "Hello."

"Ms. Engleman?"

"Yes, this is she."

"It's Sam Ryder. Is it too late to call?"

"No, no, I'm up."

"Great. Can we talk?"

Vivian mouthed, Who is it?

"Sure. Just a second." She covered the phone. "It's that pain-in-the-ass detective I told you about."

Viv grinned, mischief written across her glamour-girl face like words on a billboard. "Mr. Rubber Hose?"

"Shh."

"Ms. Engleman? May I speak to you in person?"

Warning her pal with a finger to her lips, she said, "Um . . . here? I mean, do you know where I live?"

"He's coming here?" Viv hissed. "Tonight?"

"I'm a cop, remember?" Sam interjected.

"I remember." Ellie covered the unit again. "What should I tell him?"

"That depends. What does he look like?"

Positive her face was on fire, Ellie raised a shoulder. "He's okay."

"That good, huh?"

Inhaling, Ellie stood and walked to the sink. "Ring the buzzer when you get here, and I'll let you—"

"I'm downstairs right now. Give the signal, and I'll be up in a minute."

"Just a second." She rested her bottom against the counter and stared at Viv. "He's downstairs. Right now."

"Well, goody. You can introduce us. I'll even vouch for your character."

"No."

"No?" asked Ryder.

"Not no to you, Detective." She rolled her eyes at Viv. "Be quiet so I can think."

"What's there to think about? Your apartment's decent, and you look passable enough for a woman who last wore makeup to her divorce hearing." Viv raised a brow. "Maybe he wants to torture you some more—you know, tie you to the bed and—"

"Ms. Engleman? Have you changed your mind?"

"Uh, no, but—hang on a second." She stared at Viv. "It's bad timing."

"Honey, with you, the timing will never be right. I'll leave so you and the naughty detective can be alone."

"No, don't go."

"Ms. Engleman? If this isn't convenient—"

Viv pushed the buzzer for the downstairs door as she left the kitchen.

"I'm coming up," he said. The line went dead.

"I'll be over tomorrow after work," Viv called from the foyer. "Don't do anything I wouldn't do."

• • •

"Hey," said the leggy brunette as she passed Sam on the stairway.

He nodded and continued his climb to the third floor, but instinct urged him to glance back over his shoulder. When he did, he caught the woman staring. Their eyes met, and she gave him a sexy grin and a thumbs-up, and continued down the stairs.

Not used to meeting women who stood close to his height of six feet, he shook his head. Females were something else. His younger sisters loved to tell him he was a sitting duck where the opposite sex was concerned. The only thing that saved him from a second walk down the aisle was his job. Carolanne had cheated her way out of their marriage, telling him she could no longer stay hitched to a guy in a dangerous profession who kept irregular hours and seven-day workweeks. He now realized not many women could.

When he arrived at the apartment, he found the door already open. Stepping inside, he got a good view of the hall in front of him and a spacious modern kitchen to the left. "Hello. It's Detective Ryder." Hearing a growl, he spotted one of the dogs from that morning crouched at his feet. "Hey, watch yourself. I'm an invited guest."

The dog sniffed his shoe, then took off toward the back of the apartment like a rat scurrying from a trap. Seconds later, it returned with the Engleman woman following in its wake.

"It's a bad idea to leave your door unlocked," he stated, though what he really wanted to say was "What kind of fool are you?"

"Anyone could come in and rob the place or worse."

"Hello to you, too, Detective." She glanced in the mutt's direction. "As you can see, I have a protector."

Sam tamped back a snort, knowing Ms. Engleman would be pissed if he laughed out loud at her asinine assertion. "Sorry, but I think you're misinformed. Dogs that small rarely protect you from burglars or rapists. They'd probably have a hard time frightening the meter reader."

The pooch yipped and gave another growl.

"Can it. He's friendly," she said to the pup, though her eyes never left Sam's face. "Can I get you something to drink before you bring out the rub . . . er . . . start this discussion? A soda? Water? Beer?"

"Ice water would be fine."

"I'll meet you in the living room. Make yourself at home."

He entered a large room with three windows along the back wall, a fireplace flanked by bookcases on another, and an elegant dining table nestled against a wall that opened to the kitchen. A floral-covered couch and two matching chairs faced the fireplace, while a second seating arrangement took up space under the windows.

She came in from the kitchen and caught him checking out the surroundings. "We can sit in front of the fireplace or under the windows. Whichever you prefer."

He focused on her naked windows. "You need drapes or blinds so you can close them for privacy this time of night. Anyone looking across the courtyard can see that you're alone."

"I'm not alone. I have Rudy."

As if staking his claim, the dog jumped on the sofa, growled low in its throat, and sent Ryder a glare that was both threatening and comical.

"Who is going to be very polite, or he'll go to bed early," she continued in a no-nonsense tone.

When Rudy gave another menacing growl, Ms. Engleman placed the tumblers of ice water on coasters, scooped the dog into her arms, and headed for the hall. "You're toast," she scolded the grumpy mutt. "I'll be right back," she called to Sam.

He took another survey while he waited. The honey-hued hardwood floor, covered in pastel-colored area rugs, shined in the light emitted by two brass lamps standing at either end of the sofa. A computer station took up a far corner, while a television sat on a wheeled table alongside the hearth. The dark wood furniture appeared expensive, ditto the pictures on the walls. All in all, it was a classy yet unpretentious room without a lot of feminine froufrous or annoying clutter.

"The furniture is new," she stated, returning to

the couch. "It was a present from me to me shortly after I signed my divorce papers. So was Rudy." She sat at the opposite end of the sofa, tucked her long legs underneath her, and clasped a knee with both hands. "I assume you're here to ask more questions about the professor, unless . . . Have you found Buddy?"

Sam took out his spiral notebook, wincing internally at her hope-filled expression. "Sorry, no sign of the dog."

Her lower lip quivered. "I asked the evening doorman to keep an eye out, but that was all I could manage until tonight."

"Tonight?"

"After dinner, Rudy and I took a walk and had a better look around the Davenport. I spoke to a half dozen doormen, but we didn't find a sign of Buddy."

"I take it you intend to keep looking?"

"Of course." She sat up straight. "What about you?"

"We have a call in to animal control, and they're aware of the loss. Now about the professor—"

"Was it a heart attack?"

"I can't divulge that information."

She wrinkled her nose. "Then why are you here?"

"We parted on an uncomfortable note. I wanted to remind you that I'm the good guy in this mess. I need to hear any other details you might have remembered, no matter how trivial."

Her furrowed brow told him she was thinking. "I said everything I had to say. The professor and I only met a few weeks ago. We talked sometimes, but it was always about Buddy. I thought you were here to tell me that you found him."

"No, but I spoke to the night doorman you mentioned, and—"

"Kronk? Hah, don't expect him to divulge anything. All he's interested in is money."

Sam flipped through his notebook. "Boris Kronkovitz. I plan to run him through the system, just to make sure he's legal. Told me he's keeping an eye out for the dog. Sounded as if he was already spending a reward. Any idea where he'd get a notion like that?"

She ran a hand through her unruly curls, and they caught the light from the standing lamps. "I may have mentioned something about money, but only after he assumed it was available. It makes sense that the professor's relatives would offer a reward, since Buddy's a champion. His stud fees are through the roof."

"One of the things you and Professor Albright discussed."

"That and what goes on behind the scenes at Westminster. He promised to get me a pass for next February's show and introduce me to some of the owners and handlers."

"And why would you want to do that?"

"What dog lover wouldn't? It's a thrill being

close to all that canine perfection. I'd also hoped to find new clients."

"And acquiring more clients would mean a lot to you."

"To me and every other dog walker in this town. But we're rehashing what I already told you."

"Including the fact that you were well aware of the dog's value, and knew others would pay to have him."

She squared her shoulders, and the gesture show-cased the generous breasts hiding beneath her shirt." Isn't it about time you got off that subject and started a real search?"

He raised his gaze and focused on her eyes, which were an unusual shade of blue, maybe aquamarine or turquoise. "Because if I find the dog, I'll find the killer?"

"Exactly."

"And you think he was dognapped?"

"It's an idea."

She sucked in a breath. "Then the professor was murdered."

"I can't say one way or the other while the investigation is pending, but I want you to steer clear. This is a job for professionals. It's all right for you to conduct a search for the dog, but if you think of someone we might consider a suspect, tell us and we'll handle it." The last thing he needed was an amateur Nancy Drew confronting a murderer. "Understand?"

"Was anything else missing from the professor's home?" she asked, as if oblivious to his warning.

"Not that we're aware of. His next of kin is a niece from Jersey. She's coming to town to make funeral arrangements. Then she'll go to the apartment and give an opinion on the contents."

"Poor Buddy." She thrust out her lower lip. "I don't even want to think about him with strangers."

"Then it's possible he'd go with someone he didn't know?"

"Possible, but not likely. It took several days before he'd say hello to me—"

"You mean before he came to you when called or went willingly on a walk."

"Um . . . yes, that's what I mean. I just can't see him taking off with a stranger."

"Not even if the thief had food or a toy?"

"He'd never go with anyone if the professor was ill or in danger. If we don't find him, then someone stole him, and killed the professor in the process."

"The doorman Randall intimated the professor was a creature of habit."

"And if a robber knew his schedule—"

"As well as you do."

"You can't be serious. I'd never do anything to harm that sweet old man just to take his dog." She huffed out a breath. "Is that why you're here? To see if I was harboring Buddy? I told you this afternoon that you have my permission to check the apartment." She stood. "Go on, be my guest—crawl under the bed, inspect my closets—"

"For cripes sakes, don't get so bent out of shape," he said, trying not to laugh. "I'll be honest. At first, you were top choice for a suspect, but a couple of things don't add up, so . . ."

Her eyes narrowed. "What kind of things?"

"That's something I can't divulge. Suffice it to say you're not the type to—"

"What do you mean, not the type? I didn't know murderers came in types. I could kill someone," she insisted, "if they ticked me off enough."

"Okay, fine. You're perfectly capable of inflicting bodily harm. Is that what you want to hear?"

"Yes—no—I—Oh, heck, of course not. But don't be so quick to put me in a nice-girl box and think I'll conform to your rules. Thanks to the D, I'll never do that again."

"The D?"

"Forget it." Pushing a wayward curl behind her ear, she heaved a sigh. "Sorry. I don't know where that came from."

"I apologize if I insulted you, but that's the first time I've had anyone tell me they were upset because I didn't consider them a killer." He tugged at the knot in his tie. "Have you changed your mind about looking for Billy?"

"His name is Buddy. He's a living creature, not an article of clothing or a piece of jewelry. And yes, I'll be on the hunt for him."

Sam cursed under his breath and swore he wouldn't make the same mistake twice. "Tell me again, how big is Buddy?"

"Maybe fifteen pounds. He'd fit in a tote bag or under a coat if it was roomy, and he's snow-white with a distinctive cut. There are pictures of him in the apartment—" Snapping her fingers, she jumped to her feet and headed for the computer. "Give me a second."

Sam crossed the room and stood behind her desk chair. "What are you doing?"

"I'm accessing the Westminster Web site. It has pictures of past winners." The Web site came up, and she clicked on the menu. A page of photos showcasing miniature white dogs appeared, and she hit a few more keys. While her printer hummed, she went back to flipping screens. "Here you go." She gazed over her shoulder, grinning. "That's one of the professor and Buddy at their big win. Aren't they the cutest pair?"

"Adorable," he muttered, squinting at the monitor. "You said the dog's stud fee was high?"

"Last the professor mentioned, five thousand dollars."

Sam whistled his surprise. "How often did that happen?"

"Once a month or so. Depended on where the bitch lived."

"Nice way to phrase it."

She *tsk*ed. " 'Bitch' is the common term for a

female dog. And the owner of the stud doesn't always get money. They're sometime offered pick of the litter instead."

"But the professor never took that option."

"He couldn't. He was getting up in years and making plans to retire, and housebreaking a puppy in a high-rise is hell. Besides, a new pooch might have made Buddy jealous."

"Jealous?"

"I'm aware you aren't very knowledgeable about canines, but they really do resemble humans in temperament and personality. They like or dislike other dogs, and they love, tolerate, or hate certain people. They can exhibit jealousy, anger, or pride, even if they aren't pampered."

"So you consider yourself an expert on the subject?"

"No. Well, maybe." She passed him the picture from her printer. "Let's just say I commiserate with dogs and their owners, and try to put myself in their place whenever possible."

"So even if there's a possibility Buddy was stolen, you'd still search for him?"

"Of course. In fact, tomorrow I plan to ask every street vendor I know. Then I'm going to the nearest shelter to see if someone turned him in. But it's a long shot, because if he ran away, whoever found him will probably realize he's a purebred. They might try to sell him or wait until they hear of a reward."

She stood, and he took a step of retreat, unhappy with his gut reaction to her clean floral scent and world-class breasts. "Like Kronk?"

"Like Kronk."

Out of questions, Sam nodded. He didn't have a problem allowing her to visit local shelters, because she knew exactly what to look for, and she had a lot more time on her hands than he did. His team had to keep tabs on the professor's mail and phone messages, question a few more neighbors, and try to figure out what had caused the pacemaker to short. He also had to hear from the officer he'd sent to Columbia.

"Let me know if you find him, but remember— no police work. In the meantime, we'll go at it from another angle."

"Another angle?" she asked, following him to the door.

"We'll be monitoring his phone and his mail. In case there's a ransom note or call."

"That doesn't make any sense. If a dognapper killed the professor—" She stared at him as if she'd just figured out the meaning of life. "What if whoever took him doesn't realize the professor died, and reads about it in the newspaper? If they don't think they can get money for Buddy, they might kill him."

"Right now, everything is conjecture, but either way I'm not at liberty to say."

"Oh, bull. It's the only thing that makes sense.

The robber didn't expect Professor Albright to be home, and when he opened the door and saw the professor on the floor, probably thought he'd fainted or had some kind of seizure. You're hoping the assailant will try to solicit a ransom before he reads about the death."

"I can't comment. Whatever you come up with is your idea, not mine."

"This is terrible." She fisted her hands in her hair. "Buddy could already be dead."

"Or he could turn up at the shelter, because we don't know for certain why he's missing."

"Either way, the whole thing sucks."

"Yeah, life's like that sometimes." He reached around her to grab the knob, and she stayed rooted in place, which brought him close enough to see the drift of freckles dancing across her nose. Their gazes locked, and she blushed a delicate pink.

"Don't forget to call me if you find the dog," he muttered, pulling back to a safer distance.

As if flustered, she moved aside. "I—I'll let you know."

"You do that. And I'll be in touch."

He started down the stairs, then stopped and turned, but she'd already closed the door.

Chapter 5

The next morning, Ellie found Randall in the lobby of the Davenport, pushing a broom like a Merry Maid on crack. After a few minutes of waiting, during which time she thought he might wear out the floor with his crazed cleaning routine, she tapped his shoulder.

"Randall, do you have a minute?"

Startled, the doorman jumped and spun around. When he recognized her he sighed. "Thank goodness it's you and not the police. I'm positively exhausted, answering their questions, letting them trudge through the building, allowing them to interrogate the tenants," he said in a frazzled tone. "The residents are wondering if there's a murderer living in the building, and since they know Buddy is missing, they're certain a dognapper is among them."

With Rudy sitting patiently at her feet, Ellie rested her elbow on the counter. "They should be worried, especially about their dogs, because I agree with their idea. I think the professor's killer stole Buddy."

"Then he was murdered? But how? Just about anyone going into and out of the building has to pass me, and I was at my post all morning. No stranger entered the Davenport."

"Do me a favor. Make me a list."

"Like I did for Detective Ryder?"

"Exactly like you did for Ryder, and add anyone who might have used the service elevator, too. I'll pick it up on my way out . . . unless you don't have the time."

"I think I kept a copy for my own peace of mind. I'll try to find it. You know, the police didn't ask me a thing about the dog during questioning, though they made a point of asking the names of every person on your client list."

She rested her chin in her palm. "That means trouble."

He propped both hands on the broom handle. "How so?"

"Because Ryder thinks I know something, and it wouldn't be good if he mentioned that to my customers."

Randall shook his balding head. "That's a shame, but never fear. I vouched for you. Told him you only came in once that morning, and it wasn't long before you called me about the professor. There wasn't time for you to have killed him or done anything with Buddy."

"Thanks. I knew I could count on you." She dug in her bag and brought out sheets with the bichon's picture, a description, and her phone number. "I made these on my computer last night. Think you could post one where people will see it?"

"I'll put it up, but management might take it

down. You know how prudish some of the people who live here are."

"It can't hurt to try." She slid two of the sheets toward him, then her gaze strayed to the elevator. "Is everyone gone?"

"I said a fast farewell to each of your clients, so your charges are waiting. Just don't be surprised if you find a note or two mentioning they received a visit from the police."

People with money to burn hated to be inconvenienced, and speaking to an officer of the law about their dog walker would definitely fall into the category of "nuisance."

"I guess so, but I can't imagine one of them saying something that might incriminate me. I haven't been walking in this building long enough to cheese anybody off."

"That could change once the good detective gets ahold of Eugene or Bibi."

Crap. She'd forgotten about her unpleasant competitors. "I'll just have to weather that storm when it blows in. Since it's only me and Rudy this morning, we'll go up by ourselves. That way, you'll have time to hunt up that list, and talk to the police if they stop by."

"Thank you. And you're right. I expect they'll be in and out for days. I'll simply have to do the best I can."

"Things don't look good, do they?" Rudy asked the moment the elevator door closed.

"I can handle it, pal. Don't worry about me."

"I don't like that detective guy. Like I said last night, he has shifty eyes, especially when he looks at you."

"I told you, it's because he thinks I'm a suspect. Once he's sure I'm not involved, he'll get off my case, and I'll never hear from him again."

"I doubt that. His testosterone level was in the red zone the minute he walked into our apartment."

"His testos—" The doors opened on Sweetie Pie's floor, and they stepped into the hall. "How do you know about that?" she asked, her face heating.

"Superior sense of smell. We canines can scent the big bang from miles away."

"'The big bang'? You're incorrigible." She turned the key to Barbara Jaglinski's apartment and squatted to get the leash dangling from Sweetie Pie's muzzle. "And off the mark where Ryder is concerned."

"Why are you two discussing the 'big bang'?" the Westie asked, attesting to a dog's superior hearing. *"Babs didn't get any last night, either, so I guess my ploy worked."*

"You should be ashamed of messing up the course of true love for your companion," Ellie scolded. Then she glared at Rudy. "And my sex life is none of your business."

"If you say so," he answered in a smarmy tone.

Embarrassed by both canines' opinions, she picked up Stinker and Jett and brought the troop to meet Buckley. After a few rounds of butt sniffing and play bows by the dogs, she led them to the lobby, out the door, and onto Fifth. They crossed at the light on Sixty-sixth, detoured into the park, and spent the next thirty minutes doing what dogs did while Ellie kept her eyes peeled for any sign of Buddy.

Once she tossed the waste bags, she returned her charges to their homes, stopping to write a note to each owner, something she'd had no time to do yesterday. Later, after Sweetie Pie's second walk, she'd do the same for Ms. Jaglinski. She'd learned in her first week of dog walking that a canine's family enjoyed hearing about whatever their pet did on their walk, including the condition of their BMs.

Then she stopped in the lobby to get the list from Randall and offer a final word of advice. "Please call me, not the cops, if you get any news. I don't want Buddy taken to a shelter, and Ryder said if I found him, I could keep him until they locate the professor's niece." She glanced at the paper he passed her. "You're sure this is everyone?"

"I'll tell you the same thing I told the police. No one came in or out except the tenants and the regular morning services. You know, the newspaper and dry-cleaning deliverymen, Eugene and Bibi, cleaning services, the people who are here on a regular basis, which includes you. I don't usually see those who enter via the service elevator but—"

"I forgot about that. Who goes up that way?"

"Furniture movers, people who deliver water, anyone with a product too large or bulky for the lobby. But there was nothing scheduled for yesterday."

"And none of the regulars acted suspicious or . . . off?"

"Not that I noticed. Eugene returned with his charges while you were busy with the police, and he seemed inordinately pleased when he heard the professor's death had caused the commotion. Bibi didn't say a word, but then she rarely does."

"I had a run-in with Eugene last night, when I came to talk to Kronk. He's just mean enough to find Buddy and sell him to the highest bidder."

"Do you think so?" asked the doorman, his face dour.

She sighed. "Buddy once told me—I mean the professor told me—that Eugene was rude, especially with his boy. It's the reason he was so quick to give me a chance."

Randall's brows met over the bridge of his patrician nose. "You do realize the police are going to sweep the matter of the missing dog under the rug? I know you're fond of Buddy but—"

"The cops don't give a rat's behind about him. I don't think they have a burglary team or anyone else searching, but I've been thinking: How could he escape if the door was closed when I got there?"

"Hmm. It does give credence to your dognap theory." He pulled his shoulders back. "I plan to give the police my opinion on the subject the next time they call."

"You do that, but don't say you heard it from me. Hang those flyers, and I'll talk to you tomorrow."

Still thinking about the situation, she headed with Rudy into the early-spring sunshine. Crossing the busy avenue, she stopped for a quick conversation with one of her favorite people. Marvin had been selling newspapers, magazines, candy, and lottery tickets at this stand since she was a teenager, hawking goods alongside a dozen other vendors who worked the sidewalks around her territory. She knew all of them by name, but the news seller was the most talkative. He also interacted with the locals, which could help her cover more ground in her puppy hunt.

"Hey, Marv."

"Ellie, Rudy." The elderly African-American showed a smattering of gold teeth. "Saw the commotion at the Davenport yesterday. Heard it was Professor Albright."

"Yes, and it's really got me upset."

Marvin passed a customer the *New York Times* and collected the money. "I bet. What happened?"

"It might have been a heart attack, but the police aren't saying. And there's more. Buddy is missing."

"Aw, that's a shame. He's a cute little fella."

"You didn't see him wandering the street, did you? Or maybe spotted someone with a dog that resembled Buddy?"

"I seen a hundred little white dogs bein' walked around here, but I didn't recognize any of 'em as your pal."

Ellie handed him a business card. "Do me a favor. Keep your eyes open. Ask some of the other walkers, too. And if anyone mentions they found a dog, get the info and call me."

"Will do."

She led Rudy to a hot dog vendor she frequented and waited in line. It was early for lunch, but stress always ratcheted up her hunger quotient. "One with mustard and kraut, one plain, and a diet soda, Pops."

"You sure are an easy sell," the cart pusher said, grinning. With wrinkles creasing his nut brown face, eyes that twinkled with curiosity, and a small, wiry body, Pops reminded her of a monkey who'd found a way to hide in plain sight on the busy Manhattan streets. "Saw some activity yesterday. Word is we lost Professor Albright."

She accepted the can of soda and dropped it into her side pocket. "Can you believe it? When I picked up my charges, I discovered his body."

He held out her lunch. "That's rough. How'd it happen?"

"I'm not sure, maybe a heart attack. But his pooch is missing, so keep an eye out. Buddy is my small bichon, really cute and friendly. He was one of Eugene's dogs, until the professor hired me for the job."

"Ah." He passed her the food. "I see."

"See what?" She licked a glob of mustard off her thumb.

"Eugene's probably havin' a field day, knowing the customer you stole from him is dead. He was here about a half hour ago walking his gang from the Beaumont. Guess that's why he acted so cheerful."

"He's a sicko," Ellie pronounced. "See you tomorrow."

She led Rudy to a bench and began to eat her lunch. The sidewalk teemed with people, most stepping with purpose, but many strolling while they gazed at the highrises on the opposite side of the avenue. The Upper East Side was made up of apartment buildings and condominiums, with few businesses in sight. The residents in this area didn't want the neighborhood cluttered with restaurants, shops, or bars when they paid a ton of money for a direct view of Central Park and the stately Metropolitan Museum.

Her gaze wandered to Rudy as she bit into her hot dog. He waited patiently, though his eyes never left the wiener sitting next to her in a paper sleeve. After taking a swallow of soda, she picked up the extra sausage, tore off a chunk, and tossed it his way.

"We've had quite an interesting twenty-four hours, huh?" she asked after Rudy hopped on his hind legs, caught the tidbit in midair, and gulped it down. "Have to say, you've been golden through all this—except for the way you behaved with Ryder last night."

"I did what any canine worth his kibble would do. I tried to protect my best friend. You are such an innocent where men are concerned."

Soda sputtered from between Ellie's lips. Eyes watering, she dabbed her mouth with a napkin. "Stop already with that ridiculous 'big bang' theory. And quit smelling people's hormones. It isn't polite."

"Hah! As if I could," he gruffed.

Giving him a warning glance, she tossed him a second piece of hot dog, wrapped the leftovers in a napkin, and tucked them in her coat pocket. She had the entire afternoon before she was scheduled to return to the Davenport for her second walk with Sweetie and Buckley. She had plenty of time to search the area and visit the ASPCA on Ninety-fourth, where she'd found Rudy.

It was also time she phoned the list of possible clients Viv had given her. Either way, her day was going to be productive.

• • •

Hours later, her phone battery running low, Ellie set her notebook aside on her usual park bench. Between dropping flyers at the shelter, she'd talked to doormen, spoken to guards in front of the museum, and contacted fifteen potential clients, some of whom agreed she could meet their dogs.

Rudy was now dozing at her feet, and she knew she'd nod off herself if she sat there much longer. Between the disaster surrounding Professor Albright and her visit from Ryder, she'd tossed and turned all night, alternately worrying about the missing bichon and trying to figure a way to drive the hunky detective from her mind.

Though the man was as close to her physical description of Mr. Perfect as a guy could get, he irritated the bejesus out of her. She could handle his repeat questions, though they were growing old, but what really upset her was the fact that he'd told her she was "too nice" to commit murder. Too nice, my ass, she thought as she and Ruby crossed the Avenue. Another five minutes of his double talk, and she would have committed the decidedly "un-nice" act of conking him with a fire iron.

She'd been the ideal Stepford wife for ten years, done whatever her scum-sucking husband had asked, said all the things he'd wanted to hear, worn the clothes he'd chosen for her, even lived on carrot sticks and bullion to keep her figure the way he wanted. She was done being any man's

100

idea of *nice*. She'd used the past year to become her own person, speak her mind, and stand her ground. Too bad spending time with her had convinced Ryder she was a sweet girl with no guts, no moxie. No killer instincts. Well, she'd show him.

But *how,* she asked herself as they walked to the Joe to Go nearest to the Davenport. When they arrived, she tied her dog to an outside table and told him, "Stay and be good."

"How about a little water and a biscuit? That's the least you can do for your best bud, right?"

Ellie flinched at his pathetic tone. With all the turmoil, she'd forgotten to bring the bottle of water and miniature bowl she usually carried for her pal. "Not a problem. Sit tight. I'll be right back."

The coffee shop was owned and operated by an old school buddy. Joe Cantiglia was one of Manhattan's bravest entrepreneurs: a young guy with the guts to vie for market share against the bigger national coffee chains. He lived above the business and rented out floors three through five for extra income. He'd let Ellie work a few shifts there after her divorce, but it had taken only three days for her to realize she wasn't cut out to operate machinery in tandem with hot liquids.

Keeping one eye on her pooch, she waited in line, placed her order, and asked for Joe. The barista told Ellie he was working at his second store, so she paid for a large caramel bliss and a sugar cookie, collected a paper cup of water, and walked back into the fresh spring air. After taking a seat at the table, she served Rudy a drink, gave him a bite of the cookie, and tasted her coffee.

Surprisingly, the hot, sweet liquid sent a jolt through her system, ordering her common sense to rise to the fore. What had she been thinking when she'd made that crack to Ryder? She wasn't capable of murder. She opened windows to shoo out flies and spiders. She'd never be so vile or so demented that she'd kill another human being, no matter what they did to her. But that didn't mean she'd given up on her idea of smacking the detective upside his head.

Thanks to her mother's financial assistance and Viv's moral support, she'd learned to take care of herself and live independently. Granted, she'd borrowed money from Georgette to make it happen, but she no longer answered to Ellen Lipschitz, thank God, and was proud to be back to her maiden name of Engleman. Never again would she hostess a boring cocktail party dressed in a skinny-strapped gown and four-inch heels. Nor did she have to make polite small talk with snooty people who had no interest in anything but the amount of money they'd make on their next business deal.

Intent on her musings, she didn't hear the familiar voice sneaking into her thoughts until Rudy put a paw on her knee.

"In case you've forgotten, I'm still here."

"I noticed." She ruffled his ears. "Not to belabor the point, but you were very impolite last night, growling at Ryder the way you did. I taught you better manners than that."

"You know why I don't trust him."

"Well, you're wrong, so can your observations. We have to continue seeing him until this mess is straightened out and we find Buddy."

"There's gotta be a better way," he grumped.

"I can't sit by and let whoever took him get away with it, but once this investigation is wrapped up, we'll never have to interact with Ryder again." Capping the coffee, she stood. "Come on, we have to do a second round at the Davenport. Then I have appointments. Two people at the Beaumont aren't happy with their current dog walker, and this time both of them use Bibi."

At the corner, she crossed with the light and pushed through the crowd. When Rudy tugged on his lead and jerked her forward as they reached the other side, she slammed into a skinny guy in a purple leather jacket, and knew immediately by the scent of the sickly-sweet cologne who it was.

"Well, well, well." Eugene's fingers skimmed over the garish leather as if brushing off her touch. "If it ain't Miss Wannabe again. You just can't stay off my turf, can you?"

"Trust me when I say this, Eugene, but I definitely don't 'wannabe' you."

"Yeah, well I heard about that Blackberg woman, but when I stopped by, she said I was too late. It's like I told you last night. The buildings on this block are mine and Bibi's. Find your own space, and stop poaching our clients."

Ellie stepped out of the flow of pedestrian traffic, but the creep stuck to her like dog doo to a shoe. Aside from last night, she'd had little inter-action with him since the morning he'd been fired by the professor, and thanks to Eugene, each of their meetings had been awkward. Seeing as he and Bibi were the area's dog-walking royalty, it was inevitable she'd run into him more often as her customer base grew.

"Last I heard, it's a free country. I can't help it if some dogs and their owners like me better than you."

"What'sa matter? Too scared to go out and find your own customers?"

"I simply give interested pet owners my qualifi-cations and let them make up their own minds, and it's not my fault that a couple of the doormen like me. I have a private source for referrals, and I use it, just like you do. I got to Hazel first, and her dog took to me right away."

"Maybe so, but it might not last. Especially when people know you might have taken the pro-fessor's dog."

Ellie blinked her surprise. "Why would they think such a ridiculous thing?"

"Let's just say that rumors are rampant." He dropped his cigarette to the cement and stomped it with the heel of his worn sneaker. Raising his gaze, he sneered. "You find out anything more about the mutt?"

"No." She ground her molars, sick to death of people referring to the champion bichon as a mutt. And who, she wondered, would start such a vindictive rumor about her? Since Eugene was still bitter over being replaced, would he be evil enough to take the professor's life? She'd thought him nasty and stupid. Was he really cunning and clever and vindictive enough to do Professor Albright harm?

"You sure you don't know anything about the professor?"

He gave a sly smile, showing nicotine-stained teeth. "Too bad you lost the dog right after you stole him from me," he said, ignoring her question.

"I didn't steal that dog from you, and you know it." She leaned against the building. "How about Bibi? Have you talked about Buddy with her?"

He lit another Camel and took a long drag. "That's none of your business. By the way, I got a call from a Detective Ryder. Said he wanted to ask me a couple of questions. Know anything about that?"

"Of course not." Though she wished the detective would clamp on to Eugene or Bibi instead of her.

"How come I think you're lying?"

"I don't know, Eugene. How come?"

He shook his head. "Stay out of my way, Engleman. That's all I got to say." With that, he sauntered around the corner to, she imagined, his next group of clients.

"I could still bite him for you," Rudy offered. *"Just a nip on the ankle. Might lay him up for a couple of days so you could get a few more of his customers."*

"Don't you dare. I don't have liability—" Oh, crap, she'd forgotten about the paperwork for insurance and permits. If the police found out she'd stretched the truth, she'd never get Ryder off her back. She searched her bag, happy to see her cell phone still had a slight charge. "Come on, we've got to get Buckley and Sweetie Pie. Then I have to make a call."

Ellie met Hazel Blackberg at her door when she returned Buckley to his apartment.

"How was my lamb chop today? Did he play nice with the others?" Hazel scooped the pup into her arms. "Has Snooky-wookums missed his mommy?" she asked, cuddling the Maltipoo against her tremendous bosom.

" 'Snooky-wookums'!" snarked Rudy. *"Is she for real?"*

Buckley's low growl, directed, Ellie was certain, at Rudy, made her smile. "He was great. Did his

106

business on schedule, and got along with everyone like a perfect gentleman."

"That's good to know. Now I have a question for you. Do you have time to come inside?"

Ellie checked her watch. With only three minutes left to phone the insurance company, it probably would be better if she tried tomorrow. She stepped across the threshold. "Sure. What do you need?"

"A veterinarian."

"Excuse me?"

"Buckley needs a physician."

"He does? Why?"

"In case of an emergency, of course. I never know when he might get a tummy ache or be off his food. If that happens, I'll want to reach someone competent immediately. Someone who makes house calls, in case it's nighttime or too cold to take him out of the house."

"Oh, then you want Dr. Dave," Ellie told her. David Crane was young, attractive, and vet to many of the pampered pets that lived on the Upper East Side. From what she'd heard, he made house calls, boarded special clients, even groomed them or stopped in to administer medication if the need arose. She'd met him twice in the past month, introduced herself, and talked over what she could and couldn't do for her clients. She had hoped he'd send a referral or two her way, but so far, she hadn't heard a word.

"I'm so happy his is the name you mention," Hazel said with a toothy smile. "I've asked some of the other tenants and they use him, too."

Ellie opened her Day Planner and flipped to the *C*s. "I have his number right here. Do you want me to phone him?"

"Oh, you're such a dear. Please, and maybe you could be here when he visits? Just to make sure I keep things straight. Our last vet refused to make house calls, and I'd feel so much better if I knew for certain this city air hadn't aggravated my boy's allergies or worse."

"Buckley's allergic?"

"I don't know, but you got me to thinking when you mentioned the cigarette smoke. I've managed to cut back," she whispered. "Just in case."

"Yeah, thanks for that," Buckley said, breaking into the conversation. *"I was so busy takin' care of business today, I forgot to mention it."*

Ellie winked at the dog as she spoke to Hazel. "Good for you. I'm sure it's the best thing for both of you. When do you want Dr. Crane here?"

"Sometime after six p.m. tomorrow? I'll pay for your time, of course."

"It's nice of you to offer, but—"

"No, no. I insist. Money is no object where my Snooky-wookums is concerned."

"Okay, hang on a second, and I'll make the call. That way, you can listen in and make suggestions if he isn't able to come when it's convenient."

She used Hazel's kitchen phone and left a message when she got the answering machine. "I'm sure he'll get back to me with a time. Then I'll phone you. How does that sound?"

"Perfect, and thank you so much."

Ellie waved good-bye and led Rudy into the hall. "Not a word," she said to him as they descended in the elevator. "Or I'll pop a button laughing."

"Can you beat that dame?" Rudy asked, ignoring her. *"No wonder Buck is such a crab ass."*

"Oh, I don't know. Her pet name for him is sort of cute. How about if I called you Rudykins or Snuggle puss or—"

"Hold it right there. I have limits to the amount of humiliation I'm willing to suffer to be your devoted companion."

"Limits? What kind of limits?"

"Georgette for one. She pretends I don't exist, or haven't you noticed?"

"Mother is distracted right now. The man she's dating needs special attention."

"The judge has my sympathy, but let's not forget that detective guy."

"Please don't start the testosterone thing again."

"Why not? It's true. He can't wait for me to be out of the way so he can get into your pants."

"Shut up," Ellie said as the elevator car doors opened onto a half dozen residents waiting to go home. "Hi, nice night," she muttered, hoping to cover her impolite remark.

Kronk spotted her from behind his desk and dropped down, then rushed to her side with a small pet carrier in his arms. "Look what I find," he boomed, thrusting the plastic box toward her. "Is *lee-til* white dog."

"Oh my gosh! Buddy? You found Buddy?" She brought the carrier to the counter and popped the latch. When a toy poodle hopped out, she jumped back. "Where did you get this dog?"

"I find on street. Is Buddy, no?"

" 'No' is right. This is a poodle, and he has a collar. See?" She raised the red heart-shaped piece of metal and squinted at the tiny print. "His name is Henry, and he lives with the Huntingtons a couple of doors down. How he got away, I don't know, but Henry is not Buddy."

"You are sure?" Kronk asked, his face a mask of innocence.

"More than sure." Reaching across the counter, she picked up the phone and dialed the number on the tag. Seconds later a man answered, and she gave him the good news. "That's right. He's at the Davenport. No, no, don't thank me. Thank the doorman, Mr. Kronkovitz. Yes, I'll leave him with Kronk . . . A reward? That won't be necessary. He was happy to do it."

Looking pissed, Kronk drummed his fingers on the counter.

"Yes, I'm positive," she reiterated, meeting the doorman's flinty glare with one of her own. She set the phone in its cradle, then scooted the poodle back into the carrier, but not before Henry licked her fingers in gratitude. "I took the liberty of refusing the reward in your stead. I have no idea how you got hold of Henry but do not do it again. And stop trying to fool me, because it's tacky and it's rude."

"Ah, *El-ee*," Kronk moaned.

She led her pup to the door, and Rudy snarled out his own parting shot, *"Yeah, turd ball. What she said."*

Chapter 6

Ellie hurried to her appointments at the Beaumont while pondering a way to take Kronk down a peg without getting on the wrong side of every doorman in a six-block radius. How had he gotten hold of that sweet toy poodle? He had nerve, trying to pass the dog off as Buddy. How stupid did he think she was?

After introducing herself to the Beaumont's evening doorman, she asked if he'd seen Buddy or heard of anyone finding a small white dog. When he said no, she gave him a flyer to post and requested he announce her to the Birch family. Unfortunately, her discussion with them proved to be a dead end because the Birches' dalmatian, though friendly, didn't fit her small-dog policy.

The Best family, who lived in the same building, owned a yappy Pomeranian. Bruiser was the right size, but had a disagreeable temperament and showed no interest when Ellie tried to make a mental connection. Since business was business, she agreed to escort the dog on a morning outing for the next week to see if they fit. After that, she and the Bests would reevaluate the relationship and make a final decision on continuing the project.

Now at home, she decided to lend Viv a hand and take Twink for a short walk. Using her key, she opened her best friend's apartment door and called the dog's name, to no avail.

"Where is he?" she muttered, more to herself than Rudy as she stepped into the foyer. "Twink! Twink? Come on, we're going out."

She heard voices coming from the living room and tiptoed down the hall, then peered around the corner. Twink, intently eyeing the television screen, was watching a program on the TV Land channel.

"Hey, mister. When did you learn how to turn on the television set?"

Twink kept his gaze on the screen.

She stomped in and stood behind him, noisily tapping her toe. "Twink?"

"Uh, Ellie?"

"Twink? Are you listening to me?"

"He's not gonna answer until you call him Mr. T, Triple E. I thought I told you that already."

She shot Rudy a look. "Come again?"

"It's me talkin' to you, sucka. So you'd better listen."

Ellie focused on the gaudily bedecked African-American glaring from the screen.

"Time to go, fool."

She rolled her eyes. Well, great. Now she knew for certain where Twink got his creative vocabulary . . . and his sassy attitude.

"Okay, okay. I got it." Sighing, she snapped his leash to his collar. "Come on, Mr. T. Time for a quick walk."

Instead of answering, Twink hopped to the control box sitting on the shelf below the television and nosed a button. The TV winked out, and he turned, tilting his head as he stared at her. *"Don't just stand there, fool. Let's go."*

Fifteen minutes later, Ellie returned the Jack Russell, collected her mail, and climbed the stairs. Once inside her apartment, she dumped the paltry postal offerings, unhooked her pal's lead, and headed for the kibble cupboard. It was obvious from Rudy's circling happy dance that he had supper on the brain. Still in her coat, she pulled out the extra hot dog from lunch, chopped it into small chunks, and added it to his dish. When she set the meal on the floor, he launched a full-face attack.

113

After hanging her outerwear, she dropped into a kitchen chair. With luck, she could change, eat dinner, read about the professor's death online, and tumble into bed by ten o'clock. Her cell phone rang, and she fished it out of her bag without checking caller ID. At this hour, it was probably her mother or Viv. "Hello."

"Is this Ellie Engleman?" The male voice was refined and polite, definitely not a woman.

"This is she."

"It's David Crane. Sorry I didn't get back to you sooner. Had to spend the afternoon with a sick cat. Your name is familiar. Have we met?"

A vivid picture of the veterinarian popped into her mind. On the short side, Dr. Dave had thinning wavy brown hair, hazel eyes, broad shoulders, and a flat stomach. His world-class butt made up for the male-pattern baldness, and she didn't mind staring him in the eye when they talked because she was positive he loved dogs.

"Twice. The first time was in your office, when I brought in my terrier-poodle mix. I'd just rescued him from the shelter—"

"Smallish, gray and white? He's not sick, is he?"

Wow. What a memory. "That's right, and Rudy's fine. I planned to call you after I had him a year to see if he needed vaccination updates. You and I met again three weeks ago, in the elevator at the Davenport."

A moment passed before he said, "I remember now. You're the new dog walker."

"That's me."

"Professor Albright was a customer of yours. It's a shame what happened to him." He hesitated. "Does this call have something to do with Buddy?"

"No. But now that you ask, it might. Buddy is missing, and I'm worried about him."

"Missing?"

"As in vanished without a trace." She almost slapped herself for not thinking of it sooner. "You must know all the animal gossip in the area. Any chance you've heard about someone getting a new bichon?"

"Are you saying the police think he ran away, and whoever found him is keeping him?"

"The police don't give a rat's, . . . er, . . . a plug nickel about Buddy. They've given me permission to search for him, but that's about it."

"He's a great dog, tops in his breed. There's no telling how much he's worth or—" He sighed. "What do you think happened to him?"

Beep! Beep! Beep!

Damn, she'd forgotten about her dwindling cell battery. "I'm not sure," she rushed. "All I know is he's disappeared, and the cops don't much care what happened to him."

"Keep me posted. I'd hate for any of my patients to be in trouble." He cleared his throat. "What did you need me for?"

115

Hoping to hook her phone to the charger, she jumped from her chair. "I have a customer in the Davenport. She wants a vet who makes house calls, and she's available early tomorrow morning or at six. You were the first vet I thought to ask."

"Thanks, but I'm not sure I can take another dog. My patient load is pretty full right now."

Searching the counter, she cursed mentally when she didn't find the charger. Where in the heck had she used it last?

Beep! Beep! Beep!

Frustrated, she spoke as quickly as she could. "Buckley's a Maltese-poodle mix, six, seven pounds, and he's healthy," she blathered, positive she sounded like a chipmunk on speed.

Dr. Dave laughed. "If you know anything about my practice, you'd know my four-legged clients aren't the problem."

"I don't think Ms. Blackberg will be too big a pain. She's in unit three-G."

She heard him flipping pages across the wire. "Hmm. Tomorrow morning's out, but I can do six o'clock. I'll stop by and take a look, though I'm not promising anything."

Beep! Beep! Beep!

"Great. I plan to be there, and I'll make a promise, too. I won't stick my nose where it isn't wanted."

"Not a problem, and I—"

Beep! Beep! Beeeeeeeeeeeeeeeeeeeep!

Glaring at the dead phone, Ellie heaved a breath. Then she walked into her bedroom, found the charger on her nightstand, and hooked up her cell. With any luck Dr. Dave would understand the abrupt disconnect was a mechanical failure.

Rudy ambled in and jumped next to her on the bed. Stroking his head, she met his brown-eyed gaze. "Yes?"

"He sounded okay."

"You heard him while we were talking?"

"How many times do I have to tell you, besides the superior nose, we have 'superior hearing.' And I'll let you know about his 'big bang' quotient after I check him out."

She rolled her eyes. "He's your vet, you dope. You've already met him—twice."

"Yeah, but that was right after you sprung me from the big house. And I didn't pay attention in the elevator. Too many smells to check out on that visit."

"Just remember, my love life is none of your business. The important thing is Dr. Dave's ability to give me referrals. I have no intention of checking out the 'big bang' theory with any man, and I'd appreciate it if you'd stop mentioning it."

Rudy hopped off the bed and trotted toward the door. *"If you say so."*

"I say so, and—" The pooch cocked his head, a threatening growl rumbling from his clenched muzzle. "What's the matter?"

"We're not alone."

"Who's out there?" she whispered.

"Hard tellin'. Better grab the nearest weapon."

Just her luck. With her mace sitting securely in the bottom of her purse on the kitchen table and her phone barely running, she had no choice. She picked up the baseball bat next to her dresser and tiptoed down the hall.

"It's about time you finished your call." Her mother's trembling voice hinted at disaster. "I was going to give you two minutes more, then leave a note and go home."

Ellie shot Rudy a glare. The little sneak knew exactly who'd walked into her apartment. What did he expect her to do? Bean her pushy parent with a Louisville Slugger?

"Mother, I didn't hear the buzzer." She set the bat in a corner of the living room and plopped onto the opposite end of the sofa. Maybe it was time she asked for the return of her keys? "It's kind of late for a chat, don't you think?"

Georgette appraised her through disapproving blue eyes. "Have you put on more weight?"

Ellie refused to sigh or indicate in any way that she'd heard the long-standing question. Her mother wore a size four, and couldn't understand why her only child had doubled her already-too-large size eight.

"Is something wrong at home?"

"Wrong?" Georgette's permanently sculpted eyebrows arched like two caterpillars preparing for battle. "Can't a mother stop to chat with her favorite daughter, especially since said daughter hasn't been to visit in over two weeks?"

She scanned her mother's ankle-high Roger Vivier boots, tailored wool slacks, and navy blue cashmere sweater, all visible through the parted folds of her crystal fox fur coat. Though dressed in her finest casual wear, Georgette's less than perfect makeup and wind-tunnel hairdo did not bode well.

"You don't usually leave the penthouse after dark unless—has something happened to Stanley?"

A tear brimmed from one brilliant sapphire eye, trickled down Georgette's cheek, and disappeared on the tip of her dainty chin. "I never could fool you, could I? You're right. It's the judge."

Ellie imagined all the horrible things that might occur to a wheelchair-bound eighty-three-year-old man. "Is it his heart? Did he have another stroke?"

"No, no. It's nothing like that." This time Georgette brushed away a tear before it slid past her nose. "He's—" She pulled a tissue from her Judith Lieber handbag. "He's asked me to marry him."

"Marry you?" Ellie quickly closed her mouth. Her mother was fast approaching Liz Taylor's record of seven, or was it eight, husbands. She never could keep it straight, and wondered if Liz ever had the same problem. Did Richard Burton count as a twofer? And what about—

"Honestly, Ellen Elizabeth, why do you find the idea of Stanley and me taking vows so shocking? We've lived together for over a year."

"Not shocking," Ellie fibbed. "But it is sort of— I mean, you're fifty-five and he's"—she did a fast calculation—"twenty-eight years your senior. That's quite a spread, don't you think?"

Georgette made a rude noise and punctuated it with a disdainful sniff. "Age is a number, nothing more. Plenty of men wed younger women, especially after failed first marriages. Look at Donald Trump, Kevin Costner, Kenny Rogers, Heinrich Applebaum—"

"Heinrich who?"

"Applebaum. He lived next door when I was married to Phillip. Heinz is still there, though he divorced that twenty-year-old supermodel long ago."

"What does that have to do with you and Stanley?" Ellie asked, regrouping her thoughts.

Georgette's lower lip quivered. "It's just that I never thought to marry again. And I really like Stanley. He's such a darling man."

"But do you love him?"

Her mother shrugged. "Of course, I do. But what if the same thing that happened with the others happens with the judge?"

"You think he'll cheat on you like Phillip did—"

"No, of course not."

"Drink himself sick every night or help himself to your bank account and disappear?"

"Stanley is a millionaire ten times over, and he can barely move his own wheelchair."

"Then what's the problem?"

"Don't you see?" Georgette asked after a long-suffering sigh. "For whatever reason, I'm afraid it won't work out, and he'll be devastated. I truly thought I could make his last days happy ones, but now . . ."

"You can't make him happy if you're married? Mother, that doesn't make sense. You and Daddy had a great life. You simply made the wrong choices with your next husbands." Each of Georgette's relationships had started on a joyous note. Unfortunately, after Ellie's father had died of a brain embolism at age forty, Phillip, Archibald, Preston, and Davis turned out to be bastards on a par with the D, which was one of the reasons her mother had been awarded such generous settlements in three of the decrees. "Besides, Stanley is well aware of your marital history. If he's willing to give it a go, why shouldn't you do the same?"

Her mother sniffed again, ignoring the question. "Can you believe it? The silly man doesn't even want a prenup. What am I going to do?"

"Talk him into the prenup, if it makes you feel better."

Rudy took that moment to hop onto the sofa and stretch out on her mother's fur. When Georgette frowned, he began licking his privates as if he were lapping a bowl of beef gravy. Giving a little shriek, she tugged the coat out from under him and pulled it close around her. "That animal is disgusting. I still say you should have gotten a cat."

"Rudy, off," Ellie chastised, picking the dog up and setting him on the floor.

"Told you she didn't like me."

"You're being too sensitive," she said, directing the comment to her pooch.

"That's a new one," her mother spouted. "Usually you tell me I'm not sensitive enough. Honestly, I wish you'd make up your mind."

Seemingly pleased that he'd made his point, Rudy settled on the floor at Ellie's feet while she ran rigid fingers through her curls, thinking. Georgette was insensitive, especially when it came to her only child. They might have formed a stronger bond had Ellie resembled her delicate, doll-like mother instead of her giant klutz of a dad. In fact, except for the color of her eyes, there wasn't one chromosome she could claim from her mother's exceptional string of DNA.

"Sorry. I've had a long day."

"I figured that out when you didn't return my phone messages. After I let myself in and heard you talking, I thought you might be entertaining. I didn't want to interrupt, so I decided to wait. Then I realized you were on the phone. Please tell me you were conversing with a man."

It was definitely time to change the locks. "I was speaking with Rudy's veterinarian. We're meeting at a client's home tomorrow."

"Don't tell me you're still trolling for customers to add to your dog-walking list?"

"It takes time to grow the type of business I'm starting. I need six more dogs just to pay the monthly mortgage on this place, and another eight to take care of the bills, including what I borrowed from you."

Georgette wrinkled her pert nose. "It's bad enough you're walking other people's dogs. Picking up excrement on a public sidewalk is simply demeaning."

Oh, boy. She was definitely too tired to wage this battle. "We've had this discussion a hundred times before. I perform a service people are willing to pay for. One that will allow me to be independent and live my own life."

"And how many dogs do you walk now?"

"I have four, possibly five, if things work out with a new client. I don't mean to be rude, but I'm exhausted. Maybe you should go."

"Five? Is that all?"

"I had another, but he's gone missing," she confessed. "Won't Stanley wonder what happened to you?"

Her eyes wide, Georgette skated right over the pointed question. "You lost a dog?"

"Uh, not exactly. The professor died and—"

"I tried to warn you about taking a job that required you to get personally involved with people."

"It wasn't like that—"

"What happened to the man's dog? Did it die, too?"

Sighing, Ellie filled her mother in on the situation with Buddy.

"I think I read about the incident in the paper, but the report never mentioned a dog. Just said the authorities considered the death suspicious." When Ellie didn't respond, her mother asked, "What aren't you telling me?"

Ellie had grown a set of balls since her divorce, but they shrank to the size of peas whenever her mother appeared. If she had any guts, she'd demand the return of her apartment keys, but owing Georgette for the money she'd lived on over the last year made that impossible. In fact, she was surprised the woman hadn't began her usual advice about finding a wealthy husband.

"Not a darned thing." Ellie sat upright on the sofa. "I really have to get to bed. I leave for my rounds at eight-thirty."

Georgette rose and straightened the lapels of the subtly shaded amber-and-cream fur, then fluffed her color-coordinated hair. "Very well, I'll go."

She clutched the Judith Lieber. "Maybe you can come for dinner one night this week? Say Friday? Stanley asks about you constantly, and I'd appreciate your input on our situation."

Her input? Since when? Ellie almost asked out loud. Regaining her senses, she made a demand she was certain would let her off the hook. "Only if I can bring Rudy."

"Fine," her mother replied without sparing the pup a glance. "Seven this Friday will be perfect."

"You're sure." A muscle in Sam's jaw twitched. "No one noticed a thing?"

"We talked to every resident on the floor, knocked on every door, even questioned a couple of prospective tenants in the lobby. I personally hung around until midnight so I could grill the doorman on the graveyard shift. Nobody saw jack." Liebowitz shook his head. "If the professor was murdered, a damn ghost did it."

"Have you talked to Jantzen about his contacts at the university?"

"Yeah, and it doesn't sound as if he's faring any better. Said to tell you he'd finish the questioning tomorrow and get you the details ASAP."

"Okay, fine. Drop the paperwork on my desk. I'll let you know if I need more."

The gangly officer did as requested and left. Sam frowned as he picked up the pages. Aside from his prime nonsuspect, he'd hit a dead end on every trail. He opened the file to start copying Liebowitz's findings to the pink sheets, and a vision of Ellie Engleman surfaced.

Sam cursed under his breath as the dreaded truth took hold. Whenever a female kept popping into his head, it usually meant one of two things: She was guilty of a crime, or she had horizontal potential. And since he was fairly certain the dog walker hadn't done in the professor . . .

Well, damn. If his love life hadn't been in the throes of a dry spell for the last year or so, he wouldn't be having such ridiculous thoughts. Once he caught up with work, he'd do something about it, though he had no idea what. He wasn't interested in one-night stands, and after his divorce, he sure as hell didn't want another serious relationship. Shrugging, he decided to worry about it later. He needed to go home and get some sleep.

His phone rang and he tossed the pencil on his desk. Still frowning, he figured he'd better answer it. In this business, a lead could come from anywhere at any time.

"Ryder."

"Sammy. Everyone's here and we've finished dinner. Are you going to make dessert?"

Rolling his eyes, he stared at the ceiling. "Sorry, Ma. I should have called. I'm afraid I won't be there tonight."

Her silent chastisement echoed over the line like

a bass drum. "When was the last time you ate a good meal?"

A month? Six weeks? Who the hell could remember?

"A day or so ago. Honest."

"You're lying. I can hear it in your voice."

"I'm eating all right. And I'm too busy to talk."

"I read there was a murder at one of those high-rises near the park. Did you get stuck with the case?"

"Stuck" about covered it. "That really isn't any of your business, Ma."

"I beg to differ. You're my only son. A mother has a right to know."

"I have a lot of cases. That's why I don't have time to come over." Where the hell were his sisters? "I thought Sherry and Susan were keeping you company."

"They're here. You want to say hello? Susan! It's your brother," Sam's mother screamed before he could stop her. "He wants to talk to you."

Great. Swell. Freakin' fine and dandy.

"Hey, big brother, we missed you tonight." Susan's nasal tone made him smile. "Your string of no-shows is giving Ma a weekly case of indigestion. I think Sherry's ready to kick in one of your kneecaps."

"Yeah, well . . . What'd you have for dinner?"

"Your favorite: roast beef, mashed potatoes, gravy, green beans dripping in butter, salad with

127

blue cheese dressing, and homemade apple pie fresh from the oven."

A heart attack on a plate, thought Sam. No wonder his dad had died of one. "That good, huh?"

"Fabulous. Tom's going off carbs for the rest of the week, but he says it's worth it. I'll just do a couple of extra miles on the treadmill, like usual."

Thanks to his father's health history, his younger sisters were diligent about their diet and exercise, though they avoided discussing it with their mother. The woman felt guilty enough whenever anyone brought up her husband's death.

"I'm sorry I missed it."

"You should be apologizing to Tom. As the only man at the table for the past month, he's threatening to shoot you—if he ever sees you again. With your luck, you'd probably have to investigate your own murder."

"Har-har." He hunched over his desk. "Look, tell Ma I'm sorry. Try to make her understand I'm swamped these days, but I'm fine."

"You don't sound fine. You sound tired and overworked, and I know you're underpaid."

"Tell it to the mayor." His gaze drifted to the mountain of paperwork on his desk. "I might be able to make it for Sunday brunch . . . if you and Sherry promise to show." He wasn't a coward, but there was safety in numbers. "Tom, too."

"Not this Sunday. Tom and I are going to the

Hamptons. There's a triathlon, and he's entered."

His brother-in-law was a physical-fitness nut masquerading as an attorney, while his sister worked at a local health club. Talk about a perfect match. "Great, thanks for your support."

"Sherry will be here. I think she's bringing a new guy."

"That ought to make Ma ecstatic." And keep her off his back for a while. "Tell her I'll do my best to be there."

"I'll give her the message. I have some news for you myself, by the way," she said in a hushed tone. "I wanted to tell you in person, but since you keep skipping forced family night, you'll have to hear it via the phone. You sitting down?"

"I guess I'd better be," he said with a laugh.

"You're going to be an uncle."

"Holy Christ!" Sam shot straight up in his chair. "Are you sure?"

"Three positive home-pregnancy kits later, I'm more than sure," she answered with a smile in her voice. "We haven't even told Ma yet, so keep it under your hat."

"Ma probably already knows. When?"

"In about seven and a half months. I'm seeing a doctor this week. After he gives me a due date, I'll spring the news."

"Let me know when you plan to make the announcement, and I'll be there."

"Uh-huh, sure."

"No, honest, I will." He crossed mental fingers. "Give me twenty-four hours' notice, and leave a message on my cell. I'll make it come hell or high water. Promise."

"I'm going to hold you to that. Oh, oh. Sherry and Ma are calling from the kitchen. Gotta go. Bye."

Sam hung up the phone. Well, damn. He was going to be an uncle. If nothing else it would keep his mother off his case for, say, the next couple years. If he was really lucky, she'd be so busy with a grandchild, she'd leave him alone until the kid graduated from high school. And if Susan had a few more, he'd be free and clear for the next two decades.

Standing, he eyed the Albright folder. He had an appointment with the professor's niece tomorrow morning at the apartment. When finished, he planned to hang around and have another go at the tenants. With luck, he'd catch the daunting dog walker in action, go over her story a third time, and appease his commanding officer by asking if she'd had any luck finding the mutt.

He had high hopes the niece, Ms. Victoria Pernell, would be able to tell him if anything was missing from the scene. If so, they'd have a motive that might lead to the killer.

If not, there was another theory to check out, but it was one he found hard to swallow.

Chapter 7

Ellie took Twink—make that Mr. T—off the lead and hustled him into his apartment after his morning walk. Viv was not an early riser and often had trouble giving her dog a proper outing before heading to work. Ellie didn't mind doing her friend a favor and seeing to the Jack Russell. Most of the time, the dog was a hoot, even with his new fixation on *The A-Team*.

After Viv locked her apartment door, the women and Rudy went outside and stopped in front of the building, where Viv studied Ellie's face with a knowing grin.

"Let me guess. You had a starring role in last night's horror flick, *Night of the Living Dead*."

Okay, thought Ellie, so her eyes were ringed with dark circles. Next time her mother stopped by late, she'd toss her out on her Prada-clad butt. "Thanks to a surprise visitor, I was awake past my bedtime." No exaggeration, because she'd considered Georgette's dilemma long after her mother had left for home. "You know I go to bed early."

Viv snorted before saying, "Don't expect any sympathy from me if that hunky detective decided to instigate another friendly interrogation."

"No, not Ryder. I doubt I'll have to deal with him again . . . unless I find Buddy."

"I hope he's taken you off his hit list in that

murder investigation, because I'm not looking forward to a monthly trip to Ossining or wherever the state sends felons these days."

"Cute." Ellie sighed. "The visitor was my mother."

"Really? What did the 'exterminator' want?" Viv's pet name for Georgette was a commentary on the woman's penchant for marrying men and turning them into ex-husbands as fast as Arnold had destroyed his movie victims.

"Stanley proposed."

Viv hmmphed her disapproval. "No offense, but your mom has the most unbelievable luck with men. What number will that make darling Stanley? Five? Six?"

"Six, and here's the kicker. Mother isn't sure she'll say yes. Can you believe it?"

"Not sure? Stanley's got to be a couple of years past eighty, so it's not like she'll have long to wait before she's single again." Viv turned up the collar on her trench coat. "And once he's gone, she'll be set for life."

"She's already set for a dozen lifetimes," Ellie pronounced, mentally calculating her mother's net worth. "If you want my opinion, I think she's afraid she'll be a jinx in this marriage. With Georgette, things aren't always clear."

"Thanks to her dedication to plastic surgery, the woman can be ditzy until she's a hundred, and she'll still find a man. Did that nut job painter—

Preston, was it?—ever show his face after the divorce?"

"Not that she said. Personally, I think he's living on an island somewhere in the Pacific, counting the money he pilfered from her bank account."

"Maybe. But it was spooky the way he just up and disappeared. Good thing she got rid of him before he took more than a half million, or the poor thing would be forced to buy off the rack, like the rest of us paupers." Viv slid her sunglasses to the tip of her nose and gave Ellie a look. "I have a suggestion, guaranteed to make you forget your shameless mother. How about meeting me for drinks and dinner tonight—seven o'clock at Harry's?"

The idea of another late evening sat at the very bottom of Ellie's to-do list, even if the bar was a local hangout fairly close to the apartment. "Sorry. Not a chance."

"Come on," Viv pleaded, rolling her grass green eyes. "It's been ages since we've done anything together. You need to get back into the swing of things, meet people, cut loose, and have some fun."

"I meet people when I walk my charges, and Rudy is all the fun I need right now."

"Then do it for me. We haven't had a girls' night out in forever, and I miss it."

Not spending time with Viv hadn't been Ellie's fault, so she asked the obvious question. "What happened to Jason?"

"Away on business. Please? I won't take no for an answer." Viv's discerning gaze took in Ellie's bulky jacket, faded jeans, and worn hiking boots. "And do me a favor. Wear something you didn't buy at the army surplus store. Whatever happened to that turquoise sweater I gave you for Christmas?"

The comment on Ellie's lack of fashion expertise sounded a warning bell in her brain. "It's folded neatly in my sweater drawer. And I just remembered I have an appointment."

"With who?"

"Myself, that's who." She bent to collect Rudy's morning 'gift.' "If I don't hit the sack on time, I'll fall asleep on my usual park bench tomorrow and get arrested for loitering. Not smart with Ryder on my tail."

"Then how about we forgo dinner and just have drinks at the Grotto? You can leave after one cosmopolitan."

Ellie stuffed the sealed bag in her coat pocket and crossed her arms. Viv was quite the actress. Her ploy might have worked, if she wasn't such a broken record. "I've got to hand it to you, you definitely deserve an 'A' for effort. If I didn't know you were one hundred percent Irish, I'd guess you learned how to manipulate from your Jewish mother."

Vivian huffed out a breath. "How do you consider trying to arrange a date for drinks or dinner with my dearest friend manipulative?"

"If it was just you, it wouldn't be, but I smell a rat." Ellie walked beside Viv, who wore a wounded expression as she sauntered to the subway entrance. "Let me say it one more time: I'm not interested in meeting a man, no matter how attractive they or their bank balances appear."

"How can a night out with a couple of nice men hurt?" Viv asked, her voice almost a whine. "If you don't like them, I'll even leave with you. See what a good friend I am? I'm willing to give up a free dinner to keep you happy."

Ellie stopped in her tracks. "Does Jason know you're dating when he's out of town?"

"We've yet to talk about mutual exclusivity, so it's none of his business. Besides, I'm doing this for you."

"Sure you are. What I don't understand is why my love life has suddenly become everyone's business." Ellie glanced at Rudy, who gave her the doggie version of a shrug. "It's not like I'm a thirty-year-old virgin or anything."

"You might as well be," Viv said with a sniff. "When Georgette guarantees to find you a sugar daddy, I'll stop pestering, though I really can't see you with an eighty-year-old invalid. Please, say yes. Dwayne is a lawyer, and Mark is a stock-broker. I'll even let you stake your claim first, *after* you meet them. How's that for being a pal?"

"Pals don't nag," Ellie reminded her. Since her

divorce, lawyers gave her hives, and she'd always believed that the pressure-filled job of a stockbroker had stressed her father to the max, contributing, she suspected, to his early death. "Besides, I'm seeing someone tonight, right after my last walk," she countered, stretching the truth. "Someone I met without any help from a friend."

"Oh, really? Who?" Viv asked, her eyes shadowed in doubt.

"A veterinarian by the name of David Crane."

"A vet? How old? Is he good-looking? Tall? He must have money because animal-care costs in this city are out of sight. How did you meet him?"

"Dr. Dave is a nice man, thirtysomething, my height, and he loves dogs. What more could I ask for?"

"I don't remember you talking about Rudy's vet."

"I've only met him twice professionally, once when I brought Rudy home, and again in the elevator of the Davenport. Who do you use for Mr. T?"

"You mean Twink?"

"Yeah, Twink, though we've—I've started calling him Mr. T. He seems to . . . um . . . like it better."

Viv cocked her head, much like Rudy did when he was thinking. "Hmm. I'll have to try that. The little stinker never comes when he's called these days."

"About that vet?" Ellie reminded her.

Viv stared at her Manolos. "I haven't taken him to anyone for a couple of years." Before Ellie read her the riot act, she held up a hand. "I know, I know, so skip the lecture. I'm an irresponsible owner, I don't care for my pet, yada, yada, yada."

"I don't get it. You take him to the Ritzy Canine Carriage all the way over on Fortieth when you travel, bring him to the Tomy Maugeri Dog Salon on Eighty-first for grooming, yet you can't get him to the vet for a yearly physical?"

"T deserves those pricey places."

"T deserves basic medical care with a good vet first," Ellie snapped. "I'll ask Dr. Dave if he has time to give Mr. T a quick exam and make sure his shots are current. Do you have his health records?"

"Somewhere in the apartment. I'll find them." Viv eyed her watch. "Uh-oh, gotta run. You'll take him for me, won't you?" she called as she headed down the subway stairs. "You set it up, and I'll write the check. Just let me know when. I'll phone you later."

Ellie shook her head as her friend disappeared. How could a person profess to love their dog and not make sure it had yearly checkups, or a vet at the ready in case of an emergency? Even Vivian, who knew better, was a lax parent. Now she expected someone else to handle her Jack Russell's health care. Glancing down, Ellie locked gazes with Rudy. Was he frowning?

"T deserves better."

"Oh, come on," she answered as she headed for Bruiser's building. "Viv's a good mom, just forgetful. You know that."

"T says some days his water dish is empty, and he doesn't always get a breakfast nibble."

"She has a lot on her mind. I might be the same way, if you didn't remind me." She led him to Fifth and turned north toward the Beaumont. "Now let's beat feet. We're late."

They arrived at her newest client's apartment, and Ellie pasted a smile on her face and walked in, prepared to introduce herself to the day-shift doorman. "Hi, I'm Ellie Engleman, here to walk the Bests' pom. 6-A?" She cricked her neck to meet the hulk's deep-set gray eyes, noting he topped Kronk by about three inches and fifty pounds. "They were supposed to leave the key and a permission form."

"Name's Natter. They gave the okay. You got ID?"

She dug her wallet out and waited while he read the fine print on her license. When he passed her the key, she handed him a half dozen business cards. "If you hear of anyone else in the building needing a dog walker, I'd appreciate it if you gave them one of these."

"I'll do what I can." He stuffed the cards in his pocket. "Mr. Best said this was a trial week. Guess Bibi finally wore out her welcome."

Ellie couldn't help herself; she had to ask. "What exactly did Bibi do to get on the Bests' bad side?"

"Always late, for one thing. And the family has two kids. Bibi promised to pick them up from school and escort them home a couple of times, then never showed. People might get angry when their dogs mess the carpet, but they're downright furious when their kids are put on a back burner."

"I don't blame them. See you in a few minutes." She led Rudy to the elevator, storing the bit of gossip in her brain. Once inside, her canine companion was strangely quiet. "What's wrong? Don't you like Bruiser?"

"What's not to like? He just doesn't say much."

"That's a relief. He was so quiet yesterday, I thought maybe it was me."

They trotted to 6-A and unlocked the door. "Bruiser, you ready to go?"

The ball of red-and-gold fluff didn't show, so she strode inside. Was that a doggie whimper coming from the back of the apartment? "Hey, Bruiser, It's time for your walk."

"I don't like this," Rudy announced. *"Something's up."*

Setting off down the hall, Ellie peeked into rooms as she made her way to the far end of the unit. She didn't enjoy invading a customer's private space, but the Bests were paying her to do a job, and a good reputation was important in this type of business.

Ellie froze at the sound of another whimper, and Rudy rumbled a soft but threatening growl.

"Bruiser? Where are you?"

Inching the last few steps to the final room, she peered around the doorway, prepared to care for a sick pomeranian, or maybe the little guy's collar was caught and he couldn't get free. Instead, she found a woman, dressed in overalls and a battered parka, sitting in a large wing-back chair in the corner of what appeared to be a study with the agitated dog on her lap.

"Bibi?" The pooch struggled to break free, but Bibi held him fast. "What are you doing here?"

"Waiting to have a talk with you, of course." Bibi was done up in her usual pale foundation and black-rimmed eyes; her thin lips, also lined in black, wore a scowl. "You're two minutes late. The Bests won't like that."

"I had to introduce myself to Natter and collect the key." Why the heck was she explaining her schedule to a competitor? A fired competitor, at that. "Are you supposed to be here?"

Bibi gave a nasty-sounding chuckle. "Hey, they'll never know. After all I did for this family, I still can't believe they let me go." She spat out the words. Bruiser growled and Bibi squeezed his muzzle with fingers tipped in black nail lacquer. "Shut up, you little prick."

Ellie threw back her shoulders and advanced a step. "Maybe you should discuss this with Mr. and Mrs. Best. Right now, my job is to take Bruiser for his morning walk."

"Eugene guessed you were the one who stole this gig from me, but I was willing to give you the benefit of the doubt," she answered in a sour tone. "Next time, I'll know better."

Great, now she had two enemies. "They were a referral from a friend," said Ellie, trying to play nice. "It might not work out. This is just a trial week."

"So you say," Bibi snarled, much like some of her charges. Still clutching Bruiser's muzzle, she ran her free hand through her spiky black hair. "Personally, I have a plan to get this guy and the others back."

The others? "How did you get in? Natter is downstairs, and he never said—"

"This dog isn't the only one I walk in the building. I brought up the others, then came here to wait for you. Besides, what do you care?"

"I care," Ellie told her, "because I'm the one who's now responsible." She raised a brow in question. "Didn't they ask you to return your key?"

"'Didn't they ask you to return your key?'" Bibi repeated in a mocking falsetto. "Eugene is right. You are clueless."

"Are you saying you make duplicate keys of

your clients' homes? That's illegal." And against every rule governing the dog-walking profession. "The Bests could go to the police."

"Sure they could, but I'd deny it. In fact, as far as I'm concerned we never had this conversation." She stood, and dropped the pom to the floor, and Bruiser raced to Ellie's feet. "Go on, take him out. I'll see you later."

Without thinking, Ellie stepped in front of her competitor as she sauntered past. "You'd better hand that key to Natter on the way out. If anyone knew you did this—"

"Hey," Bibi said, her brown eyes fixed in a spooky sort of stare, "don't stick your nose in my business." She stormed around Ellie, knocking her in the shoulder as she left. "And don't say I didn't warn you when the shit hits the fan."

"Any word on Buddy?" Ellie asked Randall when she entered the Davenport forty-five minutes later.

"Nothing. But a number of people are looking for him. Kronk, especially, is bent on success, though I'm fairly certain he's more interested in reaping a reward than he cares about the bichon's safety."

"Have to agree with you there," she commented. Visions of Bibi, and possibly Eugene, abusing more of their charges danced in her brain. "I met Bibi at the Beaumont, and I wonder, has she been in today?"

"Much earlier," Randall said, opening the door for a resident, "with Eugene. Neither of them said a word, of course. Just did their jobs and left, or I think they did. There's so much activity in the morning, I don't always notice. Have you had a chance to look at that list I gave you?"

She shook her head. "Sorry. I've been too busy, but I will. I assume the usual suspects have been here every day? No one's suddenly disappeared since the professor was killed?"

"As I said, I don't always see the Liquid Ice man, or the others who deliver via the service elevator. I assume the rest have been in and out."

"Come to think of it, I usually see that guy once in a while, too. Was the professor one of his customers?"

Randall walked to his desk and checked the list. "He was, and the police have his name."

"Okay, then. I guess that's good enough." She rested her elbows on the counter. "Can I ask you a question?"

He tipped his hat as another couple left the premises. "Detective Ryder has been upstairs for nearly an hour, if that's what you need to know. I believe he's with the professor's niece from New Jersey."

She'd planned to make a stop on Buddy's floor, just to check things out, but Randall's report told her now wasn't a good time. "Thanks for the warning, but it's not about Ryder. It's about Bibi

. . . and Eugene." Why not continue gathering information on the creepy gay guy, just in case he and the creepy Goth girl were partners in crime? "When they lose a customer, do you collect their keys, or is that the tenant's responsibility?"

"In the end, it's the tenant's job, but I've had to ask for the keys in a few cases." He leaned in close. "And Bibi and Eugene aren't the only walkers doing business in this building. Have you met Fred?"

" 'Fraid not. Who is he?"

"An older fellow, works mostly part-time when a few of the tenants go on vacation. The professor used him once, and so did the Burmeisters. But they were so annoyed after he walked their dog they refused to speak to Fred personally, asked me to give him their letter of termination. Touchy situation, that."

"Have you ever heard of anyone using Bibi or Eugene complain about a theft or mention objects were missing from their apartment?"

The dapper doorman tilted his head. "No. But that doesn't mean it hasn't happened. Some of these people have units full of collectibles, things they've amassed over years of living here. I doubt they'd realize anything was stolen unless they went over their inventory on a weekly basis." He crossed his arms. "Do you know something I should know?"

"Not exactly." She sidled toward the elevator

and pressed the CALL button. "I'm running a little late. I accepted a new dog a few blocks from here, at the Beaumont, and I'm scheduled to do him first."

"Congratulations," he said as the door closed.

Ellie rode up in silence, her brain working full speed. As Buddy's previous caretaker, Eugene had plenty of opportunity to make a duplicate key to Professor Albright's apartment. He'd probably returned a key when the professor let him go, but kept the copy. If so, it was plausible he could have done his usual run at the Davenport, then entered the professor's apartment without anyone's knowledge. And maybe Fred, a guy she'd never met, had kept a key, too.

"I don't know about Fred, but Eugene isn't smart enough."

Ellie started at Rudy's mental intrusion. "Are you reading my mind?"

"Duh, no. What do you think I am? Psychic?"

"Duh, yes," Ellie argued, leading her pal onto Jett's floor and marching to his unit. "What else would you call what I . . . what we can do?"

"I'd call it being in tune with each other."

She rolled her eyes. "How about we stay in tune only when asked? I don't poke around in your mind and you agree not to poke around in mine."

"Sorta takes all the fun out of life, don't it?"

Ignoring his questions, she opened Jett's door and squatted. As the Scottie neared, she caught the

145

scent of roses. "You smell great. Been to a new groomer?"

"Just Celia," he intoned dourly. *"If you ask me, I smell like a brothel at midnight."*

"Really? And you recognize the aroma because . . ."

Jett sneezed his displeasure. *"The old girl used to work in one—talk about the big bang. Of course, that was a long time ago. I was a pup, but I remember."*

At the sound of the "big bang," Ellie gave Rudy the evil eye. "Celia can't be a day past forty. And she does not resemble a hooker. Where was this place, anyway?"

"Our last apartment. Three women lived there, and men were coming and going at all hours while us dogs had to sleep in kennels in the kitchen, listening to the intimate racket—not to mention the smells." He twitched his tail. *"It's been a lot better since she quit the business."*

Celia Farnsworth—a prostitute? The woman had always appeared the height of elegance and social standing, rivaling Georgette in sophistication, expensive clothing, and perfect manners. Leading the dogs into the hall, Ellie locked the apartment door. "I thought Celia came from money, maybe through an inheritance or a divorce settlement."

"Hah! That's a good one," quipped Jett.

Conceding that Celia's past was none of her business, and if it were true, the other dogs didn't need to hear it, Ellie warned him to keep his thoughts to himself and headed for the next apartment. Her canines were already as nosy and judgmental as humans. They didn't need any encouragement.

After collecting Buckley, Sweetie Pie, and Stinker, she took the elevator to the main floor, waved at Randall, and made a beeline for the park. The brilliant blue sky and crisp spring breeze made the morning exceptionally pleasant, which helped to clear Ellie's head. Sprawling Central Park, with its budding leaves and almost-open flowers, beckoned.

A short while later, everyone had taken care of business, gotten exercise, sniffed butt, and participated in all the usual doggie dynamics.

"Okay, last snurffle, then we start for home." Ellie smiled at an elderly passerby, who shook his head when she spoke out loud. "Sorry. I can't help talking to them."

"I can see why. They're a handful, but they seem very well-behaved."

"They are." She gave the man a couple of her cards. "If you know anyone looking for a dog walker in this area, tell them to give me a call, or they can find me here about this time every morning. Most of my clients come from the Davenport, but I'm willing to travel a few blocks north or south."

He tipped his hat. "Will do."

After delivering the last of her charges and writing their progress notes, she crossed her fingers. An hour had passed. The professor's cousin and Ryder had to be through taking inventory by now. She rode to Buddy's floor and skulked down the hall. Suddenly appalled by her criminal-like behavior, she squared her shoulders. If anyone saw her sneaking around, they'd think she was guilty of something, especially Ryder.

Standing in front of the professor's apartment, she inspected the door, taped top and bottom with some kind of plastic coating. Then she put her ear to the panel.

"Exactly what are we listening for?"

Jumping back, she gasped. "I'm trying to find out if that detective is still inside, so be quiet."

"Then step aside and allow me," Rudy said, a smirk gracing his canine lips.

She opened and closed her mouth.

"Superior hearing, remember?" Cocking his head, he perked his ears. A full thirty seconds passed before he said, "The place is empty. Want me to scratch off the tape so we can go inside?"

"Are you crazy?" She dragged trembling fingers through her hair. "If anyone caught us, I'd be arrested for sure. Then where would we be?"

"Don't know about you, but I'd be home sitting on a nice cozy sofa, sound asleep."

"That's what you think. They'd probably put you back in the big house. Want to do time there again?"

Rudy shuddered. *"Okay, okay. But if we're not going inside, why are we here?"*

She raised a shoulder in an "I don't know" gesture. "I just thought that maybe the police had overlooked something in their investigation." Or maybe someone with a key, say Eugene, had found Buddy, and brought him back.

"Not in this lifetime," Rudy said. *"The jerk doesn't have enough heart."*

Leaning a shoulder against the wall, she gave the matter serious consideration. Then she decided to check the tape more thoroughly. Maybe a corner had come loose and needed to be smoothed back in place. Getting an adhesive coating to stick could be tricky, especially if *someone* scraped it with a foot. She ran the tip of her sneaker across the tape. Or there was an inordinate amount of humidity in the air. She took a bottle of water from her bag and drizzled a little on the bottom of the door. Who knew what might cause the tape to come off?

Rudy growled low in his throat, and she ignored him. After a third rub with the tip of her shoe, she poured more water on the tape.

A deeper growl made her *tsk*. "For God's sake be quiet. Can't you see I'm busy here."

"Um, Ellie—"

"Hush up and keep your comments to yourself." She bent at the waist and ran her fingers across the covering, noting it hadn't budged. Maybe a penknife would be sharp enough to break the seal.

Before she came to a conclusion, the hairs on her nape stood on end. Peering between her ankles, she spied a pair of men's dress shoes, large but not overly so, and worn but nicely shined.

The man cleared his throat and visions of her sitting in a dank, musty cell somewhere in the Big Apple danced in her brain. Swallowing, she rose slowly and rested her forehead on the door.

Chapter 8

Just when Sam thought his day couldn't get any more interesting, he stepped off the elevator and spotted Ellie Engleman, bent at the waist in front of Albright's apartment, her curvy butt reeling him in like the lure on a fishing line.

At first, he told himself he had it wrong. No way was the woman trying to break into the professor's home. When she started fiddling with the crime tape, rubbing it with her toe, dousing it with bottled water, he about shit a brick. She was a nut job. An idiot. She was insane.

She was out to get herself arrested.

Counting to ten, he made his way down the hall. Her pooch saw him coming, got an evil glint in its eyes, and glared as if to say, "Take one step closer, and I'll rip your face off." And even though the mutt's growl deepened the closer Sam got, the fool woman kept muttering as she concentrated on the door.

He stopped a yard away, angled himself directly behind her, and gave her shapely butt another once-over. "Disturbing a crime scene is a felony, Ms. Engleman. If you continue tampering with that tape, I'll be forced to arrest you for breaking and entering."

He smirked when she froze, straightened slowly, and rested her head on the door. Then she smacked her forehead against the panel a couple of times in a deliberate, measured, and totally certifiable manner.

"Hurt yourself if it makes you feel better. Just don't blame me when I haul you in."

She spun around and gave him a smile as phony as a knockoff Rolex. "Detective Ryder, fancy meeting you here."

Fancy my ass. His fingers itched to grab her and shake some sense into her. Instead, he rested a palm on the doorframe, caged her in on one side, and caught the flicker of worry in her eyes. "What are you doing here?"

The picture of innocence, she blew a stray curl from her forehead. "I was hoping to meet the professor's niece and talk to her about Buddy."

"Did you knock?"

"I did, but no one answered."

"That should have been your first clue. Ms. Pernell has already been and gone."

"Oh . . . uh . . . well, thanks for telling me." She licked her full lower lip. "Did she ask about

Buddy? Tell you how to proceed in his search, or give you instructions on what to do if . . . when you find him?"

Victoria Pernell was a thin woman with a nose that could double as a letter opener and a figure like a ruler. Her beady brown eyes had worked over the apartment at warp speed as she tallied the contents while jotting notes and snapping pictures. The disagreeable woman even warned him that she'd know if a single thing was disturbed or stolen, so the NYPD had better beware. And she didn't care jack about her uncle's prized possession.

"Not exactly."

"What does that mean?"

"It means she doesn't expect us to go out of our way to find the dog."

"Was she going to the ASPCA? The one on Ninety-second is the closest, but there are other places—"

"I doubt it."

"But what about Buddy? What if I find him and he's injured or—or—"

"She's not interested in the dog, Ms. Engleman. Seems she hated that her uncle wasted money on its upkeep and show costs. She also thinks he's dead or lost, but if he were here, she'd sell him to the highest bidder. Since he isn't . . ."

Ellie's face crumpled and tears glistened in her eyes. "That's . . . that's unconscionable. Did you check her pulse, because my guess is she doesn't have a heart."

"Just because you think dogs are four-legged humans doesn't mean everybody feels the same."

"That's the problem with this world. No one gives a damn anymore. Did you read about the thousands of dogs exterminated in China a few years ago, just because the fools didn't have sense enough to stock the right amount of rabies vaccine?" Her mouth turned prim as a grade-school principal's. "If that's how the Chinese treat their innocent animals, imagine how they treat their people."

He held up a hand, hoping to stop her before she took the rant further. "I'm not here to debate the evils taking place in a foreign country on another continent. My job is to find out how Professor Albright met his Maker."

"Quite the humanitarian, aren't you?"

When he didn't answer, she inched sideways. "Have you given any more thought to my theory—find Buddy and you'll find the killer?"

He pushed away from the door. "I'm still waiting on toxicology and the other test results before I know for certain he was murdered," he said, giving her as much info as he could. "I tie up all the loose ends before I jump to conclusions."

"Might I remind you that if the killer knows the professor is dead, he'll also realize he has no hope of a reward. That will be Buddy's death knell."

"We've checked the phone line and his mail. There hasn't been a single ransom note or phone call, so my guess is the dog's already outlived his usefulness."

"I refuse to accept that he's dead. I think someone stole him, and that someone could only have been the person who killed Professor Albright."

Sam ran a hand through his hair. Ellie Engleman might have a point, except for one thing: Why would someone commit a dognapping if there was no chance for a ransom? "Let's say I buy your theory. If they killed Albright, what could they possibly hope to gain by keeping the dog?"

"Maybe they didn't start out to steal him, but when they didn't find anything else of value in the apartment, they just grabbed Buddy and ran."

"Doesn't make sense. The professor had artwork the niece says is worth a lot of money, ditto some antique vases and a small sculpture. They would have been way easier to haul out than a squirming mutt."

"Then we have to think of a sensible reason why—"

"There is no 'we.' You have nothing to do with this case."

She rested her hands on her hips. "Can I continue to look for Buddy?"

"Be my guest." Anything to keep her out of his hair, not to mention appeasing his captain. "Just let me know if you find him, and I'll take it from there."

She jutted her chin, as if to say, "Yeah, right."

"What's his niece planning to do with the apartment?"

"After we're through with the investigation, she'll hold a tag sale. She has a friend in the antiques business who'll come in and give an appraisal. Then she'll set up a date and put out the word."

"How soon will that be?"

"In a month or so. Why? Are you interested in anything special?"

She gazed at her sneakers, then looked him in the eye. "I might want to buy a few pieces."

The woman couldn't lie her way out of a paper bag. "Your apartment appeared pretty well-stocked to me."

"You didn't see the den or my bed—the rest of the rooms." Her cheeks turned pink. "And you won't, unless you think I stole Buddy."

"I highly doubt you have the dog." *But you do have a few screws loose.* "Why were you trying to get into the apartment? And bear in mind telling the truth right about now might keep you out of jail."

Straightening her shoulders, she gave her shoes another inspection. "The professor had an original of the photo I printed off the other night, and I was hoping to borrow it and make a copy as a keepsake. Now that I know his niece is holding a tag sale, I'll buy it there."

"Maybe I can arrange for you to get the picture for free."

"That's very kind of you."

"I try." He rocked back on his heels. "I have a question. Which officer did you give your copy of the professor's key to the other morning?"

"Um, I'm not sure. I'm certain Officer Martin would remember, or maybe the other patrolman. Why do you ask?"

"It's my job." He raised a brow. "How about pulling out your key ring and letting me take a look . . . just to be sure?"

Her cordial expression closed like a slammed door. She huffed a breath.

He held out his hand.

She dug in her pocket, found the ring, and passed it over.

After plugging a few keys in the lock, he grinned when one worked. "Well, what do you know? Good thing I checked, or Martin might be in trouble for not following procedure." Slipping the key off the holder, he dropped it into his pocket. "Thanks."

Her jaw clenched. "You're welcome."

"Since we're done here, can I escort you to the lobby?"

She gave a curt nod, and they walked to the elevator, where he pressed the CALL button.

Glancing down, he frowned at her dog, who was still eyeing him as if he were a serial rapist. "Does he always look like that?"

She followed his gaze and quirked her lips. "Rudy's an excellent judge of character."

The thought made Sam cringe inside. "What's that supposed to mean?"

"Let's just say I use him as a guide."

"I smell the big bang, Triple E. And it's enough to power a nuclear explosion."

Ignoring Rudy, she wrinkled her nose. "Though he can sometimes be wrong."

"Not that I care, but I don't think he likes me."

"Whatever gave you that idea?"

The elevator arrived, and they stepped inside. "For one thing, he keeps staring at me as if I'm some kind of threat."

"You are a threat," she said, pressing the button.

"To who?"

"Me. He's very protective."

"Just so long as he doesn't decide to use his teeth."

"Unless you make a hostile move, he'll never bite, but he would show disapproval. Growling is the canine way."

"Well, he's done the canine thing the last couple of times we met. You think he'd be over it by now."

They reached the lobby level, and he let her out first. The jacket hung over her ass, but he'd already committed the curves to memory, so he followed her to the doorman's desk. "Mr. Graves, have you done as I suggested and kept a list of the people who've asked about the professor?"

Randall nodded and handed him a sheet of paper. "As you can see, I've already amassed quite a log. Do you want me to continue?"

Sam folded the pages and stuffed them in his pocket. "Sure, why not?" Turning to leave, he remembered an important point. "We collected your key to Albright's apartment, right?"

"I gave a key to Officer Martin the morning of the incident."

"Okay, fine." He directed his gaze at Ellie, who was staring at her dog in a totally nutso manner. "Remember what I said, Ms. Engleman, and let me know if you find Buddy. That's all you're allowed to do. Just look for the dog."

She bit her lower lip and nodded, and he headed out the door, fairly satisfied with the way the morning had gone. Things would be damn near perfect if only Ellie Engleman would get off this case and stick to walking her charges.

"At least he got Buddy's name right," Ellie commented after Ryder strode from the building. "That's one plus."

Randall expelled a breath. "Are all officers of the law so—so—anal?"

"I think it's a requirement of the job," she

answered, propping an elbow on the counter. "If it makes you feel any better, Rudy doesn't care much for him, either."

"Most dogs are excellent judges of character."

She shrugged. "Too bad about your key. I was kind of hoping I could use it to go inside the apartment and take a look around. You know, just to see if anything was out of place."

A grin radiated from Randall's ruddy face. He offered her his palm. "Perhaps this one will work just as well."

"You have an extra?" she asked, her heart skipping a beat.

"It's only prudent I have extra keys, in case a tenant misplaces theirs. The good detective merely asked if I'd returned a key, not *every* copy." He tucked the key inside his jacket pocket. "I took it upon myself to fudge the truth . . . in case something was amiss."

"There's tape covering the professor's door. If I went in now, Ryder would know it was me."

"Then wait a day or so. I'll phone you the minute I'm certain the coast is clear, and you can take a look-see yourself." He sniffed. "Who knows what a cleaning crew can do in a hallway late at night? If the detective asks, I'll simply pass that along, and he can draw his own conclusions."

Ellie beamed in approval. "Why, Randall, who would have figured you to be so devious?"

"Who, indeed?"

She turned from the counter, her smile still firmly in place. "It's lunchtime, and I have work to do. Last night, I printed Buddy's picture from his MSG win on my computer. I'm bringing a couple more flyers to the ASPCA, but I'll be back later. See ya."

She didn't get more than three feet out of the Davenport before Rudy pronounced, *"Be careful around that cop, Triple E. Besides the rampaging pheromones, he has shifty eyes."*

Shifty no, smoldering yes, Ellie thought, then tamped down her thoughts on Ryder's eyes. Eyes that had appraised her from head to toe and back again in what had seemed like a purely male manner. Recalling the way his full-body inspection had made her warm all over, she filed the impression away for later scrutiny and glanced at her furry pal, trotting obediently at her side.

Rudy had protecting her on his brain, but she could take care of herself, even though it was nice to know he looked out for her the way she looked out for him.

Filled with a warm, fuzzy feeling for her pal, she led him across the street to their favorite lunchtime vendor. "Hey, Pops, one plain, one with kraut and mustard, and a diet Coke."

The wizened street merchant made change and passed her the order, then nodded toward the Davenport. "I see things have quieted down since the other day. Any word on Buddy?"

"Unfortunately, no." Ellie picked a clump of sauerkraut from her wiener and popped it in her mouth. "I guess you haven't seen him on the street?"

Pops scratched his stubbled chin. "Nope. Sorry. You been to the shelter?"

"Once, but I'm going again, after I eat. Anything can happen in twenty-four hours. Just keep on the lookout, okay?"

She and Rudy went to their usual bench, and she set his treat beside her. Rudy cocked his head, his expression pleading, and she rolled her eyes in return. "You're a dog. The rules say you're supposed to eat second."

"Rules, schmools. We're buddies . . . like Timmy and Lassie, Rusty and Rin Tin Tin, Asta and Nick Charles—"

"In case you haven't noticed, I'm a female."

"Ryder's noticed."

"Forget Ryder, and concentrate on Buddy. Where would you go if you ran away?"

"Me, I wouldn't. Maybe Buddy got sick of the high life, saw the open door, and went looking for adventure."

"Something tells me that's not what happened." Breaking off a section of the extra wiener, she tossed it in the air. "Here, and try chewing this time."

Rudy caught the treat on the way down and swallowed it after two bites. Ellie was about to throw him another hunk when a familiar shadow fell across her knees. Raising her head, she locked gazes with one of the homeless residents of Central Park.

"Hey, Gary. What's up?"

Gary, a man of indeterminate age, focused on the remainder of the hot dog. "Not much. Is Rudy gonna eat that?" His dour expression, crusted in dirt and bits of vegetable matter Ellie didn't want to think about, screamed of starvation. " 'Cause I'm hungry today. Maybe you could ask Rudy for me?"

She raised a brow in Rudy's direction.

"Sure. Fine. Whatever."

She passed Gary the wiener. "He says you can have it."

"Tell Rudy thank you." Gary wolfed down the hot dog, then dropped onto the bench, stretched out his legs, and gave a toothless smile. "He's a good friend."

Ellie glanced at Gary's sneakered feet, the biggest she'd ever seen on a normal-sized man. The worn red Nike high-tops had to be a size fifteen, maybe more, even though he stood eye level with her five foot eight. Then again, they could have been three sizes too big and wadded with newspaper, but they were all Gary could find in the way of footwear. Guys like him didn't have the luxury of being choosy.

"Rudy's the best. Did you ever own a dog?"

"Nuh-uh, not me," he confided. "My mama

used to say dogs were dirty and full of fleas."

If only your mama could see you now, thought Ellie. "Not my boy," she told him instead. "I give him a bath, clip his nails, and douse him with flea repellent every month. He's probably cleaner than you—er—most people."

"That's good, 'cause fleas aren't nice." He scratched his chest in an intimate demonstration. "They bite."

Ellie moved a few inches away. "Good thing for you the weather got warmer, huh? You were probably freezing in your cardboard shelter."

"Not after you gave me that blanket." He flashed his gums a second time. "You're a nice lady, Ellie." He rubbed his nose, and she spied a bit of skin peeking out from behind the grime. "Say, I got me a pair of almost new curtains for my window from a Dumpster behind the Duane Read. You wanna come see 'em?"

"Maybe some other time. I have to go to the shelter and ask about Buddy." She couldn't believe she'd forgotten to ask the homeless man about the bichon. "You know Professor Albright is dead, don't you? And his dog is missing?"

"The little white one with the funny haircut? The one you said was a champion?"

"That's him. Have you seen him inside the park or on the street? He's been missing for a couple of days, and I'm worried something bad's happened to him."

"If I did, I woulda brought him home with me until I saw you and given him to you—honest I would have. I know he's one of yours now, and not mean Eugene's."

"That's good to hear. Keep a lookout, okay?"

"Uh-huh." Gary's mud brown gaze darted across the street to a pair of young men arguing loudly as they stood side by side on the corner. When a police cruiser pulled up, he mumbled, "Them guys is nothin' but trouble."

Ellie peered over the traffic. "Do you know those two?"

"I just seen 'em around. I don't like people who are mean or do bad things."

"Bad like how?"

The men joked with the cops, then crossed Fifth and headed into the park. Gary jumped to his feet and walked in the opposite direction. "I gotta go now, but the next time you're here, promise you'll come to my house. I got lots of new stuff to show you." He walked backward as he spoke. "Okay, Ellie? Promise?"

"Sure, fine, just be careful in there. I hear guys still deal drugs in some out-of-the-way places."

Gary shuffled off as if he hadn't heard the warning, his clown-sized sneakers slapping the pavement. Ellie had only been to his foliage-covered cardboard box once this past winter, and remembered he lived somewhere in the bowels of the park. Wondering what brought a man to such a sorry state, she made ready to go to the animal shelter.

"If you ask me, his mama was a real ball buster," chimed Rudy, again reading her thoughts.

"Some mothers are like that," she agreed, thinking fleetingly of Georgette. Her mother hadn't always been so judgmental and interfering; those charming personality traits had only surfaced after Ellie's father died. Obsessed with the state of their finances and her ability to put a daughter through college, she'd made it her personal quest to marry a wealthy man. Archie Brewster, their attorney and family friend, had been more than happy to fill the bill as husband number two.

His and Georgette's divorce two years later, coupled with her own unhappy marriage to the D, only supported Ellie's belief that money wasn't the most important thing when searching for the right man.

Hands on her knees, she stood and asked, "You ready to visit the ASPCA?"

"I hate that place."

"Me, too. Whenever I'm inside, I get this crazy urge to free all the prisoners and bring them home." She sighed. "Totally stupid, I know."

"You got that. Our apartment won't hold another dog."

"Not even a cute little girly-girl poodle or shih tzu?"

"You had me snipped and clipped, remember?" he grumped. *"Thanks for that, by the way."*

"I did what any responsible pet owner should do if they don't plan to breed their dog."

"Maybe so, but it might be nice if someone made a condom for us canines. Then we could keep our manhood intact and experience the big bang whenever we wanted, just like humans."

Canine condoms. Ellie smiled at the possibilities. They had doggie diapers and female pads, so why not?

"If we find Buddy, he could be the first test subject. He was already scheduled to live out the rest of his life enjoying the big bang whenever the professor arranged it."

"He was, wasn't he?"

"Lucky son of a gun."

The light changed to green, and she stepped off the curb with Rudy's question nagging at her brain. A split second later, a speeding taxi careened around the corner, coming so close she felt it brush the tips of her shoes.

"Hey! We're walking here!" Passersby didn't raise their heads, not even when she flipped the driver the bird. Then, taking a calming breath, she checked to make sure they still had the right of way and charged through the crosswalk.

"That was a close one," Rudy said when they arrived on the other side of the intersection.

"No kidding. Now where were we?"

"On our way to the shelter to ask about Buddy."

"Right, exactly right. Come on, let's go. I still need to call the insurance and bonding companies, and I'm going to make a another round of the neighborhood. Then we'll take Sweetie Pie and Buckley on their second walk, and meet Dr. Dave at Hazel's."

Ellie headed for the shelter, though her mind continued to process. There had to be something she'd missed about Buddy's disappearance. But what?

Chapter 9

Ellie and Rudy returned to the Davenport in silence. Visiting the place of their first meeting, the East Ninety-second Street ASPCA shelter, was a sobering experience, so intense neither of them had a thing to be happy about. Though the well-maintained building was staffed with dedicated animal lovers, seeing so many homeless dogs, cats, puppies, and kittens angered them both. As usual, Rudy clammed up on the subject, while Ellie stewed as she walked briskly to her afternoon appointments.

Why was it that humans lost all common sense when it came to dealing with one of the more important aspects of caring for their four-legged friends? Every year hundreds of supposedly intelligent people bought pets unsuitable for cramped city dwellings, then abandoned them when the animals didn't fit their lifestyles or apartments. Worse, the owners weren't smart enough to get their dogs or cats neutered or spayed. She'd heard one horror story after another about garbage bags holding unwanted kittens and pups tossed into Dumpsters or thrown in the river, and the unconscionable acts enraged her to tears.

Scooping poop wasn't rocket science, but it was a service Ellie knew helped keep owners and their canine companions together. Without competent pet walkers, there was no telling how many New Yorkers would tire of taking their dogs out and cleaning up after them, which could lead to dropping them in the nearest alley or park.

Striding south on Fifth Avenue she crossed Eighty-third, recalling the volunteer's advice. There were still no reports of a stray bichon, but the woman was certain the adorable and friendly breed would go to anyone with a calm demeanor and soothing voice. That type of canine always found a home.

Unfortunately, the police were monitoring the professor's number, which was on Buddy's tag, so they'd get word before she would. More important, there was no guarantee that the person who found Buddy would phone the number at all.

On this visit, the volunteer accepted Ellie's card and allowed her to post a second flyer in the window, which had her name and phone number as the contact. The volunteer also promised to call if they received any leads, but doubted the dog would turn up.

Believing he'd been found and taken in by a kindly stranger gave Ellie a smattering of hope, but she'd rest easier when she was absolutely certain Buddy was safe. The not knowing drove her crazy, and she didn't need any more insanity in her life.

Now at the Davenport, she and Rudy entered the lobby where they met Kronk, who gave them a wide, menacing grin.

"*El-ee*, my friend. Is good to see you. I have big surprise." He disappeared into the holding area behind the front desk before she could comment and returned seconds later with a quivering, mountain-sized cotton ball in tow. "See what I find. Is *lee-til* white dog."

The behemoth, possibly a Great Pyrenees, jumped up and rested its ham-sized paws on her chest, laying a trail of slobber with its huge pink tongue. She gave the enormous head a pat, ordered the animal down, and glared at the doorman. "This dog in not Buddy."

"Is white dog, no?"

"He's white, yes, but he weighs about a thousand pounds, and Buddy was fifteen, tops. Where did you find him?"

The doorman hung his head. "I want to help, so I look for missing dog."

"Well, you aren't helping. Now where did you get this handsome boy?" She ruffled the dog's shaggy ears, and the fur haystack moaned in pleasure. "I'm sure his owner is hunting high and low for him."

The friendly beast gave her a drippy grin. *"Home is the German beer joint about ten blocks south of here. My owner hooks me in the alley on cool days, where I was minding my own business, I might add. Next thing I knew, this guy was leading me down the street."*

She smiled at the pilfered pooch. "You do realize I can hear and understand you?"

"Same here, and it's kind of spooky, if you ask me."

"I know you hear me, *El-ee*," whined Kronk. "I found him in alley near where I live. Is not missing dog?"

"I just told you no, didn't I?"

Kronk's raised eyebrows and open mouth telegraphed his surprise. "Is impossible!"

"You are what's impossible." She picked through the fur, found the animal's collar, and searched for a tag. "Great, no identification." Raising her gaze, she shot him a look of dismay. "You'll have to take him back to where you stole him from. Right now."

"Not stole . . . I rescue. Poor dog was chained, so I liberate. Was not the right thing to do?"

"If you don't bring him back I'll—I'll call the tavern and tell his owner."

170

"Tavern?" The doorman blinked. "How you know is tavern?"

"I know plenty," she blustered. "Now take this dog home."

He shrugged. "I cannot leave Davenport."

She gazed at the empty lobby, then the newspaper Kronk had been perusing, open on the counter. How difficult could manning the desk be? She held out her hand. "Give me your keys. I'll take over while you're gone."

"You want I desert my post?" He shook his head. "If anyone knows, I am fired."

"What's worse, getting fired or going to jail for grand-theft canine? His owner has probably called the cops by now."

"*Nyet!* No police." Kronk frowned, his expression grim as he studied the Great Pyrenees. "I take, but I need cab fare."

Ellie ground her molars, fished in her tote bag, and pulled out a twenty. "Here, and I want change. Now hurry up."

After stuffing the bill in his pocket, he fussed with whatever he could find behind the desk. She drummed her fingers on the counter, wishing there was some way to warn every pet lover in Manhattan who owned a white dog to keep it under house arrest. Finally, sulking like a three-year-old, Kronk wrapped the leash—a yard of worn clothesline—in his hand, and led the dog away without a backward glance.

Just her luck, the surly doorman would probably be gone for hours, and she still had to take two of her charges on a second walk, then meet Dr. Dave at Hazel's. She gazed at Rudy, sitting patiently at her feet.

"What do you have to say about this?"

"Plenty, but it's all four-letter words."

Before she could say more, an older gentleman wearing a bowler hat, fancy suit, and jauntily knotted ascot sauntered to the counter. "Godfrey Harcourt in 2A. I'm here for my dry cleaning, if you please."

Between his British accent and overdone outfit, it took a second for Ellie to realize he was speaking to her. "Um, hang on. I'll check." She gave Rudy a pleading glance. "Watch the desk, okay? I have to take care of business."

Entering the storage area, she surveyed the twelve-by-twelve-foot room. A couple of dozen dry-cleaning orders hung on a rolling garment rack, and she wondered if Randall had curtailed the apartment delivery service after what had happened to the professor. She thumbed through the plastic bags, found Mr. Harcourt's items, and carried them to the front desk, where she was met by several more tenants.

She handed the man his clothes and a business card, just in case he had a dog. Before she could address the next person, a Bette Midler clone pushed her way to the front of the line.

"Darleen Frank. I'm looking for an overnight envelope," the frumpily dressed woman wheezed. "Do you have it?"

"I'm ahead of you, Darleen," said an obviously harassed mother holding a squalling, dark-haired six-month-old. "Be considerate and wait your turn."

"Evan Gold, and I was here before either of you," groused a short man wearing a George Hamilton tan and a scowl. "I need my dry cleaning."

A few more tenants joined the fray, elbowing to get Ellie's attention. She let them squabble while she ducked down and snagged Darleen's envelope from a shelf under the counter. "Is this what you want?"

The woman swiped the packet and disappeared.

The baby wailed again, louder. "Please. There should be a package from Amazon," insisted the mother, her face as red as the screaming child's. "Bethany Jordan. 4C."

"My dry cleaning," the George Hamilton clone reminded her in a clipped tone.

Ellie rolled her eyes, rushed to the storage room, and snared Mr. Gold's clothing. Spotting a box bearing the online bookseller's name sitting on a shelf, she tucked it in her other hand, hurried to the lobby, and set both items on the counter.

"Thanks." The frazzled mother swept up the parcel and Ellie's card, and hurried off. The tanning bed devotee ignored her offer of a card, grabbed his plastic-shrouded hangers, and turned without a word.

Before she knew it, a throng of restless residents crowded the desk, all speaking at once.

"Where's Mr. Kronkovitz?"

"Who are you, and where'd you learn to do this job?"

"You sure don't look like any doorman I've ever seen."

"I'm writing a letter. The service here is abominable."

Insulted by the accusing comments, Ellie brushed a curl from her forehead, stuck two fingers in her mouth, and gave an ear-shattering whistle, leveling the racket to a whisper. "Okay, everybody, listen up! Form a line and pretend you're reasonable human beings, or no one is getting a thing."

Amazingly, the mob obeyed. Slapping on a gracious smile, she found her rhythm and cleared the testy tenants in fifteen minutes. Pleased with the peace and quiet, she decided she couldn't wait any longer to take care of her real job. Searching the lower shelf, she grabbed a piece of poster board and folded it in half, wrote BACK IN FORTY-FIVE MINUTES in block letters on one side, and propped it on the counter.

She had just enough time to collect her charges, take them out, and return before Dr. Dave's arrival. If he showed up while she was gone, she'd meet him at Hazel's, where she would ask if he'd heard anything about Buddy's disappearance in the last twenty-four hours.

Ellie delivered Sweetie Pie to her apartment and dropped Buckley at his, assuring Hazel she'd be back up soon and so would Dr. Dave. Now back in the lobby, she asked Rudy to stand guard while she inspected the note she'd left on the counter. She bit the inside of her cheek when she saw that a disgruntled tenant had scrawled MANAGEMENT WILL HEAR ABOUT THIS on her makeshift sign while, in different hand-writing, someone had added DITTO FOR ME.

Positive the past disastrous hour would not have occurred if Kronk hadn't stolen the Great Pyrenees, she tore the sign in two and dropped it in the wastebasket. Let the big idiot field questions and comments from the tenants' association. It served him right for being so dishonest.

She checked her watch. Where the hell was the devious doorman? With nothing else to do, she gazed at the newspaper still open on the desk and skimmed the first few pages, hoping to find a follow-up story on the professor's death. Knowing Ryder, he'd slip details of the investigation to a nosy reporter before he'd share a shred of information with her, even though Buddy was at risk.

"Don't tell me you're the doorman on duty," a voice from across the counter asked.

Prepared for more problems, she raised her head and was captured by the beguiling brown eyes of Dr. David Crane, vet to many of the dogs and cats on the Upper East Side.

"Only temporarily," she answered, returning his smile. "It's nice to see you again."

He set a black leather bag on the desktop. "Same here. Am I interrupting something?"

"Not really. Kronk, the evening doorman—"

"Big guy with an accent and an attitude?"

"You got it. He's running an errand, and he asked me to give him a hand." She took another look at her watch. "Ms. Blackberg's expecting you, so go up if you want."

He rested his elbows on the counter. "I thought you were supposed to join me."

"I'll be there eventually, but I'm sure you'll do fine. Hazel's over the moon about Buckley. She just wants someone sane to make sure she doesn't go off the deep end with demands, if you get my drift."

"Oh, I get it all right," said the vet, his eyes twinkling. "She treats her dog like her only child and expects everyone else to do the same. Believe me, about seventy-five percent of my clients act that way. I'm used to it."

"I hear it a lot, too," Ellie confessed, embarrassed to admit the vet had just described her, as well. "My customers give me detailed instructions on how to walk their darlings, as if I was a babysitter and their dog a newborn. I don't know how you get a thing done with them watching your every move."

"You take it in stride." He ran a hand through his thinning hair, then slung the strap of his bag over a shoulder. "So, you'll meet me up there?"

"It's 3G. I shouldn't be too long."

He walked to the elevator, and Ellie took note of the way his snug jeans cradled his butt. His face was as handsome as she remembered, his smile as unassuming, his demeanor as warm. A totally nice guy. And he loved dogs. She sighed. Too bad there was no tremor of excitement when she talked to him, the way there was when she locked horns with Ryder.

Then again, Dr. Dave wasn't out to send her ass to jail.

A couple walked into the lobby, nodded in her direction, and reached the elevator as the door was closing. Dr. Dave held the car, impressing her even more. Most New Yorkers didn't have the patience to allow others on ahead of them, never mind hold the door.

Moments later, a gust of air swept through the foyer, and Kronk charged in like an enraged bull. Stomping to the desk, he set his hands on his hips. "Is done."

"Good." Ellie stretched out her palm. "My change?"

"No change." Moving to her side of the desk, he folded his arms and nudged her out of the way. "You go now."

She narrowed her gaze. "What did you do? Ride to Battery Park and back?"

"Is far. I add my own hard-earned money to fare."

"To go ten blocks?"

"Who said is ten blocks?" He furrowed his brow. "You spy on Kronk?"

"Never mind." Aware the conversation would go nowhere, she reined in her temper, grabbed Rudy's leash, and skirted the front desk. "Don't let it happen again."

"I only want to help," he said, his tone less challenging.

Just then, Eugene and Bibi plowed through the front door and swept past the counter in a rush. Not thrilled with having to share the ride up with them, Ellie waited while they pressed the CALL button and gave her nasty sidelong glances.

When the door closed, Kronk muttered, "Those two big trouble."

Could the thieving doorman actually be a decent judge of character? "Why do you say that?"

"They go up with dogs and don't come down for long time. Is, how you say, suspicion?"

"I believe the proper word is 'suspicious,'" Ellie corrected, remembering her morning encounter with Bibi. "And you're probably right." When the floor indicator stopped, telling her where Bibi and Eugene were picking up their first customers, she hurried over and hit the button. Let them wait while she rode to Hazel's apartment.

She and Rudy arrived at 3G, saw the partially open door, and accepted the obvious invitation to come inside. In the foyer, she heard voices drifting from the living room and made her way down the hall.

"I'm not available during the day, and my little man just loves Ms. Engleman to pieces. If any treatment is necessary, I want her to have full authority, after she confers with me via telephone, of course."

"If that's what you want, I'll draw up a waiver and have you sign it," Dr. Dave said. "I'll mail it to you, and you can send it back."

Ellie heard paper rustling and sighed. Hazel had just tossed a huge responsibility in her lap without asking permission. If something went wrong with Buckley and she made a bad decision . . .

Too late now, she figured, and stuck her head around the corner. "Hi. Sorry I'm late," She led Rudy into the neat and stylish living room, and guessed Hazel must have used a cleaning service to put things to right since moving day. The well-endowed woman, wearing a voluminous dress covered in what appeared to be purple and green flowers, sat on the sofa while the vet lounged in a wing chair with Buckley on his lap. "Are you two getting acquainted?"

"Sure are," said Dr. Dave. "I've already given Buckley a quick exam and pronounced him in perfect health, but he's on the hefty side. Ms. Blackberg now has the name of a low-calorie dog food, and I'd like Buckley to have a little extra walk time each day, if that's not too much trouble."

"Can you believe it? He's puttin' me on a friggin' diet," whined the Maltipoo.

Ellie smothered a laugh. "It's not a problem. All my charges could use a few more minutes on their feet."

"I'm not doing any wind sprints. Remember that next time we're out."

Dr. Dave stood and passed the dog to Hazel, then shook her hand. "And go easy on the treats. One a day, if he's been a really good boy." The vet stroked the Maltipoo's head, ignoring the petite pooch's threatening growl. "I'll send my bill with the waiver. You have my card, so call me if you have questions. Ms. Engleman and I will see ourselves out."

Ellie held her tongue until they were in the hall. "I can't believe she's giving me power of attorney over her boy."

"So you heard part of our discussion?"

"I heard. What was she thinking?"

He chuckled good-naturedly. "She was thinking

you're a fine caretaker. She sees you as competent and thoughtful, probably from the way you handle your own dog. And I'm sure she's talked to other tenants in the building."

Though still a bit miffed, Ellie couldn't help swelling with pride. "I've only been walking their dogs for a month, some less. How do they know I'm treating their pet right? And the police didn't help, grilling my customers about me after the professor died."

He pressed the elevator CALL button. "I doubt any of them think you had a thing to do with Albright's death. I don't."

She met his smiling face. "What, exactly, have you heard about me?"

"Word is you're prompt, you don't invade a client's space, and you perform additional services without charge. None of your customers have any complaints." He let her enter the elevator first. "Besides, I know how worried you are about Buddy. I'm sure they do, too."

She gave herself a mental reminder to take her charges on an extra-long stroll tomorrow. "It's nice to know, but I don't have that many clients."

"The street vendors talk, too, as does Randall. And I've already spoken to a police detective—"

"You talked to Ryder about me?"

"Yes, and don't panic. He called me in for questioning this afternoon. Apparently they found one of my bills in the professor's apartment and realized I'd examined Buddy a few days before the incident. He just wanted to go over a couple of things." The vet leaned against the car wall. "Detective Ryder made it clear he knows your main concern is Buddy's safety, and asked my professional opinion on your theory."

"I suppose I should be grateful he's even considering my dognapping scenario."

"He's considering it, especially since I gave him reason to see it your way."

"What have you heard that I haven't?" Ellie asked, trying for calm. "Does someone you know have information on Buddy?"

"Not Buddy, specifically, but after you and talked, I spoke to a vet pal of mine, and he said one of his patients, a miniature schnauzer, was stolen a week ago, in pretty much the same way as our missing bichon."

"You mean someone else was killed?" Jeez, things were getting dangerous for dog owners in this town. "How come it wasn't in the papers?"

"Because no one died. But the owner was knocked flat on her butt when she answered the buzzer. She woke up twenty minutes later with a massive headache and her champion schnauzer gone. Since there was no need for Homicide to get involved, Ryder hadn't been informed. It seems Manhattan detectives have their hands full. If one case isn't directly linked to another, they're kept separate."

"Who handled the other dognapping?"

"Someone in stolen property. And according to my friend, the police aren't doing much. Missing dogs, even best-in-show winners, aren't as important to them as stolen jewelry or other private property." They entered the lobby. "If you've got time for a cup of coffee, I can go over the rest of it."

This is not a date, Ellie told herself, merely a meeting to exchange information. "There's a Joe to Go a couple of blocks from here, on the way to my apartment."

"Sounds good to me," he said, opening the Davenport's front door. "My treat."

Sam hung up the phone and muttered a curse. If there was one thing he hated, it was looking like a fool, but that was exactly the way he felt. Good thing David Crane had given him the skinny on another vet's patient, or he wouldn't have known to contact Ragusa and Taylor, a pair of detectives working Stolen Property.

But the pieces were finally falling into place. According to Ragusa, a week earlier one of their victims answered the door before leaving for work and didn't remember a thing until she woke up twenty minutes later and found her dog missing.

He scanned his notes. The kidnapped dog, Forsythe's Valor of something or other, was a champion best in show, the same as Albright's mutt, and though not a winner at Westminster, he was small enough to hide under a coat or carry in a tote bag. Heartsick over the loss, the woman hadn't received a ransom request, which she gladly would have paid if asked.

The detectives had found a charred area around the doorknob and sent the sample to forensics, and were still waiting for results. Other than that, they had no leads.

Sam flipped through his in-box, noting the toxicology results for the professor had yet to arrive, but he doubted they'd turn up anything unusual, and it was too late in the day to talk to Bridges. Besides, the ME did her job. She'd send him a report the moment she finished it.

He checked the name and number of the new victim. Her apartment was about fifteen blocks south of Albright's, in a nice but not exclusive neighborhood, and he imagined she'd be home from work by now. After pushing from his desk, he shrugged into his coat. None of the other officers assisting on the professor's case had turned up a thing. The victim's neighbors respected him, his associates at the college admired him, and his students worshipped him. His niece had insisted no one would have a reason to do her uncle harm, and Sam had to agree.

Much as he hated to admit it, Ellie Engleman's theory was sounding more and more like the motive for his murder.

He signed off on the duty board and walked outside. The evening was cool, but spring was definitely in the air. The sidewalks were still teeming with people, and the street was clogged with vehicles. Before long every nutcase in Manhattan would be out in the evening, causing the police more trouble.

He'd joined the force right out of college, after majoring in criminal justice. Originally, he'd hoped to become a lawyer, but found he lacked the patience to deal with the backed-up judicial system and the mountain of red tape needed to prove someone innocent or guilty of a crime. This case was the kind he enjoyed. He liked the brainpower needed to put the pieces together. He looked forward to the hunt and the actual capture of the bad guys, and savored the satisfaction of knowing he'd arrested the right party.

He even liked the people he met. Some were interesting, a few certifiable, but every once in a while someone fascinating came along, someone who intrigued him, challenged him, and made him wonder. The analogy so perfectly fit Ellie Engleman, he had to smile.

Though she seemed to thrive on sticking her nose where it didn't belong, she had a unique sense of humor and wasn't afraid to give her opinion, even if it was somewhat nutty. If he had a few free moments, it might be worth spending a little personal time with her instead of giving her grief. He was relieved she wasn't the missing schnauzer's dog walker. That would have been way too coincidental.

Leaving the parking lot, he headed south. After a quick interview with Rita Millcraft, he'd be through for the day. Too bad it wasn't family-dinner night, because he actually had time to stop at his mother's for a good meal.

Chapter 10

Ellie's nondate with David Crane was relaxing, pleasant and to use a familiar phrase, shorter than a New York minute. Though his personality was amicable and his looks appealing, he was also a tad boring. After they'd shared information on the missing canine, they had little to discuss except the weather. But two positive things came out of the meeting: Ellie got a free cup of coffee, and she found out more about the kidnapped schnauzer than she ever would have learned from Ryder, including the name of the dog's owner and his vet.

She fed Rudy, left him home to snooze, and headed for Rita Millcraft's apartment, her fingers crossed that the woman would agree to speak to a stranger. Any bit of information she received might add a piece to the puzzle of Buddy's disappearance and the professor's death, and that would bring her a step closer to solving this case.

Solving this case? She marveled at the realization of what she was doing. In her year of searching for a meaningful career, she'd never thought of becoming a private investigator, yet it seemed to be her latest undertaking. Perhaps she'd bitten off more than she could chew in her quest to find the missing dog, but *somebody* had to move things along, especially since Ryder didn't seem to be making headway.

She rehearsed opening lines as she walked to her destination, where she planned to introduce herself to Ms. Millcraft without frightening her or giving her false hope. But Ellie was positive of one thing: If Rudy had been stolen, she'd want to know there were people committed to locating her missing pal—people who understood how devastating the loss of a beloved pet could be.

After climbing the steps of an attractive brownstone, she peered at the row of mailboxes in the foyer. Pushing the button marked MILLCRAFT, she waited.

A few moments later, a female voice answered, "Yes?"

"Ms. Millcraft?"

"Yes."

"If you have a minute, I'd like to speak with you about your schnauzer."

The buzzer sounded immediately. Ellie opened the foyer door and took the stairs to the second floor, still mulling over a possible introduction. How much should she reveal about Professor

Albright? Should she mention how she'd found out about the woman's missing dog? Would Ms. Millcraft speak to her if she knew her visitor was a regular citizen, not a member of the police force?

A door at the far end of the hall opened and a woman stepped out, wringing her hands. Rita Millcraft had short curly brown hair, a pretty face, and a look of weariness in her forty-something eyes that suggested she hadn't slept in several days. Dressed in hospital scrubs, she also wore a worried frown.

"Please tell me you have news about Jimmy," she said in a rush of words. "I've been so despondent. I can't thank you enough for—"

Ellie shook her head. "I don't have any information on your missing—on Jimmy—but I do have a theory I want to discuss. Do you have some time?"

Ms. Millcraft propped herself against the doorframe and raised a brow. "What did you say your name was?"

"Ellie Engleman." She held out her hand. "I'm a professional dog walker, and I heard about Jimmy from my vet."

The woman accepted the gesture, but didn't make a move to invite her inside. "You talked to Dr. Lepitsky?"

"My dog's vet, David Crane, is a friend of Dr. Lepitsky's. I saw Dr. Crane today, and he told me he and your dog's doctor had a discussion about the incident."

Rita Millcraft continued to appraise Ellie warily. Suddenly, her brown eyes filled with tears, and she began to sob. Ellie pulled a tissue from her bag and passed it over, waiting while the woman blew her nose and composed herself.

"Forgive me. I'm trying to be strong, but I can't seem to get it together." She took a shuddering breath. "Just when I think I've accepted the fact that Jimmy is gone, something triggers a crying jag and I lose all control." She sniffed. "If I knew what happened to him—that I'd never see him again—I could grieve and move forward, but that's not possible as long as no one has any answers."

"That's why I'm here." Ellie offered a sincere smile. "I have a story to relate and a theory to run by you. I'm hoping you'll help me make sense of it all. Maybe together, we can find those answers."

Moments later, she sat on the sofa in a drab apartment with worn furniture and the faintly acrid smell of dog piddle. Ellie resisted wrinkling her nose as she filled Rita in on Buddy and the professor. "I'm positive the two incidents are connected, especially since your front door was charred, exactly like the professor's."

"You're right. It's too much of a coincidence," Rita agreed, dabbing her watery eyes. "But it's bizarre to think that someone out there is zapping

189

people in order to steal their pets. And I can't imagine anybody killing over one."

"Both dogs were—are champions," Ellie reminded her. "And that could be the key."

"Jimmy finished at a show in Connecticut last year. I put him up for stud through one of the popular breeder magazines, just to see if I could earn a little extra money. Owning a top-of-the-line canine is so expensive these days." She sniffed again. "Not that I mind, of course. Jimmy was—is—worth every penny I spend on him."

"Of course he is," said Ellie, patting Rita's hand. Was it possible the professor had advertised in the same publication? "Can you give me the name of the magazine?"

Rita picked a periodical from a stack on her coffee table. "Here's a copy you can have. My ad is in the back."

Ellie tucked the magazine into her tote for future reading and passed Rita another tissue. "Do you use a dog walker?" she asked, expecting to be told no.

"I take Jimmy out in the morning, after work, and before bed, but a woman named Bibi Stormstein stops by every day around three to give him a nice long walk, even on the weekends." Stifling a sob, Rita heaved a breath. "Of course, I don't need her now that—that—"

"I understand," soothed Ellie, though her heart began a kettledrum pounding. From the *eau de dog* pizzle scenting the air, she'd bet money Bibi was doing a piss-poor job. Biting the inside of her cheek at the pun, she debated sharing what she knew of the Goth weirdo with Rita and decided to put the news on hold. The poor woman had gone through enough trauma over the past week. If she thought someone she'd hired had a hand in the dognapping, Rita would never forgive herself.

"How long has Bibi been walking Jimmy?"

"About a year now. She's not very friendly, but she came highly recommended." Rita wadded her tissue into a ball and set it on the table. "Do you think she knows something?"

"I'm not sure. What about the actual break-in? Did you let whoever it was inside the building?"

"They must have been inside, because I never heard the buzzer. I thought the knock might be a neighbor. I remember reaching for the knob, then wham. Next thing I knew, I was on the floor, and Jimmy was gone." She rubbed her right arm. "It was an electrical jolt of some kind. I'm sure of it. But what it was exactly, I haven't a clue—and neither do the police." She bit her lower lip, holding back another volley of tears. "After I came to my senses, I searched the entire complex. When I finally figured out what happened, I called the authorities."

"And you haven't learned anything since? There hasn't been phone contact or a ransom note?"

"Nothing. I even printed a reward poster on my

computer and hung it around the neighborhood. Called the shelter, too. But there's been no word."

"And the police haven't helped?"

"Not really. I phoned the officer in charge just this morning, but he hasn't returned the call."

Ellie wasn't surprised that the detective working Rita's case was ignoring her. She knew firsthand how uncooperative the city's police were when it came to a missing dog. "Your building doesn't have a doorman. What about a security camera that records whoever comes in and out?"

"The officers asked the same question. Unfortunately, we're not that lucky. The tenants have pestered the owner, but he's come up with every excuse in the book to avoid the expense of installing cameras."

"Other than the people who live here and the landlord, who else is able to come and go as they please?"

"A maintenance crew shows up a couple of times a month to mop the halls, vacuum, that sort of thing. Some of the other tenants have dog walkers or a cleaning or delivery service. But there's no telling which individuals gave out keys to whom."

"Do you use one of those services?" Maybe a cleaning service that deodorizes?

"No. Jimmy and I didn't need help with the cleaning, and the tap water is okay." Rita's shoulder's drooped. "It's all I can do to pay someone to walk my boy. This city's getting so pricey I won't be able to live here if things keep going up."

Ellie couldn't think of anything else to ask, so she stood and handed the woman a business card. "I'm going to mull over what you told me and see if I come up with something. In the meanwhile, you do the same. I'll check back with you in a couple of days."

The downstairs buzzer rang, and Rita raced to answer it. Ellie picked up her tote bag and followed, only to find that the woman had already let her guest in the building. "You have company, so I'll be going."

"Please wait. That was a detective. He's on his way up. He might have news about Jimmy."

Ellie suppressed a groan. What were the chances someone from the NYPD, a detective no less, would pick tonight to stop and discuss the case? "I'd really better leave," she insisted. "My own dog is home alone and—"

A knock on the door sent a chill down her spine.

Rita smiled and fluffed her hair. "I'm sure it'll only take a minute, and it might be positive."

She swung open the door, and Ellie, who had expected to see a strange detective, blinked. Sam Ryder's cocky gaze swept over her from head to toe and back again. Heat surged upward from her chest to her face, embarrassing her further.

Continuing to grin, the devilish detective introduced himself to Rita and held out his shield.

"Officer Ryder," Rita gushed, "this is Ms.—"

"There's no need for introductions," he supplied, his expression locked in a completely out-of-character smile. "Ms. Engleman and I are friends. Isn't that right . . . Ellie?"

"Sure we are," she agreed, biting back a sharp retort. "Thanks so much for talking to me, Rita. Like I said, I'll be in touch."

She stepped around Ryder, but he danced in front of her and grabbed her elbow. "Don't leave on my account, Ellie. Better yet, join me while I ask Ms. Millcraft a couple of questions. From where I stand, the conversation might prove interesting."

As if oblivious of her new friend's discomfort, Rita headed to the living room. "Follow me, and I'll fill you in on the fascinating theory Ms. Engleman's come up with on Jimmy's disappearance. I'm sure it will help in the investigation."

Sam gave Ellie's arm a yank, sat her down next to him, and unclenched his fingers from around her elbow. The expression on her face, a mixture of horror and derision, was almost worth the rise in his blood pressure. He should have figured the faux Nancy Drew would be here, seeing as she kept turning up like the proverbial bad penny.

"Ms. Millcraft," he began, taking a breath. Holy

Christ, what was that smell? Rubbing his offended sniffer, he tried to concentrate on the woman he'd come to see. "I've been talking to Detective Taylor." *And I wish to God the idiot had warned me to bring a gas mask.* "He suggested I speak to you."

"He's one of the policemen who came here when I reported Jimmy missing. I phoned him this morning, but he hasn't called, back. Did he send you with information about my baby?"

"Sorry, no. That is, I'm not sure how much progress the detectives have made. I'm here to get a few details on what happened that morning because it might connect to a case I'm working on."

"You mean the one where that poor professor died protecting his dog? Such a sad story. Ellie just told me all about it."

Protecting his dog? He gave his personal "bad penny" a sidelong glance. "Did she now? So I guess you know what I'll need from you."

Ms. Millcraft wasted no time reciting a recap of the morning in question, going over it point by point while Sam scribbled in his spiral notebook. Every once in a while, he cast Ellie a pseudo-grin, meant to let her know just how much trouble she was in. Finally, the woman ran out of steam.

"Thanks for your time." He tucked the notebook in his pocket and held back a gag. He didn't remember Albright's apartment stinking like this, or Ellie Engleman's. "If you think of anything else, give Taylor or Ragusa a call, and they'll pass the information on to me."

Ellie jabbed him with her elbow, and he scowled. Did she want him to comment on the stench? When she arched a brow, he got the message. "Oh, and I'm sorry for the loss of your pet." And the fact that you're living in an outhouse.

Ms. Millcraft gave a strangled hiccup and started crying all over again.

"Nice move, Ryder," Ellie whispered. She passed the woman a tissue. "It'll be all right. We're going to find Jimmy."

"We are?" Sam asked, glaring at her.

"Of course we are. It's what the police do," she said brightly. "They solve mysteries, and that's what this is."

Standing, Sam pulled Ellie to her feet. "That's it. We're outta here."

Wrenching from his grip, she heaved her tote bag over her shoulder and flounced from the room.

"Don't get up. We'll see ourselves out," he called to the still-weeping woman. Striding away, he muttered under his breath as he slammed the apartment door and walked into the hall, where he took a gulp of stale but mercifully piss-free air. Damn it to hell and back, when he got ahold of Ellie Engleman he was going to—to—

He spotted her on the stairs, scurrying away as if

her pants were on fire, and envisioned himself stalking after her, spinning her around, and putting her at his mercy. He'd lean into her, and she'd gaze up at him, flames sparking from those big turquoise eyes, daring him to touch her . . . taste her. And he'd be more than happy to oblige, running his hands under her sweater, skimming her creamy flesh, cupping her breasts and teasing those suck-me nipples to tight buds of desire.

A gust of outside air fluttered his hair, and Sam realized the object of his lascivious thoughts had escaped through the front door. He shook his head as he jogged down the steps. He had to stop thinking like a marauding Viking, or a pirate bent on ravishing a damsel on a hijacked ship.

Ellie Engleman made him hot as a blowtorch, both above and below his belt. Next thing he knew, he'd be imagining them on the cover of a paperback novel, Ellie draped over his arm while he drooled on her barely covered bosom.

He caught up to her on the sidewalk and ordered his hands to remain at his sides. He didn't need the kind of trouble she so obviously was capable of luring him into. But she did need to be taken down a peg or three.

"Turn in here." Sam nudged her with his shoulder, steering her into a deli with a chalkboard out front advertising several specials of the day.

Instead of obeying, she spun to face him. "What the heck are you doing?"

"Buying you dinner," he ground out. "A nice quiet meal where we can talk over a few things without fainting from urine overdose." He continued encouraging her inside without touching her. "I promise it'll be painless."

She stuck out her lower lip. "I'm sure that poor woman has tried to train her dog, and he's resisted. Spoiled animals often test their owners in that manner, and from the sound of it, Jimmy was definitely spoiled."

"Isn't there a drug they can take or something? How can you people live with that stench?"

"By 'you people' I assume you mean dog lovers."

"I mean dog fanatics," he corrected. "Now let's talk."

She stiffened her posture. "We don't have anything to say to each other . . . unless you found Buddy."

"One more time, I'm looking for a killer—not a dog." He stopped at a table in the corner and nodded toward a chair. "Sit while I enjoy the scent of Manhattan's carbon monoxide–tinged air. It's got to be better than inhaling the toxic atmosphere in Ms. Millcraft's apartment."

To his surprise, she did as he asked and hoisted her bag on the empty chair beside her. He weighed his options: sit across from her and lose himself in her tempting blue eyes, or sit next to her, where his hands might prove impossible to control.

He opted for simple eye contact.

"Why are we here?" she asked, glancing around the deli.

He passed her a menu. "Because I haven't eaten dinner yet, and reaming you out on an empty stomach could prove dangerous to both of us."

"You don't have any right to ream me out." She folded her arms and leaned back in her chair. "I don't answer to you."

"What do you want to eat?"

"I'm not hungry."

"The pastrami looks good. So does the soup."

"For some reason, I seem to have lost my appetite."

"Anyone who stayed in that apartment more than five minutes would. The soup of the day is split pea with ham, by the way."

"Since I'm already sitting with a pea brain, I'll pass on the soup."

They were experts at firing one liners, Sam thought, as if they'd done so a hundred times before. "Tell you what. If you promise to eat something, I'll promise to go easy on you. How does that sound?"

"It sounds ridiculous. You have no right to hold me here or anywhere else." She cocked her head and pursed her lips. "Unless . . . Am I under arrest?"

He thought about saying yes. It just might shut her up long enough for him to eat in peace.

"Well, am I?"

"Not at this moment." But I'm considering it.

"What's that supposed to mean?"

The waitress, a college-age cutie wearing braces that rivaled the grillwork on a sixty-nine Buick, came to take their order, and he tossed her a flirty grin, just because he could. "I'll have a bowl of the soup and a pastrami on rye. The lady will have the same."

"You got it," the girl said with a giggle.

Sam watched her walk away, her hips swinging to the gritty beat playing overhead. When he turned to Ellie, her pinched expression spoke volumes.

"You're disgusting."

"I'm a guy."

Her *tsk* echoed in the room. "That's no excuse."

"Sure it is. All men look. We can't help ourselves."

"Now you're the one making excuses."

"Why are you so uptight? I didn't mean any harm."

She arched a brow. "Did it ever occur to you that some women don't appreciate being treated as if they work at Hooters."

"I don't think it bothered our waitress."

"She's a child. No real woman wants to be ogled as if she were a stripper on the runway."

"So besides sticking your nose in police business, you're now speaking for all women?"

"Of course not, but most intelligent women

want respect, and that's not what they get from men like you."

He had no idea why, but he enjoyed ruffling her feathers. "What makes you such an expert on 'men like me'?"

She opened and closed her mouth. "Never mind." The waitress brought their water and arranged place mats and silverware. Instead of ogling her, he realized he'd rather tempt fate and converse with Ellie. "I'm not such a bad guy, but I have a tough job to do, which sometimes makes me testy. Having you show up in places you shouldn't only adds to my annoyance quotient."

"Then you're not planning to arrest me?"

"Not unless you've done something illegal."

Her ramrod posture relaxed a little. After shrugging out of her dark green rain slicker, she hung it on the back of her chair, but that only called attention to her bountiful breasts encased in a formfitting gray sweater.

"I'm a law-abiding citizen," she reminded him, following his wayward gaze. "And the part of my anatomy you're supposed to be focused on is up here."

He grinned. "Just checking out the scenery. And I already figured you for law-abiding."

"That's right. You decided early on I was too *nice* a person to commit murder."

"Yeah, I did. And you went off on me when I said so. What was that all about?"

Ellie took a sip of water, then exhaled a breath. "I apologize if I was harsh."

"You mentioned someone called the D?"

"My ex. It's not a fun topic."

The waitress served their soup and sandwiches. "Anything else I can get for you?"

"Not right now," he answered. "I've been there," he added when the girl shuffled away. "And I agree. A failed marriage is never a laughing matter."

They ate in silence for a few minutes. Sam took a bite of his pastrami, caught her watching him, and realized he was eating with gusto. "Sorry. This is the first decent meal I've had in a couple of days. Under better circumstances, I do fairly well at carrying on pleasant dinner conversation."

She dabbed her mouth with her napkin. "So am I really in trouble for talking to Rita Millcraft?"

He thought while he chewed and swallowed. "Investigating a murder isn't for amateurs. Ask the wrong person the right question, and anything might happen. That's the reason I told you to stay out of it."

"Any chance you can tell me what you found out so far?"

"Only if you promise to retire from the PI business."

"I'm not—that's not—" She sighed. "All I'm trying to do is rescue a missing bichon."

"So you checked the shelters?"

"I did. I also hung flyers with Buddy's picture, spoke to most of the doormen in a three-block radius, and all the street vendors. Nobody has a clue. I only went to Rita because I heard from David Crane that someone stole her dog under circumstances very much like the professor's. I'm hunting for anything that could lead to Buddy's return."

"How do you know the vet?" And why do I care?

"Rudy is one of his patients, and you already know he was Buddy's vet, too."

"So he told you I called him in for questioning, and he let me know about Ms. Millcraft."

She nodded but kept mum.

"His info convinced me to talk to the detectives working Ms. Millcraft's case, see if there's a connection."

"Have you made a decision? Because I think there is."

"Well, guess what. So do I."

Ellie rewarded him with her first real smile of the night. "You do?"

"It might surprise you to learn I'm even considering your theory. I'm starting to think Albright was killed because of his dog."

" 'Surprise' is putting it mildly," she responded, sliding her empty plate to the side. "Guess I was hungry after all."

"My mother says it's good to have a healthy appetite." It was a nice change, sharing a meal with a woman who actually ate instead of counting calories or fat grams. "Think you have room for dessert?"

"You've got to be kidding."

"I don't kid. Besides, half the fun of eating is knowing there'll be something sweet at the end."

She rested her chin on a fist and stared at him. "All right, now I know you're joking."

"About what?"

"First you act as if you approve of my packing away as much food as a man. Then you ask me about dessert." She ran a finger around the edge of her water glass. "Women are supposed to eat like birds so they stay slim and delicate."

"Who the hell passed along that bit of wisdom?"

"My ex, my mother, the fashion magazines, Hollywood, and just about every designer and style expert on the planet." She raised a shoulder. "If you ask me, it's a conspiracy."

"Well, what do you know. I agree with you there, too. Personally, I enjoy women with curves. What's the fun in snuggling with a stick, when you can snuggle with a pillow?"

She rolled her eyes. "You are so full of it."

"Think what you want, but I'm serious." He signaled for the check. "Sure you don't want coffee or something else?"

Standing, she shrugged into her coat. "No, thanks. It's late, and I have to get home. I'm an early riser."

Sam signed the charge slip, left a tip on the table, and tucked the paperwork in his billfold. "Me, too, though it's not always by choice." He followed her out the door, where they stood on the sidewalk.

"Thanks for dinner," she began. "And for sharing what you know about the case."

"And thanks for your promise to stay out of my way while I do my job. Come on, I'll give you a ride home."

Chapter 11

Ellie flinched when Ryder caught her arm a second time. Though his grip was less threatening than it had been at Rita's, it was still proprietary and definitely made her uncomfortable. And what was his last comment? Something about her promise to "stay out of his way and let him do his job." She hadn't agreed to any such thing, but this probably wasn't the best moment to point out his error.

When he steered her toward a tanklike gray sedan parked in a TRUCKS ONLY zone, she guessed his intentions and planted her feet. "I can walk myself home."

Clenching his jaw, he opened the passenger-side door. "Not on my watch, you can't." He spotted a paper tucked under a wiper blade, muttered a string of curses, and snatched it off the glass. "Get in and buckle up."

The set of his shoulders told her there was no point in arguing. Besides, she could think of just one thing someone would tack to a windshield, and giving him grief for the way he'd treated her at Rita's seemed only fair.

Biting back a smile, she took her seat and strapped on her belt. "Is that by any chance a parking ticket?"

He slammed her door, trotted to the driver's side, and slid behind the wheel. Then he reached to open his glove box, but she grabbed the paper from his fingers before he did the deed.

"Oh, my God. It is a ticket! You *are* on a par with the rest of us mortals." Her chortle eased to a snort, then a cough as she caught the devilish glint in his eyes. "Sorry, but it's difficult imagining you, Mr. Big Shot Detective, breaking the law in such an everyday-citizen manner."

Swiveling on the bench seat, he made a grab for the ticket. "Oh, really? Who says?"

When she held the ticket overhead and opened the glove box, a raft of identical pages fluttered out. "Holy crap. You're one of those people who ignore their parking citations—a—a scoffer or whatever the term is. The city publishes an annual list of their most wanted, and I bet you're their number-one culprit."

"Not even close," he insisted, leaning toward her. "Now give it over."

She turned on the map light, gathered a stack of

loose citations, and shuffled through them with her free hand. "Jeez. Some of these go back three years." Returning the pile to the glove box, she added, "They're going to throw the book at you, Ryder. You might even get a write-up in the *Times*. I can see the headline now: *Local detective named one of Manhattan's biggest scoffers!*"

Edging closer, he blew out a breath. "Not unless I pop in the system, and that's not going to happen."

"Oh? And why not?"

He edged a few more inches in her direction, and the interior of the sedan shrank to the size of a Volkswagen Beetle. "I have a buddy in Violations, and we have a deal." He moved closer still. "Now stow tonight's with the rest of them."

When his breath fanned her cheek, Ellie's heart skipped a half dozen beats, and she acted without thinking. Like a pigmy warrior taunting a hungry lion, she shook her head. "I don't think so."

Light from an overhead streetlamp cast shadows on his handsome face, but those damn eyes still smoldered with danger. His lips curled into a smile that should have frightened her but instead set her insides dancing to a rhythm she hadn't felt in several years.

He sidled over another inch, pressed his chest against her shoulder, and made a grab for the lone ticket. "Then I guess I'll just have to take it."

The little air she managed to inhale caught in her

throat, and she stumbled into gear. "I . . . um . . . ah . . ." Pushing the paper at him, her hand met a wall of muscle. "Here. There's no need to get physical."

"Physical?" he asked, as if he enjoyed the idea. His long fingers circled her wrist, and he focused on her mouth, staring as if he still longed for a taste of the dessert he'd denied himself earlier. "Maybe I should arrest you, have you remanded into my custody."

She gasped. "You wouldn't dare."

His thumb skimmed her skin in gentle yet insistent circles. "Who's going to stop me?"

The thought of closing her eyes and willing him away was tempting, but a sixth sense told her he'd move in for the kill if she did. She had no intention of starting something it would be stupid to finish. She pursed her lips in disapproval, but that only seemed to intrigue him further.

"You have an interesting mouth," he said, getting so close his nose bumped hers. "It reminds me of pink rose petals, but that little pout gives it a certain edge."

Rose petals from the dastardly detective? She squirmed backward and found herself plastered against the door. "You don't mean that."

"I don't?"

"Nu-huh."

"Care to tell me why?"

"Because—because—you're an officer of the

law. That means you're too much a gentleman to take advantage of a defenseless woman."

His hungry expression shifted to amusement. "Believe me, sweetheart, with that mouth, you're the least defenseless woman in Manhattan—probably all five boroughs."

She bit her lower lip, realized it again called attention to the object of his fascination, and sighed, too confused by the insistent two-step tapping in her belly to continue baiting him. "How about if I remind you that we're working together?"

He stared at her as if she'd grown a second head. "What in the hell gave you that idea?"

"I just thought—"

"I already have a partner—a professional who knows this business as well as I do. The only reason you haven't met Fugazzo is because he's on family leave, and the department's too short-handed to give me an interim partner."

Ellie remembered the medical examiner, Dr. Bridges, asking him if someone had had a baby, but didn't think to connect the dots. "You might have mentioned it before all this," she said, giving a wounded sniff.

He gazed at the ceiling, then back at her. "You are, without a doubt, the most obstinate, hard-headed, contrary, disobedient, hardheaded—"

"You said that already."

"Don't remind me—the most frustrating woman

I have ever met. What will it take to make you understand this isn't a game? Albright was murdered, and whoever did it is still out there. The killer is interested in dogs. You own a dog—"

"I have a worthless kennel hound no one wanted. Of course, Rudy's not worthless to me—he's the most important thing in my world, and I'd fight to the death if someone tried to—"

"Get to the point," he ground out.

"The killer's only interested in champions, canines that proved they can win big in a ring."

"And what makes you so sure about this theory?"

"Isn't it obvious? Jimmy's a best-in-show winner. Buddy's won the most megacanine prize of them all. I bet if you ask some of the other detectives working stolen property, you'd come up with a couple more missing pups, and they'd all have top-of-the-line pedigrees and successes."

He smirked. "Too late. I already put out the word."

She said, "Oh," though she wanted to say, "Thanks for telling me, you big idiot" in the worst way. "Good."

"I've been at this job long enough to know how to get things done."

At a loss for words, she raised her nose and stared out the window. He settled behind the wheel and turned the key. The engine powered to life, purring like a high-performance racing machine. Okay, she conceded, the iron tank was a disguise so people would only *think* it was a reject from a used-car lot. He pulled into traffic and stepped on the gas.

"I thought all cops had a roof thingy. You know, a light that reminds regular folks of the specials running in one of those big discount stores?"

"Official use only," came his terse reply. Dodging a taxi, he took a right at the next corner.

"So your visit to Rita wasn't official?"

"It was."

"Then . . ."

He crossed two lanes and hung a left, leaving a trail of blaring horns in his wake. "I parked too far away to justify the light, plus I have a sticker. A beat cop is supposed to pay attention to the department decal, but it's a good bet he was a rookie, maybe even a patrolman buddy who thought it would be fun messing with my head. I'd have to interpret the scrawl at the bottom to see exactly who wrote the citation."

"Mess with your head?"

"Yank my chain. It's probably somebody who already knows I have a couple of tickets, and thinks adding another is cute."

She found it hard to believe an officer would be so devious. "But it's childish, and it could get you in trouble."

He stopped the car at a light and glanced in her direction. "Who are you—Mary Poppins? Guys on the force pull practical jokes all the time, even on television cop shows."

"I don't watch cop shows." Too bad if he thought her the personification of a fictional Goody Two-shoes. She hated the cruelty, the violence depicted these days on both the small and large screens. "Too much bad stuff."

"The writers make up most of the shit on TV, but some of it is real. There's a lot of *bad stuff* out there, and they use the best of it for their stories. Look what happened to your pal."

What *had* killed Professor Albright? "Not to belabor the point, but are the test results in? Do you know exactly what caused the professor's death?"

Ryder drove past her apartment building, found a spot with a sign marked DELIVERY ONLY. VIOLATORS WILL BE TOWED, and pulled into the space. Reaching under his seat, he retrieved the blue-light special, climbed from the car, and slapped it on the roof. By the time he arrived on her side, she was ready to beat a fast retreat.

"Thanks. I can take it from here. My apartment's just around the corner." After their close encounter in the tank, she wasn't sure she could handle more private time with him. "This neighborhood is perfectly safe."

"Not so fast." He caught her by the elbow again. "It won't take long."

Ellie breathed a sigh of relief. He said the dome

light was for official business only, which meant he thought of this escort as part of his job. Now he announced he wouldn't be long. The tiny zaps of electricity his touch sent zinging through her veins and the "dying-for-dessert" look in his eyes were merely her imagination running wild. Viv was right—she'd been celibate too long. All she needed was a serious bout with a vibrator . . . once she grew brave enough to buy one.

They covered the distance in silence and reached her building in minutes. Aware she was almost free of him, Ellie tried for bright and breezy. "Good night, and thanks again."

"If I remember, you live *inside* the building."

Anchoring her feet, she put her hands on her hips. "You're going to be a pain about this, aren't you?"

"What's the problem? Afraid of what'll happen if I walk you to your door?"

"Afraid? Me? Of course not."

"Then prove it," he dared.

Feigning nonchalance, she shrugged, fished the keys from her shoulder bag, and took the stairs. Moments later, they were at her apartment. Before she used the key herself, he pulled it from her fingers and unlocked the door.

"Want me to come inside and check things out?"

"There's no need. I have Rudy, remember?"

"Oh, yeah. The ten-pound dragon slayer."

"Twelve pounds," she corrected. "And he can

be a regular Cujo when the situation calls for it."

Ryder made a rude noise, then clasped her upper arm and pressed her against the doorframe. "I doubt it. Besides, there are things I'm pretty certain he can't do for you."

His honey-colored eyes focused on her mouth. His fingers skimmed her neck and captured her jaw, while he slid a knee between her legs. Inching forward, he claimed her lips, and the kiss ignited her insides like a match to kindling. In seconds, the joining burned as hot as an out-of-control forest fire, searing her blood and turning her muscles to candle wax.

She opened her mouth to protest and he slipped his tongue inside, then moaned as if he was tasting his favorite after-dinner treat. Lost in the warmth of his body and the pressure of his upper thigh nestled intimately into her sweet spot, her head slumped against the wall and her knees buckled.

Just as she was about to wrap her arms around him and beg for more, he drew back. Seconds passed before she found the courage to raise her eyelids and look at him. When she did, he was grinning.

"Let me know if your fuzzy pal can make you melt the way I just did, okay? Because if he does, I'm going to retire."

Breathing as if she'd run a four-minute mile, Ellie licked her swollen lips as he sauntered down the stairs. Ryder's tart, provocative taste lingered on her tongue, calling to mind strawberries and champagne, fine wine, and a chocolate cream doughnut all rolled into one.

She only had herself to blame for the sexually charged atoms bouncing through her nervous system. From the moment she'd climbed into his metal-plated tank, she'd had an idea something impossible might happen, yet she'd sat there thinking she was smarter than he, had more self-control, was strong enough to take whatever he dished out.

Sad to say, he'd proven her wrong. His mouth had been demanding, seeking more than she was ready to give, yet gentle enough to turn her bones to butter. A kiss to remember.

A pity it had come from Sam Ryder, a man with a big ego and an even bigger attitude.

Inhaling deeply, she willed her heart to slow its erratic pounding, gathered her composure, and turned to enter her apartment. A door downstairs slammed, and she guessed it was Vivian returning from her double date. Slipping inside, Ellie shrugged out of her coat, kicked off her shoes, and carried everything to her bedroom. That was when she caught Rudy staring. "What do you want?"

His brown eyes appraised her knowingly, and he gave a soft growl. *"I see that cop again, I'm gonna lock onto his ankle so hard he'll need the jaws of life to pry me off."*

She ignored the comment, tugged free of her clothes, pulled a sleep shirt over her head, and stuffed her feet into fuzzy pink slippers. Plopping on the edge of the mattress, she imagined Vivian would be at the door in a few minutes. Since she'd turned down Viv's offer of a date, she had to act as if she'd been home all night doing nothing more taxing than reading or watching television.

Jumping on the bed, Rudy gave her one of his are-you-for-real looks. *"What do you have to say for yourself?"*

"I didn't know I had to answer to you when I went out for the evening."

"We had a deal, remember? You take care of me, and I take care of you. It's hard to hold up my end of the bargain when you're out on the town with a caveman, and I'm locked here in the apartment."

Sometimes his mind-reading act was uncanny. Even more amazing was the expertise with which he piled on the guilt. "Have you been taking lessons from my mother?"

"Georgette hates me."

"She's never been an animal lover. I wasn't allowed to have a dog when I lived at home, and even after I had my own place, she disapproved. I was shocked when she agreed to keep you—the old you—after the wedding."

"And look how that turned out."

Ellie narrowed her eyes. "She swore to me it was an accident. Is she lying?"

Rudy gave his version of the doggie shrug. *"It's water under the bridge."*

"Fine, but be aware I'm wise to your manipulations."

"I'm just reminding you of our agreement. And warning you of the despicable detective at the same time."

"I know we have an agreement, but I explained before I left why I couldn't bring you with me tonight. And I didn't expect to see—Hey, how did you know I was with Ryder?"

"Pheromones. When he's around you, they roll off him like stink off a skunk. I smelled him through the door, heard him, too. He has some nerve, too, saying he can protect you better than me."

"He wears a gun, though I don't want to be around if he has to use it."

"Big deal. I can grab a mugger's butt and hold on like a steel trap. I'd protect you, Ellie, and I wouldn't expect a thing in return . . . not the way that dime-store dick does." He snuggled beside her and placed his head on her thigh. *"You shouldn't trust him."*

"He's an officer of the law."

"I don't care if he's the pope. He's still a man."

A knock echoed from the hall, and Ellie jumped. "How do I look? Relaxed? Sleepy? In control?" Leaving the room, she muttered, "Viv can read me almost as good as you can," and hurried to the foyer.

The moment the door opened, Vivian's smile faded. Dressed in the identical outfit she'd worn to work that morning—a black cashmere turtleneck under a red DNKY jacket and matching pencil skirt with black hose—she appeared professional yet ready for anything the night had to offer. Staring, she opened and closed her mouth. "Oh my God. You had sex!" Her gaze narrowed a fraction. "Oops. Not quite, but you did suck face."

"For the love of— Is sex the only thing you ever think about?" Ellie stepped back and motioned her inside. "Talk about a one-track mind."

Ellie marched to the kitchen, opened the freezer, and brought out two pints of Caramel Cone. Was there an ice-cream company that made a flavor mimicking strawberries and champagne, she wondered, or one that tasted like the creamy filling in a chocolate doughnut?

After smacking Viv's container and spoon on the table, she wrestled with the plastic seal on her own fresh carton. "Here, finish this tonight. It's taking up room in my freezer."

"No need to be such a grump," Viv said. "If I had to guess, which I do because it's obvious you're not going to tell me, I'd bet you were canoodling with that detective." She stuffed a glob of ice cream in her mouth. "How'm I doing?"

"You're right. I'm not talking," said Ellie around the lump of chocolate and caramel melting on her tongue.

"Is that the thanks I get for trying to fix you up with a white-collar type? It would have helped if you'd told me you went for swaggering NRA members instead of professional men."

Viv's observation had Rudy yelping with laughter.

Ellie sent him a glare, then said, "A simple ride home isn't enough to tell me if Sam Ryder is an NRA member. I mean, I don't have any idea what kind of guy he is."

"Uh-huh." Viv glanced at Rudy, who was sitting at Ellie's feet wearing an I-told-you-so expression. "Why is your pal staring like that?"

"He's hoping to snag a taste of Häagen-Dazs," Ellie lied.

"So, Rudster," Vivian began, "what do you think of the big, bad detective?"

"Don't answer that," Ellie snapped, then quickly recovered. "Stop asking my dog questions. You know he's not capable of a response."

"Says who? I chatter to Twink most days, and sometimes I swear he's ready to comment. And don't deny that you talk to Rudy when you think no one is listening, because I've heard you do it."

"It's a habit I developed when the D worked late. I babbled to myself. Now I babble to Rudy. That's all."

"Get back to tonight," Viv ordered. "If it wasn't the detective you kissed, then who?"

Ellie swallowed another spoonful of ice cream.

"Wait. Was it that veterinarian guy? The one named after a bird. Dr. Crow? Or was it Swan?"

"Dr. Crane, and no, it wasn't him." No sense lying. Viv would probably hunt down Dr. Dave and give him the third degree, which would be totally embarrassing. "Much as I hate to admit it, you were right the first time."

Vivian put down her container and sat back, a grin gracing her cover-girl lips. "And . . . ?"

"And what?"

"How was it?"

"How was what?"

Viv leaned forward and rested her arms on the table. "Cute does not become you. You're not the cute type. Now was it a kiss? Or was it a *kiss*?"

Heat rose from Ellie's chest and inched to her neck. "It was . . . okay."

"How did it happen?"

"Lips met lips in the usual manner."

"There you go, trying to be cute again. You know what I mean. Did he sneak up on you and make it quick, or ram you against a wall and plant a big, wet one? Was there lots of tongue, or just a lot of spit? And what about his hands?"

"You're gross." And it was *so* not sneaky or quick, but it had been good enough to make her panties wet—something she would never admit to anyone. "How about if I say it was good, and leave the rest up to your imagination?"

"Did he grope you in the hallway or inside the apartment?"

Ellie *tsk*ed. "All right, can your imagination. There was no groping, just hands holding me steady while we shared a moment at the door."

Viv folded her arms across her formfitting black sweater and shook her shoulder-length fall of hair. "You are such a liar."

Yeah, I am, Ellie admitted to herself. "Since when do you kiss and tell?"

"I'd spill my guts if you asked me, but you never do. Want to know about the last time Jason and I did it? It was in the kitchen, and he sat me up on the—"

Ellie slammed her palms over her ears. "Stop. I don't want to hear."

Viv's smile grew wide. "See what I mean?"

"Change of subject. Want to go to dinner at my mother's tomorrow night?" *Please say yes.* "I'm bringing Rudy, so you can bring Mr. T."

"A night with the exterminator? No, thanks. I have an appointment for a root canal."

"Very funny."

"Okay, then I have a date. The attorney from tonight asked me out."

"You're cheating on Jason," Ellie said without inflection. "That's not nice."

"I keep telling you, we have an agreement. Jason can see other women if he wants, just like I can see other men."

"But he doesn't."

Viv capped her carton. "Not my problem."

"It's your life." Ellie frowned. "And mine is mine."

"All right already, I get the hint." Viv stood. "One more question, then I'm out of here."

"Okay, shoot."

"Are you going to sleep with him?"

"Him . . . you mean Ryder?"

"No, I mean Hannibal Lecter. Yes, I mean Ryder."

"That's not a good idea."

"Because . . ."

"Because he's not—we're not going to—we're not right for each other. We met at a woman's apartment by accident tonight. Her schnauzer was stolen the same way someone took Buddy."

"You're kidding."

"Wish I was. I got to her place first, hoping to get info that would help me locate Buddy. Ryder arrived as I was leaving. Needless to say, he didn't approve of my snooping."

"And that led to his kissing you?" Viv propped her backside against the counter. "Sorry, but that's a stretch, even for me."

"He bought me dinner first," she confessed.

"Somewhere fancy?"

"A deli."

"Big spender."

"That's why it wasn't a date. Besides, we did a

lot of arguing. When things got personal, he insisted on driving me home and walking me to the door."

"And then things got *really* personal."

"It just sort of happened. Took me by surprise, or I would have ducked and made my escape."

"Uh-huh."

Ellie hated trading punches with Viv, because it was worse than arguing with Rudy, who was curled in a ball under the table watching with interest. "Okay, so maybe I was hoping something would happen . . . just to see what it was like. It's been a while since my libido's seen any action. I wanted to make sure it still worked."

"Now we're getting somewhere. And does it?"

"Oh, yeah."

Vivian nodded. "That means you're ready."

"I'm almost afraid to ask—ready for what?"

"To jump back into the dating pool. We'll start slow, coffee or drinks. That stockbroker was cute, in a nerdy sort of way. He mentioned he was free, said he'd still like to meet you. Blow off your visit to Georgette tomorrow night, and I'll call him." She headed for the door. "Okay?"

Ellie stood. "Not okay. According to mother, Stanley wants to see me, and I'd hate to disappoint him. Besides, once I go over there, I'm off the hook for at least a month. Then we'll see."

Stopping at the front door, Vivian spun on her heels. "You're serious?"

"Yeah, I guess so."

"Praise Jesus and all the saints." She grinned. "But I have a question."

"It had better be your last," Ellie warned her.

"If Ryder asks you out, will you say yes?"

Ellie opened the door and shoved Viv into the hall. "I doubt it. See you in the morning."

Vivian's steps faded, and Ellie locked up. Ready to hop into bed, she practically stumbled over Rudy, holding his leash in his mouth, when she turned. "Oops, guess you need to go out. Just let me get my coat."

He peered up at her through sad brown eyes. *"Did you mean what you said about that cop?"*

Ellie shrugged into her jacket, glanced at her fuzzy slippers, and decided it was too late to worry about fashionable footwear. She led him out the door. "I meant it."

But she was a terrible liar.

Chapter 12

Sam stuffed his fists into his trench coat pockets and squared his shoulders, focusing on the local action as he walked to his car. Except for a few pedestrians and a trio of teenagers playing hand-held video games on a front stoop, the area was quiet, or at least as quiet as was possible for Manhattan at nine o'clock in the evening. The only other citizens of note were a couple on the steps of a brownstone, their mouths and bodies fused together so tightly he doubted there was room for a sheet of paper between them.

The X-rated sight sent him reeling like a prizefighter KO'd in the first round. Was that the way he and Ellie had looked only moments ago—lips locked, hips joined, legs entwined as they wrestled against the wall in her apartment hallway?

He'd been a cop for a lot of years, and not once had he lost it, even when his fingers itched to slam a punk against the bricks or immobilize a killer. He believed himself to be a sane, sensible adult male working a stressful job, able to keep his act together and stay in control . . . until he found himself within ten feet of the buttinsky dog walker tough-girl-in-training. So what was it about her that sent his testosterone level soaring and made him lose his cool?

Good thing he'd escorted her into the building before he'd jumped her bones. Then again, if he'd been thinking straight, he wouldn't have gone near her to begin with. Thanks to her uncanny knack of being where she didn't belong, she'd forced him to break one of his personal rules concerning members of the opposite sex: Never strong-arm a woman, unless in the performance of his duty and, even then, curtail the rough stuff.

She wasn't a criminal, yet he'd manhandled her in his car, and hoisted her against a wall in an attempt to tame her sassy mouth. Though it was

225

only a single kiss, it had been so heated, he was still sweating, and surprised they hadn't set the building on fire. The erotic interchange had left him so damn frustrated he'd probably be up all night, reliving the experience while his cock enjoyed the instant replay every time it ran.

And what the hell had possessed him to throw out that last crack about her dog? He shook his head. When Fugazzo got off family leave, he was going to make a couple of phone calls, then take a weekend off. There had to be a few ladies he'd dated in the past who were still available and willing to end his drought between the sheets.

Reaching his car, he inspected the paper-free windshield and grunted in approval. One ticket a night was all that his buddy in Violations had promised to make disappear. After removing the flashing dome, he slid behind the wheel and stuck the light under the front seat. Now what?

Stay away from Ellie Engleman, the logical part of his brain advised. Far, far away.

He could follow his own advice, provided she stopped sticking her nose into police business. Unfortunately, something told him that trick wasn't in the cards. He'd probably have to do something drastic, maybe arrest her for obstructing an ongoing investigation to keep her from showing up like that friggin' bad penny wherever he went. The woman was everything he'd accused her of and then some.

Obstinate? Hell, she was stubborn as a mule.

Contrary? He expected to see her picture next to the word in the dictionary.

And it went without saying that she was disobedient. She ignored his orders at every turn, and he'd bet his bullets she had no intention of obeying the last one. No doubt about it, she was hardheaded to a fault . . . but damn, she could kiss.

Steering the car into the street, he aimed for home. He had a lot of thinking to do, about both the case and the exasperating dog walker. Besides her tenacious demeanor, she had a gift for putting the pieces together. Though she swore she didn't watch cop shows, she also seemed to have an instinct for talking to the right people, ferreting out the particulars, and drawing a logical conclusion.

But she was a civilian with no training, no knowledge of procedures, and absolutely no idea what she might be getting herself into. Finding the professor's killer was his job—not hers. He had too much on his plate to babysit amateur detectives, even if they were on the right track.

On a positive note, talking to Rita Millcraft had given him a thread that could lead to Albright's killer. He might even find a third or fourth link, once the boys in Stolen Property heard he was interested in anything they had on missing mutts. When that happened, things would fall into place and he'd catch his man.

His cell phone rang as he climbed from his car. Glancing at the readout, he groaned. His ex-wife was the last person he wanted to speak with tonight.

"Ryder," he said as he took the stairs to his apartment.

"Would it hurt to be civil? I know you have caller ID."

"I'm busy, Carolanne. What do you want?"

"I thought you might appreciate knowing that my father passed away early this morning. I left a couple of messages, but as usual, you haven't returned a single one."

Frank Jeffers had been a good man, someone Sam admired. The retired dockworker had been well aware he had a flake for a daughter, and had commended his son-in-law for sticking with the marriage for as long as he had. Sam had seen Carolanne's number earlier in the day and, as accused, ignored it, unwilling to get involved in their normal war of words.

He blew out a breath. "I didn't know he was sick. I wish you'd told me."

"Really? So you're saying you would have taken time from your busy schedule to see him?"

"Maybe . . . yeah."

"Then he must have meant more to you than I ever did."

He refused to be taunted into an argument over his ex-wife's standard excuse for her many affairs.

"Where's the wake?" he asked instead. "And the funeral?"

"You mean you'll make the viewing? You're not just being nice to get rid of me?"

Her tone was skeptical, almost biting, and exactly what he'd come to expect since confronting her about the men she'd slept with during their five-year marriage. Sam did want to get rid of her, but he also had an obligation to her mother. "How's Patricia holding up?"

"Okay, all things considered." She gave the name of the funeral parlor and the hours. "He's being buried the next morning. I'm sure she'd appreciate your being there."

"You have my word I'll be at the viewing," he promised, but he ignored the funeral crack. His schedule was packed, but he owed Frank and Patricia Jeffers for taking his side in the divorce. "It's late. I have to go."

"Of course you do." Her smirk slithered across the wire. "I wouldn't expect anything else."

He didn't bother with a polite good-bye. Carolanne would appreciate his hang-up, just to prove she was right about dumping him. The fact that she knew exactly what he did for a living when they'd tied the knot held no weight, nor had her encouragement when he'd passed his test for detective. She'd been aware of the extra hours he had to work, but it had taken him a while to figure out why she didn't care. It gave her more time to fuck their downstairs neighbor and God knew how many other men she met at her job or her health club.

His mother would probably want to know about Frank's death, as well. Though she had nothing good to say about her ex-daughter-in-law, she'd always thought Carolanne's parents were the salt of the earth. Maybe he'd call his mom and offer to take her out before the viewing. That way, he could make up for missing their weekly dinners and fulfill his obligation to Patricia at the same time.

Inside his apartment, he hung up his coat, loosened his tie, and dialed his mother's number.

"Sammy, it's you."

His lips twitched. "You're finally getting used to the new phone, I see."

"I still have to stop and remember to look at that tiny screen and figure out the numbers, but I'll admit it does come in handy. Just today, I had three calls from telemarketers or people I didn't want to talk to. In fact, I'm thinking of getting a cell phone, like you and your sisters have."

His mother and a cell phone? The idea simply didn't compute. "You're kidding?"

"I'm serious. Then I can assign a different ring tone to each of my children. I'm thinking of—"

"Uh, Ma, I didn't call to shoot the breeze."

"I hope you phoned to tell me you miss me, and you're coming to dinner next week."

"I'm not sure about next week, but I have news about someone, and I think you'll want to hear it."

"News? Is it Tommy? One of your sisters?" His mother's voice rose as she spoke. "Oh, wait. Sherry's upstairs studying in her room. Is it Susan—"

"Calm down, Ma. It's not one of the girls or anyone in our immediate family."

She exhaled a breath, and he imagined her making the sign of the cross. "Don't frighten me like that again, young man."

"Sorry. I just got off the phone with Carolanne."

He waited through the long silence.

"What did she want?"

"To tell me that Frank passed away this morning."

"Oh, Lord, how terrible. What was it? A heart attack? A stroke? Cancer? He used to be a smoker, you know."

"I remember, but Carolanne didn't say, and I didn't ask. The obit will probably run in tomorrow's paper." His mother had been reading the death notices every day since his dad passed away. "I didn't want it to come as a shock."

"I appreciate you telling me." There was another pause before she asked, "Are you going to the viewing?"

"I'm planning on it. I thought maybe you'd come with me. I'll buy you dinner first."

"Buy me dinner? When you could eat here?"

"I know I can eat there, but I want to take my favorite girl out. Just the two of us."

She laughed before she said, "That's sweet, Sammy. I'll be happy to be your date, even if it is to a funeral."

"Pick you up around five? We'll go to Provenzano's. How's that sound?"

"Fine. It'll give me a chance to wear my new hat. I bought it yesterday, but I had no idea why. I guess I must be psychic or something."

Or something, is right. "Swell, Ma. I'll see you tomorrow at five."

The next morning, Ellie woke with a pounding headache. She'd tossed and turned most of the night, in the throes of an erotic dream that returned to haunt her every time she closed her eyes. Though the face of her tormentor had been shrouded in smoke, she suspected Sam Ryder was the cause, but it could have been good old Dr. Dave, or some hunk she'd seen on the street who made her thighs ache and her blood run hot. One thing was certain: Her reaction to the invasive sexual fantasy had proven her libido wasn't dead—just . . . dormant?

After swallowing two ibuprofen with her break-fast orange juice, she dressed for the evening, in case there wasn't time to return to her apartment when she finished her last walk. Taking a final glance in the mirror, she was certain Georgette would approve of her tailored black slacks and matching jacket. She even wore the turquoise sweater she'd received from Vivian this past Christmas, the one that matched her eyes and showed off her reddish-gold hair and other attributes to full advantage.

When she arrived at Viv's condo to take Mr. T on his morning constitutional, she was relieved to find her best human friend gone for the day. Last night's grueling inquisition had drained her dry. She didn't have the patience to go another round with Vivian, especially when she had to be at the top of her game to avoid arguing with her mother.

On the way to her first stop, she and Rudy dropped by the nearest Joe to Go and ordered a regular coffee. Because walking Bruiser wasn't a done deal, it seemed prudent to bring Natter a hot beverage on the off chance it would persuade him to recommend her to a few more residents in his building.

"Thanks," said the burly doorman when she handed him his drink. "By the way, new tenants are moving in over the weekend. Two women, and they each have one of them small naked-lookin' dogs with big ears and buggy eyes."

"Chihuahuas?" asked Ellie.

"Them's the ones. I handed the ladies your card, and they promised to give you a call."

"I appreciate it." Ellie gave herself a mental

high-five for bringing him coffee. "What's their apartment number?"

"Penthouse suite. My guess is Patti and Janice are big tippers, so there ought to be some hefty bonus money come Christmas, if you play your cards right." His expression turned thoughtful. "One's a supermodel, and the other's supposed to be a singer at some fancy supper club, but I can't remember which is which. Either way, they have to be well off to sublet the top floor of the building."

Ellie penned a welcome-to-the-neighborhood note, added another of her business cards, and passed the letter to Natter. "Could you slip this in their mailbox for me? I'll stop over soon for a face-to-face meeting and see what they have to say." She pressed the elevator CALL button. "And thanks again. I really appreciate it."

The doorman saluted her with his coffee, and she and Rudy rode to Bruiser's apartment. Inside the Bests' foyer, she crossed her fingers and called for the Pomeranian.

"He's coming," yipped Rudy. *"And I don't smell that Bibi person, so the coast is clear."*

Before Ellie could comment, Bruiser trotted out from the back of the condo and sat at her feet. "Good morning," she said, hoping for a response.

The ball of fluff grinned, but said nothing.

"How are you today?" she asked, thinking the Pom might need a nudge in the verbal-exchange department.

When he continued to stare, she grabbed his leash from a key board on the wall, squatted, and clipped him to the lead. "I think you and I have something in common," she teased, looking for a reaction. "We have the same color hair."

The Pom licked her fingers, but didn't utter a sound.

"Ever hear that saying 'The lights are on but nobody's home'?" Rudy asked with a snort.

"That is so impolite," Ellie chastised. The poor little guy was probably still traumatized from his frightening encounter with Goth girl. "Okay, don't talk to us," she said as she made her way into the hall. "Just relax, and we'll have you out and back in a jiffy."

Thirty minutes later, she stopped at a second Joe to Go, where she picked up a large tea for Randall and a caramel cappuccino for herself. She'd have to locate Joe soon and tell him how much money she spent in his shops these days. It might be good for business if he started one of those frequent-buyer cards. A lure like "Buy eleven, get the twelfth coffee free" was sure to win him a few more customers.

"I brought your regular," she said as she passed the tea to Randall, who was standing in the Davenport entryway. "Anything happening I should know about?"

"Thank you." He uncapped the cup and took a sip. "There are no police present, if that's what you're asking. But the professor's niece is scheduled to arrive later today with an appraiser." He stuck his free hand inside her jacket pocket. "Perhaps now is the time to take your . . . um . . . survey?"

She didn't have to check to know it was his extra key to the professor's apartment. "I'll see to my charges first and do the deed after I deliver them home."

"Sounds like a good idea," the doorman said, tipping his hat to a passing tenant, who entered the building carrying a newspaper and a bag from a local bakery. "Morning, Mr. Seltzer."

Mr. Seltzer, a silver-haired gentleman well past the age of retirement, nodded politely, then spotted Rudy and grinned. His brown-eyed gaze moved over and upward, taking in Ellie's black flats and wool slacks, then lingered at her breasts. When Randall coughed, he raised his head.

"Frederick Seltzer, at your service. I don't believe we've met." He sketched a bow. "Are you a tenant here?"

"I'm Ellie Engleman, and no, I don't live here," she answered as she followed him into the elevator. How much trouble could a seventy-year-old lech be? "But I do walk a few of the building's four-legged occupants."

He pressed the button for the tenth floor, which also happened to be her first stop. "Ah, I see."

"Do you have a dog?"

"Not at the moment. But now that I know you're business is walking pets, I might be coerced into getting one."

He winked and Rudy sneezed on her feet. *"His pheromones are in good working order, Triple E, so be careful."*

"That's very sweet of you to say," she answered, ignoring her pal. "Here's my card. If you hear of someone in the neighborhood who needs a dog walker, please pass this on."

He read the card and deposited it in the pocket of his Burberry raincoat. "Are you the woman who attended to Professor Albright's Buddy?"

"I was. Did you know the professor?"

"We met with a group in the building once a month to play bridge. He was an excellent partner and a challenging opponent. What happened to him was a shame."

"I assume you've spoken to the police."

"Several times. But I didn't have word one to add to the investigation. Aside from bridge, the only thing the professor and I had in common was our water."

"Water?"

"Gil delivered Liquid Ice to both our apartments, still does to mine." The elevator stopped and he held the door to let her out first. "Are you going to Ms. Jaglinski's unit? If I remember correctly, she has a charming white canine with excellent manners, just like your friend there."

Ellie gazed pointedly at Rudy. "He's a good guy, when he remembers to behave. And picking up Sweetie Pie is always my first order of business. She gets walked twice a day."

"Then I'm sure we'll see more of each other." He turned in the opposite direction. "It was a pleasure meeting you."

An hour later, Ellie stood in front of the professor's door, noting that the crime scene tape had been removed. After inspecting the hallway to her right and left, she inserted Randall's key and entered the apartment foyer. Aside from a hollow feel to the air around her, she didn't notice anything odd. Apparently a company specializing in crime scenes had already taken care of the mess she'd heard was usually created by the investigators.

Once inside, she checked her cell phone to make sure it was on. Randall had promised to call if he saw Victoria Pernell or a police office enter the building, and she planned to be prepared. "Do you want to wait or follow me?" she asked Rudy.

The Yorkiepoo planted his butt on the hardwood floor. *"I'm staying put."*

Dropping his leash, she threw back her shoulders, took a deep breath, and muttered, "Here goes nothing," as she strode down the hall to the rear of the unit.

Unsure of what to look for in the bedroom, she opened dresser drawers, checked under the bed, and gave the closets a once-over. Moving to the professor's office, she again searched a closet and rifled through the bookcases, careful to return things to their proper place as soon as she finished. Then she quickly inspected his desk. A folder on the blotter caught her eye, and she opened it, surprised to find an invoice adorned with a familiar-sounding name on top of a pile of bills.

Reaching into her tote bag, she pulled out the magazine Rita Millcraft had given her last night, *Breeder's Digest*. Thanks to her erotic encounter with Ryder, she'd completely forgotten to check the publication for a link to Buddy. Scanning the invoice, she noted it was a bill for an ad, and the name on the letterhead was the same as that of Rita's magazine.

Her phone rang, and she jumped. "Hello."

"Ms. Pernell is on her way up with an appraiser. I suggest you leave now. Take the freight elevator down and slip out through the service entrance."

"Gotcha." She stuffed the phone into her pocket, stuck the invoice in the magazine, and returned it to her bag as she raced down the hall. "We have to get moving." She dragged Rudy out the door and locked it. The elevator signaled its arrival, and they disappeared around the corner at the same time as she heard voices. Holding her breath, she stood unmoving until the voices faded and a door slammed.

Flooded with relief, she jammed her finger on the freight elevator's CALL button. Moments later, the conveyance shuddered to a stop, and the door jerked open. Before she could step inside, a man backed out pulling a dolly loaded with plastic water bottles.

"Hey, sorry," he said when he realized he'd almost run her down. "I didn't see you there."

She read the brand of water on the side of the container and guessed the tall, thin deliveryman was Gil. "My fault. I don't usually take the back way, but I thought I'd do a bit of exploring today."

"Not a problem." He grinned at Rudy. "Nice-lookin' pooch. What kind of dog is he?"

"A Yorkie-poodle mix," she said, always willing to talk about her canine friend. "You like dogs?"

"You bet." He wiped a hand on his coveralls and offered it to her. "Name's Gil Mitchell."

"I'm Ellie." She accepted his hand, then pulled out a couple of business cards. "Would it be too much trouble if I asked a favor?"

"Uh, sure. What do you need?"

"If you go into an apartment that you know has a dog, would you mind leaving a card on the kitchen counter? I'm new to the job and it's hard finding customers."

"Sure." He tucked the cards in his breast pocket and tilted the dolly. "I'd better be going. Have a nice day."

She led Rudy onto the elevator and waited until

the door closed before speaking. "He seemed like a nice guy."

"Personally, I didn't much care for him. And you know what else? Either my sniffer is on the fritz, or Buddy's scent was all over him."

"Of course it was. He delivered water to the professor's apartment. He probably patted Buddy's head, and the odor is on his uniform."

"Maybe. But there's something else going on with him. I just don't know what."

"You're being silly. He seemed perfectly normal."

"So says you," Rudy chided.

"Yes, I do. And it's time for lunch. I have a magazine to read over, and I'll need peace and quiet to do it."

"Fine by me, because I plan to take a nap. Thanks to Ryder, you kept me up all night. I need my beauty sleep, especially if I have to make nice with your mother later."

She ignored his crack about Ryder and concentrated on the evening to come. "I don't expect you to do anything more than be yourself at dinner. Don't beg, and whatever you do, sit on the floor, not the furniture." She led them off the elevator into a hallway and followed it to a stairway and a ramp. "And no licking—anywhere. Georgette hates when you do that. So do I, by the way."

"Talk about taking the fun out of a social situation."

"That type of crass conduct isn't right for any situation. It won't hurt you to exercise some self-control. Oh, and be nice to Stanley."

"Stanley's an okay guy, for a lawyer."

"He's more than a lawyer. He's a retired judge."

"Lawyer, judge, what's the difference? Hey, you wanna hear a joke?"

"Not another one of your dopey lawyer snipes."

"Jeez, you really know how to hurt a guy."

"Okay, go ahead and say it. But don't get mad if I groan."

"Why don't snakes bite lawyers?"

Ellie rolled her eyes. "I give. Why don't snakes bite lawyers?"

"Professional courtesy." He snickered. *"Get it? Snakes and lawyers are cut from the same cloth."*

"I get it, and you're terrible." She tamped back a smile and opened the door to the outside, where she sagged against the bricks and inhaled a lungful of fresh air. Between the stale atmosphere in the professor's apartment, the institutional smell of the freight elevator, and the pounding of her heart, her adrenaline was bubbling. She needed to eat lunch and study the bill she'd pilfered from the professor's apartment.

Walking to Pop's hot dog cart, she stopped in her tracks when the reality of what she'd done slapped her upside the head. "Oh my God. I'm a thief."

"You? A thief? Hah!"

"No, really, I am. Wait till you hear what I just did." She staggered to a bench, plopped down, and held her head in her hands. "If Ryder finds out about this, I'm toast."

Rudy put a paw on her knee. *"Okay, so what did you do?"*

She pulled the magazine from her bag and flipped it open. "I stole this invoice from Professor Albright's desk. It doesn't belong to me. I had no right to touch it. I could be arrested for tampering with evidence or—"

"That's doubtful. My guess is they already took everything they needed from the place."

Rudy's sensible observation sent a wave of calm coursing through her veins, giving her the courage to thumb through the pages. She found the advertisement section and familiarized herself with its layout, noting the ads were arranged by state. She ran a thumb down the list and scanned the columns.

"We're in luck. New York City is advertised by boroughs. The Bronx . . . Brooklyn . . . Manhattan . . . And here's the ad for Buddy's stud services, with Rita's query about three boxes down from his in the column."

"There's your connection. Now you have to tell Ryder."

"Tell Ryder? And how do I explain the invoice?"

"He doesn't have to know about it. Just say the Millcraft woman gave you the magazine, and you forgot to tell him. After all, it's his fault you weren't

yourself last night and didn't do the research."

"And let him know how much he got to me? Not a chance. Besides, I'd rather come to him with something more concrete than these two ads. And I'm still waiting to hear if more champion dogs were stolen."

"Okay, but don't say I didn't warn you when the doodoo hits the fan."

She slid the magazine back into her bag. "All right already. I'll think about it. Come on. It's time for lunch."

"And then I nap?"

"As if I could stop you. Besides, I have to phone the bonding and insurance companies before I get into real trouble. Then we'll need to take another walk through the neighborhood, check with the Humane Society over on Fifty-ninth, and go to the ASPCA again. Someone might have found Buddy since the last time I asked about him."

"You really think he's out there somewhere?"

Ellie heaved a sigh. "I have to stay positive, and so do you. I'll continue to ask questions while you and the others keep your noses to the ground. If he's on the streets, imagine how frightened he must be. How alone. How sad."

"And if somebody stole him?"

"Then it's up to us to find him, no matter what the police say. I keep thinking we've missed something. Maybe if I sleep on it, I'll figure out what it is."

Chapter 13

That evening, Ellie walked through the entry of the elegant Fifth Avenue high-rise, impressed, as usual, by the building's ambience and aura of refinement. Georgette had lived in the imposing structure for the past three years, ever since her last divorce catapulted her from the ranks of the well-to-do into the land of the obscenely wealthy. Though she came from a healthy family bankroll, their affluence paled in comparison to what Georgette had accumulated over the past four divorces.

"Go right up, Ms. Engleman." The doorman greeted her and Rudy with courtesy. "Mrs. Fuller is expecting you."

Ellie nodded as they passed on their way to the elevator. She made it a point to speak to everyone in a friendly manner, but Orlando scared the bejesus out of her. Though his union insisted on regular days off for its members, he was at his post no matter what time of day or day of the week Ellie stopped by, which made her wonder if he slept or had a personal life. According to her mother, the stalwart doorman guarded the high-rise like his personal kingdom, scheduling cleaning crews, coordinating deliveries, organizing the freight-entrance doormen, and handling anything else needed to keep the building running smoothly.

Thanks to years of city living, she'd learned that each building on the Upper East Side ran things its own way. Some had only a single doorman, like the Davenport and the Beaumont, some a small staff, and many, including Georgette's pricey high-rise, a contingent of men and women who lived to serve their residents every minute of the day.

The D had always thought a condo on Sixty-sixth and Third a step up in the world, especially because of the unit's high six-figure purchase price. In contrast to these stately edifices, it was a mere gardener's cottage on the estate, with no doorman and no special services. From the way Rita Millcraft had talked about her own very nice complex, Ellie felt lucky to have cameras, monitored by an off-site security firm, strategically placed throughout the building.

"Hey, Corinna," she said when her mother's live-in housekeeper, a petite woman about the same age as Georgette, opened the door. "What's new on the home front?"

"Ms. Ellie." Corinna's café au lait skin creased in a smile. "I was wonderin' when you'd show that pretty face of yours. Ms. Georgette, she's been beside herself about this business with the judge. It took a lot for her to swallow her pride and visit the other night."

Ellie stepped closer and lowered her voice. "So you know about the proposal?"

"Sakes, yes. Your mama and me share everything. 'Course, it's not like telling you, you being her daughter and all. She values your opinion."

"Yeah, right," Ellie answered with a roll of her eyes.

"Don't be like that. She let you bring your best man tonight, didn't she?" Corinna bent and scratched Rudy's ears. "How you doin', little boy? You taking good care of your mistress?"

"He's doing an okay job. And he's promised to be on his best behavior while we're here." She gave the terrier mix a warning smile. "Haven't you?"

Corinna's deep contralto soothed her worry over the evening, making her again wonder why the personable and intelligent woman agreed to work for a pain-in-the-butt snob like her mother. She'd finally come to realize Georgette needed the nurturing companionship Corinna gave her, while Georgette filled the hole in Corinna's life due to the death of her husband.

"You're something else, the way you talk to that dog. Mark my word, one of these days he'll answer back, and you're gonna faint in surprise."

"If that happened, I probably would," Ellie told her, biting her tongue at the prophetic statement. They walked from the ornate foyer into the living area. "Where is everybody?"

"Your mama's fussin' in the dining room, and the judge is in the library watching one of his favorite game shows on the flat screen. How about you and Rudy go see him, and I'll tell Ms. Georgette you're here?"

"Fine, but there's no hurry. If you have something else to occupy your time—say, taking a nap or finishing the ironing—feel free to do it."

"You are a pistol," Corinna responded, shaking her head as she disappeared into the bowels of the apartment.

Ellie tiptoed into the library, fearful of startling Stanley into a heart attack or a second stroke. Not that she'd been the cause of his initial attack, but she was concerned about his fragile health. She breathed a sigh when she saw the eighty-three-year-old former superior court judge sitting in his wheelchair, loudly participating in a popular TV game show.

"*W.* You want a *W,* young lady," he ordered the contestant spinning the wheel.

"A *C,*" said the young woman on the screen after she'd landed in the five-hundred-dollar slot, which prompted, "Sorry. There's no *C,*" from the host, and a resounding raspberry from the judge.

Sauntering behind him, she planted a kiss on his shiny hairless head.

"Corinna, how many times do I have to tell you, I'm not here to satisfy your crazed sexual desires? You simply aren't enough woman for me."

Ellie bent and whispered, "Ah, but I'm just your

speed, you old faker. Mentally impaired, pathetic, and dog-tired."

"Oh, Ellie, it's you," he answered with a smile in his voice. "And you're much too young to be dog-tired."

Ignoring the fact that he hadn't quibbled about her being mentally impaired or pathetic, she took a seat on the sofa next to his wheelchair. Rudy stood on his hind legs and rested his front paws on the judge's knee, and was rewarded with a lively ear rubbing. When the greeting ended, the pooch took his place at Ellie's feet.

"You look good, Judge."

"I'm fit as a fiddle, these day, thanks to your mother." His gray gaze appraised her jacket and sweater in a manner that bore no resemblance to Mr. Seltzer's leering assessment. "And you're lovely, as usual. That color suits you." He turned down the sound on the flat screen. "Georgette will approve."

"I certainly hope so." Unlike the other men in her mother's past, the judge was caring, understanding, and sweet. From the moment Ellie met Stanley she'd felt a kinship of sorts, as if he'd been sent to replace the father she'd lost as a teenager. After she connected with Rudy, she'd become a staunch believer in destiny. The judge's insightful comments and uncanny way of knowing how much she desired to please her mother only added to her belief.

"How's the daring new business venture coming along? Still planning to make a living walking dogs for the privileged patrons of Manhattan?"

"I'm trying. And I'm grateful for the encouragement. Your support means the world to me."

"Last time we talked, you were in the process of obtaining insurance and a business license. How's that shaping up?"

"Funny you should ask. I took care of it today," she reported, relieved she'd remembered to make those phone calls. "If the background check pans out, I'll be fully bonded by the end of the month. I gave your name as a reference, by the way, so be sure to tell them what an upstanding citizen I am if the company gets in touch with you."

"Of course. I want nothing more than to see you succeed." He reached into his jacket pocket and pulled out a folded paper. "And before I forget, this is for you."

"For me?" She opened the thick cream-colored sheet of stationery. "Names and phone numbers?"

"They're friends and acquaintances. I've already spoken to each one personally. They live in the vicinity you want to set up business, and all of them have canines. I've asked them to consider you if they're unhappy with their present dog walker or are planning to buy a dog. The starred names are those of people who intimated they were looking for a change. They expect a call."

Ellie swallowed back tears. "I—you—you didn't have to do that for me."

"It was my pleasure. Besides, I'd love to see your mother's face when you pay off your debt. I'm aware of how much you hate owing her money." He winked. "My original offer still stands, you know. I'd be happy to lend you the amount needed to repay her, with no strings. She'd never hear the truth about how you got the cash."

"Thank you, but no," Ellie answered, as she had a dozen times before. "I'm managing, and I'm building a clientele base. I'll be off her list soon enough."

"Good. And speaking of Georgette . . ." His jovial expression turned questioning. "I assume the two of you have discussed my proposal, and I have your blessing."

The hope radiating from the judge's eyes tugged at her heart. "I did everything I could think of to encourage her, though I can't imagine what you see in my egotistical and totally self-absorbed mother, when you know I'm the right girl for you."

His cherubic face lighted with a smile. "And if you were thirty years older, I'd be honored to make you mine. Since that isn't the case, your mother is my second choice."

Ellie clasped his hand and entwined their fingers. "It's the lack of a prenup that's sticking in her craw. On a happier note, I do believe she loves you."

"Then there won't be a divorce," he said with a *humph*. "And no need for a prenuptial agreement. But if it will make her feel more secure, I'll comply with her request."

"Good. You ready for me to wheel you into dinner?"

He heaved a sigh. "In a moment. First, I want your opinion. How much, do you think, will she accept?"

"How much? Jeez, I don't have the faintest idea. Mother's set for life, so it could be a smallish amount."

"Yes, but how small? One million? Two? Ten?"

One, two . . . ten! "Good Lord, Judge," Ellie blurted. "How wealthy are you?"

"I've done quite well for myself over the years," he replied. "And while we're on the subject, you should know that once your mother and I are wed, I intend to treat you exactly as I do my own sons where the matter of my estate is concerned."

"Me? Nuh-uh." Ellie could tell by the heat creeping up her neck that her face was beet red. "No way."

"Nonsense. You're like a daughter to me already. I have plenty of money, and I won't need it when I'm gone."

"It's enough of a burden being Mother's heir. I don't want to be one of yours," she answered, unable to process the idea of profiting from someone's death. "Besides the fact that your two sons wouldn't approve, I wouldn't have the faintest idea what to do with all that green."

"Give it away." He nodded at Rudy. "I'm sure your local ASPCA could use the boost, and they deserve it for rescuing this handsome fellow."

"I'd do anything to help the shelter, but you can leave them money on your own. Better yet, make the donation now—you can do it online. I'll be happy to investigate the details. Just don't mention me and your millions in the same breath. It's morbid. Sick. It's—it's—"

He skimmed his jaw with thumb and forefinger. "Not to worry. I'll figure it out for myself. As long as I have your approval regarding your mother, things will work out fine."

She heaved a breath, embarrassed at her outburst. "Okay, then, no more talk of money."

"No more talk. Now about your offer to bring my chariot to the dining room?"

"Great." She stood and so did her pup. "And remember, our goal tonight is a united front. You, Rudy, Corinna, and I are the four musketeers." Ellie clasped the wheelchair handles. "Hang on, in case I decide to pop a wheelie."

Sam detested wakes, funerals, and anything else that had to do with the deceased. Being comfortable around dead bodies was the most difficult part of his job. He'd had to inspect, study, and write reports on so many strangers who had died under catastrophic circumstances that the idea of viewing those he knew casually or, worse, loved had become more a painful chore than an act of sympathy. And though he'd attended plenty of services for fallen comrades, he always had to prepare himself. Death was a natural part of the circle of life, but he didn't have to like it.

Tonight was no different. He hadn't spoken to Carolanne's father in more than two years, but he recalled the man's fatherly goodwill. When Mr. and Mrs. Jeffers had condemned their daughter for her infidelity, they had caused a family rift that his ex, for reasons known to her alone, believed was Sam's fault. Her unwillingness to take responsibility for her actions was only one of the reasons they hadn't been right for each other.

He and his mother paid their respects at the casket, then approached Patricia Jeffers and her daughter. "Patricia, I was sorry to hear about Frank. He was a good man." He shook the woman's hand. "You remember my mother, Lydia?"

Carolanne greeted them with a frown. "Hello, Sam. Lydia, it's nice to see you again. I only wish it was under more pleasant circumstances."

"Carolanne. Patricia," his mother acknowledged. "We're sorry for your loss. Frank was a wonderful human being. I'll never forget the way he treated my son when—"

Sam squeezed her fingers hard.

"When we were at that . . . that Fourth of July barbecue you threw back in 2003. Frank never did give me the recipe for his . . . his baked beans."

Clutching her daughter's hand, Patricia nodded through her tears. "Thank you for coming."

"Is there anything we can do for you?" Sam's mother asked.

Leave it to Lydia Ryder to offer assistance to an ex-in-law she hadn't seen in several years, and bring up baked beans in the process, Sam thought. His mother was a firm believer in the healing properties of food for any and all ailments, be they of the mind, body, or heart.

"Ever since my husband passed, I have a lot of free time on my hands," Lydia continued. "Come for coffee. I'll make my special cinnamon pecan rolls, and we can sit and talk. You never know when you're going to need a friendly ear."

"Your mother sounds lonely," Carolanne whispered, giving him a tepid smile. "But then, I don't imagine you have time to sit with her."

"Leave it be, Carolanne. This isn't the place to scrape old wounds."

"It never is," she countered. "Dating anybody these days?"

Ellie Engleman's captivating face and wide turquoise eyes popped into his mind, and he quickly suppressed the image. "No. How about you?"

"Two guys," she said with a smug smile. "One's a podiatrist, so he keeps regular hours. He's there for me whenever I need him. The other's a personal trainer." She took a step back and twirled in place. "Notice anything new?"

What I notice is a bag of bones. Carolanne's once respectable figure was now reed thin, her gaunt face troweled with makeup, and her lips plumped to double their usual size. Again, he compared her to his "bad penny" and grinned in spite of himself. "You've lost some weight," he said tactfully.

"I'm a four, official runway-model size," she answered. "I'm thinking of trying to work a few fashion shows."

Before Sam could comment, his mother said, "Carolanne, you're father's illness took its toll on you. You're positively wasting away. When was the last time you had a decent meal?"

His ex frowned, but her facial muscles didn't move. "I've been dieting, Lydia. This is the new me."

"Come on, Ma," Sam advised. "We're holding up the line."

Neither spoke until they were outside.

"Oh, my God. Did you see Carolanne?" his mother asked. Then she began what Sam suspected would turn into a diatribe of mammoth proportions. "She's skin and bones. And her face. Too much makeup, too much—"

"I saw her, Ma."

"But she's a skeleton. I swear, what's up with the women of today? Susan is thin, but she has muscles . . . boobs . . . a butt. She'd never allow anyone to inject that bo-sox stuff into her."

"I think it's called Bo*tox*."

"Bo-sox, Bo-tox. Whatever it is, it's dead cow cells or some other disgusting additive." She shuddered. "And Carolanne used to have breasts. Don't you remember her breasts?"

Sam gazed at the star-filled sky. "I remember."

"Fried eggs. I bet they look just like fried eggs."

"Enough," he ordered. "I don't give a rat turd about the chemicals she's using."

"I heard the two of you whispering. Is she still hoping to break into fashion?"

"She mentioned it." He opened the car door and helped his mother inside, then jogged around and slid behind the wheel. "Buckle up."

"What aren't you telling me?" Lydia went on, as only his mother could. Then she gasped. "Oh no. She wants you back, doesn't she? I knew she had an ulterior motive the moment I saw her all tarted up—"

"She doesn't want me back, Ma." What woman in her right mind would? "She's dating someone, two someones, in fact."

"Two? Hmmph. That figures. The woman will

never change. It wasn't enough she cheated on you; she's even cheating on her boyfriend with another boyfriend."

His phone rang and he jumped to answer it. "Ryder."

"Pellicone, over in the Twentieth, Sam. I'm working a robbery, and I heard through the grapevine the case might interest you."

Sam pulled into traffic. "I'm on the road. How about a quick overview?"

"We're handling a dognapping. Warren Taylor, a detective out of the Nineteenth, said you'd want the particulars."

Another dog gone missing? Well, damn. "I do." He headed toward the Sunnyside section of Queens and his family home. "Give me thirty minutes. You on your cell?"

"Yep. I'll be waiting."

Sam closed his phone and set it in a cradle on the dash. "I can't stay. The caller has information linked to a case I'm working, and it sounds important."

"I understand." Lydia placed her hand on his forearm. "This was nice, Sammy, even if it took a funeral to get us together. Will you make dinner this week?"

"I'll try," he answered, turning a corner.

"That's what you always say."

Her wounded tone raised his guilt quotient a couple of notches. "Honest, I will. I don't miss on purpose, Ma. It's the job."

Her "I know" was followed by a heaving sigh.

He pulled in front of the house. "Want me to walk you to the door?"

"That's not necessary. Just stay here until I'm inside." She leaned over and planted a kiss on his cheek. "You know this neighborhood is safe."

Sam waited while she walked through the gate and onto the porch. Turning, she waved and let herself in. The porch light flickered and went dark, and he sat there until he saw the upstairs hall light go on. Then he hit a button on his phone and returned Detective Pellicone's call.

The perfectly prepared dinner, complete with sterling silver and Georgette's finest china and crystal, was one of her mother's usual lo-carb affairs. The meal, accompanied by a vintage sauvignon blanc which Ellie guessed cost a hundred dollars a bottle, and a caviar and lobster appetizer, had been chosen to impress, and they did.

She dropped a second pat of butter onto her baked potato, then added a heaping spoonful of sour cream. Corinna had made the potatoes especially for her and the judge. She'd also provided a creamy, homemade blue cheese dressing along with Georgette's standard balsamic vinaigrette, to go on the endive-and-pear salad.

"Do you really need all that butter?" Georgette asked, staring at Ellie's plate.

"She's starting again," came a voice from under the table.

Good thing Rudy couldn't see her mother's raised brow or pursed lips, or he'd probably nip Georgette's ankle, thought Ellie. Refusing to acknowledge the pointed jibe, she rubbed the pooch with her toes. Thanks to Stanley's clever manipulation of the conversation, her mother hadn't gone overboard on comments concerning her daughter's invisible love life, lack of fashion sense, dubious profession, or her less than stellar figure.

"The broiled sole was fabulous, as were the string beans. What's for dessert?" Okay, so she was begging for trouble. "Please tell me Corinna made one of her special pies."

"Dessert?" Georgette asked. "I thought you'd be too full for another morsel, what with all the calories you just inhaled."

Ellie rarely ate the amount of food she'd had tonight, but doing so gave her a chance to show her mother she'd bid her old life good-bye for good. "I don't count calories anymore. The D is dead to me, and so are his rules."

"What about your health? You've stopped going to the club, and I'm certain all that fat is doing disastrous things to your cholesterol level."

"I can't afford the club, and even if I could, I don't have the time." Ellie swallowed a final forkful of potato and scraped up the last of her green beans. "I had a physical about a month ago. My cholesterol is well within normal range, and thanks to my profession, I get plenty of exercise. I wore a pedometer last week, and it registered almost ten miles a day."

"What did the doctor say about your weight?"

"My weight?" she asked, purposely obtuse. "What about it?"

Her mother *tsk*ed. "You must have put on thirty pounds since the divorce."

"Thirty-seven, but who's counting?"

"And?"

"And I'm healthy in every way I need to be. If you check the charts, I'm on target for a large-boned woman of my height."

"Large-boned? How can you say that when the women in my family are just the opposite?"

"I take after dad's side, remember?"

Georgette's pinched expression telegraphed her displeasure.

"You never did answer the girl's question," Stanley interjected. "What's for dessert?" He leaned back and burped behind his napkin. "Excuse me. The meal was wonderful."

Corinna took that moment to stride into the dining room carrying a tray holding a lemon meringue pie, dessert plates, a sterling silver coffee urn, and cream and sugar. "Finish up now, 'cause this pie isn't waitin' around," she ordered. "And who wants coffee?"

"Corinna, there's no need to rush us." Georgette dabbed her lips with her French linen serviette. "And the sole was exceptional. Thank you."

"I hope that's decaf," said the judge.

"Of course." Corinna passed a full cup to him. "How about you, missy?"

"Not for me." Ellie glanced at her watch. "I can't stay much longer, so let's get down to the nitty-gritty while we dig into that pie."

"Yes, let's," said the judge. "Georgette, when are you going to accept my proposal?"

Corinna grinned as she cut pieces of pie and set a plate in front of each guest. Then she pulled up a chair and joined them as if she were an old family friend. "Yes, Ms. Georgette, when are you going to put the poor man out of his misery?"

Ellie's mother blanched, gazing at everyone around the table. "I don't believe it. Who's idea was this planned attack?"

"Not an attack," Stanley answered, forking up a bite of pie. "Merely an intervention. The three people who love you most are sitting here, hoping you'll use your head and do the right thing. I'm too old to wait any longer, my dear. Who knows how many good years I have left?"

Tears sparkled in Georgette's blue eyes. "Don't say such things. There are plenty of good years ahead of you."

"Of course, there are, Mother. But think of the stress you're putting on the judge's heart. He loves you and wants to spend as much of his life as he can with you."

"Amen to that," Corinna added.

As if three years old, Georgette stuck out her lower lip. "We're already living together—"

"In sin," he added.

"You're not being fair. I need more time—"

"It's you that isn't being fair, Mother. Time is the one thing Stanley may not have."

The judge straightened in his wheelchair, then grinned at Ellie. "Do me a favor and wheel me over to the lady of the house, if you please."

Eager to do his bidding, Ellie stood. It was good to see her know-it-all mother at a loss for words. When they arrived beside Georgette's chair, the judge pulled a pale blue box from his pocket and held it out to her.

"Georgette, I love you. I'll even sign a damn prenup, if it will make you happy. Please marry me."

He opened the box, and her mother inhaled a breath while Ellie stared in shock. The square-cut diamond was the size of a postage stamp. All Ellie could manage was a whispered, "Way to go, Stanley."

Georgette held out her hand and allowed the judge to slip the ring on the proper finger. Ellie pushed the wheelchair closer, and her mother bent and placed her lips on her fiancé's.

Corinna swiped at her eyes. "Allow me to be the first to congratulate you."

"And I'm second." Ellie bent and kissed Stanley's cheek, then her mother's. When her phone rang, she walked to her seat and dug in her bag. "Hello?"

"Ellie? It's David Crane."

She turned her back on the happy couple. "Hi. What's up?"

"I just finished talking to my vet friend, Dr. Lepitsky. There was another dognapping."

"No kidding? Where?"

"The west side of town. A miniature poodle bitch. It happened yesterday morning." He gave her the name and address of the owners. "Hope it helps in your hunt for Buddy."

"I'm sure it will. Thanks."

She snapped closed the phone and tucked it away. It was too late to visit someone she didn't know, but tomorrow was Saturday. The Marinos would probably be home. She only hoped she didn't upset them by asking questions while they grieved for their missing dog.

The thought of phoning Sam flashed through her mind, and she balked. She had yet to inform him of the ads in the breeders' magazine. When she added this third dognapping to the list, it was too much to explain over the phone, but she wasn't keen on spending any more personal time with him than was necessary. Better to mull it over and do something about it in the morning.

In the meantime, she'd take another gander at

those advertisements. If she found one announcing the Marinos were looking for stud service, she'd have a real lead.

And a plausible lead was what she needed to convince Ryder she knew what she was doing.

Chapter 14

"So. How long are you gonna keep me a prisoner here?"

Ellie fluffed her hair in the bathroom mirror while Rudy sat at her feet. They'd returned from his morning walk, and she'd just informed him he would not be tagging along on her visit to the Marino family.

"I'll only be an hour or two. Use the time to catch up on your sleep."

"I slept plenty last night," he grumped.

"Well, I didn't." She studied her reflection, noting that a swipe of peach-colored lip gloss and a couple strokes of mascara were all the fussing she planned to do in preparation for her day. She'd worn a full complement of makeup yesterday, and had hated every minute of it. "Would you rather I turn on TV Land? Twink seems to love it."

"Only because he's obsessed with that guy who wears all the gold jewelry. He's keepin' his paws crossed that Viv buys him the same kind of collar for Christmas."

Ellie grinned. She'd seen a lot of canine wear,

both cute and ridiculous, at the PetCo on Eighty-sixth as well as at Bark Place on Seventy-second, but never a collar bedecked with gold chains. She couldn't imagine anyone being stupid enough to buy one for their dog, even if they were available. The dangling chains could get caught on a dozen things around the house and create a choking hazard for the poor pup who wore them.

"Remind me to talk some sense into him, next time we're on the topic of doggie fashion, okay? He's taking this Mr. T business a bit too far."

"Yeah. Whatever."

She sat on the commode lid, and he rose on his hind legs for a scratch. "I could turn on a classical station. It's your favorite type of music. Soothing and mellow are good when you're in a grouchy mood."

Leaning into her stroking fingers, he snorted. *"How about a nice long walk in the park? I met a friend yesterday, and maybe she'll be there today."*

Ellie racked her brain for a clue. "Are you talking about the little Havanese that got loose in the afternoon?" Owned by an elderly woman, the petite pup had broken free of its leash and gravitated toward Buckley, Sweetie Pie, and Rudy. She'd hung around long enough for Ellie to gather her up and return her to Mrs. Steinman, to whom Ellie had also given a few of her business cards. "The one we rescued? Lulu?"

"That's the one." He made deep panting sounds. *"She's hot for me and vice versa."*

"I hate to harp on the subject but you're . . . um . . . not intact, remember?"

"So you keep saying. It doesn't mean Lulu and I can't engage in a bout of friendly humping. You humans do that all the time."

"We do not!" Ellie stood, embarrassed. The denial was a lie, and her pooch knew it. Though she wouldn't exactly call what she and Ryder had done the other night *humping,* Rudy had heard and smelled their raging pheromones through the door. "I'm late. I have to get going."

"Sure, run away when you're caught with your pants down," he shouted, trotting behind her. His nails clicked a pointed "guilty, guilty, guilty" on the hardwood floor as he followed her into the kitchen.

Refusing to look at him, she went about the task of making amends. "Here's fresh water." She filled his bowl at the sink and set it on his place mat. "And here's something special." She pulled a mini-Dingo bone from its red-and-yellow package. "Because you were such a good boy at Mother's last night."

His eyes darted from hers to the rawhide chew and back again. *"If that's hush money, I'm up for it,"* he told her, and snatched the chew from her hand.

Ellie straightened her black turtleneck sweater,

slipped on a lightweight denim jacket, and headed for the door. With luck, Rudy would sleep for the morning after devouring his treat, giving her plenty of time to talk to the Marinos and do a little snooping for Buddy, too.

She left the apartment and strolled into the nearest Joe to Go, smiling when she spotted her old school buddy working the counter. A handsome, dark-haired Joey Tribianni look-alike with an attitude to match, Joe Cantiglia had two things in his favor: a mind for business and a warm personality that reeled everyone to his side.

"I'll have a half-caf skim latte, extra hot, hold the whip but add cream, and one packet of the blue stuff," she chimed at him across the counter. It was a barista's coffee order nightmare, and she'd done it on purpose. "Oh, and throw in a splash of that amaretto flavoring."

Joe raised his head and peered around the customer standing at the register. "Look, lady, you have to wait your—" His scowl morphed to a grin when he saw her. "Damn, Engleman, I should have know it was you by that pain-in-the-keester order. Is that really what you're drinking these days?"

She opened her wallet and pulled out a five. "Heck, no. I'll take a large caramel bliss, extra hot. I can add my own crap at the bar."

Joe scribbled on her cup and passed it to a helper. "So how you doin'?"

"I'm good. I've stopped at both stores and haven't seen you in a couple of days. What's up?"

"I'm opening a third Joe to Go over on Park and Eighty-first."

"Wow, nice address."

"It's costing me a fortune, but it'll be worth it. I've got sidewalk privileges, with a half dozen umbrella tables and extra chairs."

"Just in time for summer. Lucky you." Ellie stepped to the side and waited while he took another order, then grabbed the cup the barista set on the divider. "How's Bev?"

He heaved a sigh. "We broke up. She said I was too busy to give her the attention she and the relationship deserved. What about you? No more hassles from the D?"

She rested a hip against the counter. "Not a one. It's just me and Rudy now."

"Guess that means you're still walking dogs."

"I have six regulars, and the possibility of a couple more." She sipped the drink, savoring the rich caramel flavor. It needed more cream, but she wanted to spend another minute with Joe. "Know anyone around here who could use a walker?"

"You're too expensive for my friends, but I'll hand a card to whoever comes in."

She dug a few business cards from her bag and passed them over. "Thanks. And tell them to call for my rates. They're comparable to what everyone else charges. The difference is the extra care."

He rang up another order. "Extra care?"

"You know, the special handling. I treat each charge like I do my own baby. Plenty of walk time, scratches, and tummy rubs, even a little ball playing in the park. And a price break for two walks a day or two dogs from the same owner. And speaking of breaks . . ."

"You want free coffee? Jeez, Engleman, are you that bad off?" he joked.

"Not me, you dope. I have an idea your competitor doesn't, and I'm sure it will improve sales. What about offering one of those punch cards with a 'buy eleven, get the twelfth cup free' motto printed on it. Hell, I buy so much coffee at your stores you already owe me a free pot."

"Hmm. Might be something to think about." He pursed his lips. "Thanks for the idea."

"In return, maybe you can do me a favor?"

"I'll try."

She pulled two flyers from her bag and passed them over the counter. "Hang these in the window of both shops, and ask your customers if they've seen a small white dog on the loose. If they say yes, tell them to copy my number off of here and give me a call."

"Going into search and rescue, are you?"

"Not exactly. The dog belonged to a client, but

the client died and the pooch disappeared. If I don't find him—"

"No one else will bother. I get the picture. Okay, count me in. I'll have them up by noon."

Outside, Ellie caught a cab and gave the driver the Marinos' West Side address. Leaning back in the seat, she sipped her drink and thought about Ryder. She hadn't called him on this lead, but if she phoned him now, he'd never get there in time to meet her. And there was a possibility she wouldn't find a connection to Buddy and Jimmy. Better to catch him after she talked to the Marino family. She could tell him about the breeders' magazine at the same time.

Twenty minutes later, she'd paid the driver, tossed her empty container in a trash basket, and climbed the steps to the Marinos', where she pressed the buzzer under their name.

"Yes," said a child's voice.

"I'd like to talk to Mr. or Mrs. Marino, if they're home."

"Mom," the kid shouted, "it's for you."

Seconds later, a woman answered the intercom. "This is Sylvia Marino."

"Good morning. My name is Ellie Engleman. I just need a minute of your time. It's about your missing dog."

The buzzer sounded immediately, and Ellie pushed into the building and glanced at the layout. It appeared to be two apartments per floor, which meant the people living here had plenty of room for both pets and children. She climbed the stairs and steeled herself at the door, then raised her fist to knock. She'd learned from her discussion with Rita Millcraft this was the hardest part of the interview.

When a hand clasped her shoulder, she shrieked.

Though it was his first free Saturday in a month, Sam had too much on his plate to bag everything and relax. Detective Pellicone's phone call had been interesting, definitely worth consideration, even if the crime had been committed on the opposite side of town.

He hated to lose the prime parking spot he'd snagged last night, so he hopped the subway while he thought about the latest missing dog. The details were too on-target to be ignored. There had to be a connection between the three dognappings, but what? Flipping open his spiral pad, he scanned the pages. Each of the dogs was small, which made them easy to handle. Each was a champion, something canine aficionados admired, and each was stolen after the owners had been zapped as they'd answered the door. With luck, this interview would point him in the direction needed to close this case.

He climbed the subway steps and set out for the Marinos' building, taking in the bright sunshine, cool, dry air, and clear blue sky. One of these days he was going to find the time to book a plane at that small airfield in Far Rockaway and spring for some fly time. Flying was his only hobby, but he hadn't been in a plane since the previous fall. A little R & R in the clouds might relieve some of the tension he'd been immersed in of late.

It was either that or find a lady friend and get in a couple rounds of exercise between the sheets.

Fat chance, his mind nagged. A few hours of fly time would never take the place of hot and heavy sex with a willing woman, especially Ellie Engleman, with her killer body, full lips, and wide turquoise eyes.

Acting on those "below the belt" impulses would be a good idea—if the woman in mind was anyone but his personal "bad penny." The sex he wanted right now had to be uncomplicated, no strings, and just a step up from a one-night stand. He had a gut feeling that wouldn't be possible with the frustrating dog walker, no matter how much he wanted to jump her bones.

He took the stairs to the brownstone's entry, found the Marinos' mailbox, and rang the bell.

"Hello," said a woman.

"Detective Sam Ryder, New York City PD. I'm here to discuss your missing dog."

"Didn't I already ring you up? Come on in," she said in a sharp tone. The buzzer went off, and he opened the door to the inner foyer. Mrs. Marino sounded short-tempered. Then again, she'd lost a

family pet. Remembering Ellie's silent chastisement when he'd spoken abruptly to Rita Millcraft,
he agreed he might not be the most sensitive guy
on the planet. Add that to the fact that he had a
hard time relating to dog people, every one of
whom seemed to be addicted to their canine companion, and he understood the disconnect.

The stairs led to a hallway with a single door on
each side. The area was dark, so he didn't immediately notice the person poised to knock at one of
the units. When he did, his breath caught, and his
stomach clenched.

Going for surprise, he tiptoed down the hall
until he reached his destination and placed a hand
on Ellie Engleman's shoulder. When she jumped
and let out a scream, he released her, and she
turned, giving him a disdainful stare. Would the
woman never learn?

"I don't believe this. Next time I make an
appointment with a lead, how about I just pick you
up on the way? It'll save you cab fare."

Her expression morphed from shocked to
annoyed in a half second. "What are you doing
here?"

"You're kidding, right?"

"No—yes—I mean—you—you scared the crap
out of me. Are you wearing shoes or moccasins?"

He quirked up a corner of his mouth. "Shoes,
but I'm light on my feet." Placing a palm on the
door-frame, he leaned toward her. "Want to tell

me why you're here, or are we going to play twenty questions?"

"I meant to call you." Her face flushed. "I heard about the Marinos and—"

"Thought to beat me to the punch."

"No, of course not. That vet friend of mine, Dr. Crane? His pal Dr. Lepitsky heard about another dognapping, and they talked about it. I got the message late last night and figured you probably wouldn't work on a Saturday. I didn't want to bother you on your day off."

"So you decided to keep me out of the loop as a professional courtesy? That's a good one." Hanging on to his temper, he asked, "Any idea why he'd contact you instead of me?"

"Because he knows I'm looking for Buddy," she lectured, jutting her chin. "I want to find Professor Albright's killer as much as you do, but Buddy's the one who's still got a chance at salvation, which makes him a priority."

"I see." Time to have a talk with the veterinarian, he decided, just as soon as he took care of Ellie Engleman and her continued interference. "Who do the Marinos think you are?"

"I gave my name and asked if I could speak with them about their missing dog. They let me come right up. It's funny she's taking her time answering the door."

No wonder Mrs. Marino sounded annoyed. He was her second caller in a minute, only she thought he was with Ellie and still hadn't let himself in. "Smart girl, 'cause I'd hate to add impersonating an officer to the charges I'm going to level if I find you sticking your nose where it doesn't belong again."

"You wouldn't dare."

She had some nerve acting indignant when he was the wounded party here. "What else do you know about the missing mutt?"

"Gemma's hardly a mutt. She took best in breed at Madison Square Garden a couple of years back."

He straightened. "I already know that."

"Then you see the connection?"

"That's why I'm here."

"Well, there's something you don't know. It's about—"

Before she could continue, the door opened and an attractive woman, Sylvia Marino, he guessed, stared at them. "I heard you mumbling through the door, and didn't want to intrude. What's going on?"

Sam whipped out his badge and raised it for her inspection. "I'm Detective Ryder, Mrs. Marino, and I have a few questions about your missing dog."

"Did the man find Gemma?" asked a dark-haired girl of about five, who was hanging on to the woman's knee.

"I don't know, honey." Ignoring Ellie, she gazed at Sam through serious brown eyes. "Did you?"

"No, but—"

The child burst into tears and fled down the hall. Mrs. Marino sighed, then stepped back and let them in. "I'm not sure what more I can add to the story. My husband and I gave the detectives every bit of information we had." She led them into a large living room strewn with toys. A baby wailed in the background, adding to the din her daughter created.

"Take a seat. I'll be back in a minute."

Sam recognized one of those skinny, big-busted dolls little girls seemed to dote on, perched on a toy truck, along with building blocks and a few books scattered throughout the room. His gaze slid to Ellie, and their eyes locked. "I don't want you to say word one. Is that clear?"

"But I haven't told you everything yet."

"You told me all I need to know. I'm going to call Dr. Crane as soon as we leave here, and instruct him to put me first on his speed dial, or he'll be joining you in that jail cell."

Her eyes opened wide. "You're joking."

"Try me."

Mrs. Marino returned with baby on her hip, and sat in a chair across from them. Balancing the kid on her thigh, she proceeded to unbutton her blouse, pull down her bra, place the child to her breast, and conceal the motherly action with a pale blue blanket. Sam felt like a voyeur, though his being there didn't seem to bother Mrs. Marino in the least. Pellicone had hinted that the woman was "out there," and he figured this was the reason why.

Once the baby settled in, the woman raised her head. "What do you want to know?"

He cleared his throat. Where the hell was he supposed to focus now? Was this what he had to look forward to when Sherry had her kid? "Um . . . I understand your missing poodle is a champion? Worth a lot of money?"

"Even though Gemma had tremendous success in the show ring, she was a family pet first. My grandmother bred toy poodles, and Gemma was pick of the litter so we could keep the bloodline in the family. My daughter, Kayla, loves her to pieces, and Ben here was coming to love her, too. I was in bed when it happened, nursing my son, and Kayla was asleep. Phil heard a knock, thought it might be one of our neighbors, and left to answer the door. Gemma followed him out. A minute or two later, I heard a thud and the slamming of a door." She peeked under the blanket, then raised her gaze. "I called to him, but didn't get an answer, so I put the baby in his crib and went to investigate. Phil was flat on his back in the hall."

"Then what?" Sam asked, scribbling details on his pad.

"At first, I thought he'd been knocked out. After a few minutes' encouragement, he came around, and I helped him up. He claimed he'd been hit with a stun gun or something like it, because the second he grabbed the knob to open the door an electric shock laid him out flat." Sylvia swiped at a tear. "It was then we realized Gemma was gone. Phil ran into the hall but didn't see her, so he told me to call the police while he scoured the building."

The baby made a noise, and she peeked under the blanket again. Sam glanced at Ellie and smiled when he saw her pink cheeks and embarrassed expression.

Stop that, she mouthed when she caught his teasing grin.

He wrote another line in his notebook, then said to Sylvia, "So there was no trace of the dog?"

"No, and it took another hour for the detectives to show, during which time my husband continued to scope out the building and the street in front of the apartment. He referred to it as a 'hit and run,' because whoever took Gemma knew their way in and out of the complex."

"Do you use a dog walker?" Sam and Ellie asked in unison.

He shot Ellie a scowl meant to quell the most persistent of pests, but she paid him no mind.

"I'm only asking because it's usually easy for them to get inside a building unnoticed," Ellie said, making a point of concentrating on Mrs. Marino.

"I'm a stay-at-home mom, so Gemma got walked when I escorted Kayla to preschool and when I picked her up, but a couple of the other tenants use walkers. We gave the police their names, and I assume the officers checked it out."

"Would you mind giving me their names? I'm a dog walker, too, and I might know them."

Mrs. Marino raised a winged brow. "A dog walker? I thought you were with the police?"

"I lost a client the same way you lost Gemma, and I—"

"It's a long story," Sam interrupted. "And I'll get the names from Pellicone." He gave Ellie a warning frown, and she had the nerve to toss him a dirty look. "Where's your husband right now?" he asked Sylvia.

"At his office. He's a writer for a local television program." Mrs. Marino named a popular afternoon talk show, then took her time shifting the baby to her other breast. "The theft has taken a toll on our daughter," she added in a quiet voice. "On all of us, if you must know."

Sitting forward on the sofa, Ellie asked, "Have you received a ransom note or a phone call asking for money?"

"No." Sylvia paled. "Do you think that's what this is? That someone is holding Gemma for ransom?"

"I don't know, but here's another question."

Sam put his hand on Ellie's knee and squeezed, but she kept on chatting.

"Did you plan to breed her?"

"We were considering it. We put an ad in a breeders' magazine, just to see what kind of offers we got. If the dog was worthy of our line, we were going to let my grandmother handle it, but she's getting up in years, so I thought it might be fun to try doing things on my own."

Sam stood and took Ellie's hand, pulling her to her feet. "I think that's all the questions for now." Sylvia fiddled with the blanket, and he raised a hand. "Don't get up. We'll see ourselves out."

Steering Ellie ahead of him, he turned in the living room doorway. "And I'm sorry for the loss of your dog. We'll do everything in our power to see that she's returned."

As soon as they were out of Sylvia Marino's sight, Ellie wrenched her elbow from Sam's grasp and marched out the apartment door. It was bad enough he'd caught her disobeying a direct order; watching Sylvia Marino, a very pretty woman, nurse her baby in front of him was mortifying. And he'd had the nerve to grin at her, as if he was thinking . . .

It didn't matter what he'd been thinking, she told herself. The important thing was that she'd tried to tell him she had more information, but he wouldn't listen. When she had brought it up with Sylvia, he had acted as if she didn't know what she was talking about. After his overbearing treatment, she'd throw snowballs in August before she filled him in on the magazine and anything else she deemed pertinent to the case.

Trotting down the stairs, she heard, "Engleman! Wait a second," but kept going. Unfortunately, Sam caught up with her as she slammed out of the building.

"You got a problem taking orders?" he asked, clasping her elbow a second time.

Spinning around, she jerked from his grip. "This isn't a branch of the armed forces, so I didn't think 'taking orders' is the proper term." She jogged to the sidewalk and headed for home. Hiking a couple of miles would help work off her anger and frustration, plus keep her from whacking him on the head if he touched her again.

"Hang on," he shouted, catching up to her.

She kept on walking.

"Hey." He two-stepped in front of her, and they danced from side to side. "Ellie, wait."

Blowing out a breath, she stood still and met his heated gaze. "What?"

"What do you mean, what? I'm trying to talk to you."

"I don't think we have anything to say to each other. In fact, the sound of my voice seems to get you so angry you won't let me finish a sentence."

He stuffed his hands into the pocket of his leather jacket. "Sorry about that."

When he moved over to clear the walkway, she

moved with him, waiting for the tirade to continue. A breeze ruffled his blond curls, and she noted he'd gotten a haircut. He grinned boyishly and she sighed. At least he'd stopped yelling.

"I thought we had ironed out your part in all this," he began.

She focused on his broad chest, remembered how hard and demanding it had felt under her fingers, and met his whiskey-colored eyes again. "I do understand. My job is to find Buddy. I can't help it if our paths cross in the process."

"I asked you politely—"

"You demanded. There's a difference."

"You mean all I had to do was say, 'Pretty please, Ms. Engleman, keep your nose out of my case,' and you wouldn't be here right now?" He raised a brow. "Why is it I doubt that?"

She opened and closed her mouth. Damn, but she hated being wrong, even when she was. "I'm not doing anything dangerous, so what's it to you?"

"It's my responsibility to look into matters. When you show up and run an inquisition, it appears as if I'm unable to do my job. I'm trained to take statements, examine what was said, and come to a conclusion. And no matter what you say, you could be in danger."

"How?" She put her hands on her hips. "We've already agreed my dog is not the breed that would interest a kidnapper."

"So you admit you're looking for the kidnapper, which translates into a murderer?"

"Believing there's a kidnapper is the only thing that's allowed me to fall asleep at night since this episode began. Because if there isn't—" Her head started to spin. What didn't the man understand? "Buddy just has to be alive."

He frowned and gazed skyward, then looked her in the eyes. "What if I said I thought you were right?"

"You do?"

"I hate to admit it, but yes, I do. I'm also riding your bandwagon—find Buddy and I'll find Albright's killer."

Her shoulders slumped. "Then what's your problem?"

"My problem." He shook his head. "You don't get it, do you? I'm paid to do a job, and you're interfering. Plus, I don't want you to get hurt." He took her hand, and she forgot to whack him for it. "You're an okay lady."

Uh-oh. She tugged, but he'd entwined their fingers. When she started to speak, he headed up the street bringing her along with a determined stride. "How about lunch?"

He was talking food? "We did that the other night."

"That was dinner. This is lunch. We can sit and eat while you tell me what you were trying to tell me in the Marino's apartment. I'll listen and consider."

They were halfway across the park before she realized it. "Where do you want to eat?"

"Anyplace is fine. You must know a few good restaurants."

"I like burgers and fries."

"Who doesn't?" he asked, smiling.

"The Wickery is good. It's nice enough to eat outside, and it's just over on Lexington."

"Sounds good. Lead the way."

Chapter 15

The Wickery, one of Ellie's favorite restaurants, was located next to a day spa she'd frequented when the D insisted she be polished, painted, and primed for his business functions. Someday, when she had extra cash and free time, she'd return for a facial or— Heck, no. What was she thinking? There was a new man in her life—one she cared for deeply.

Instead, she'd bring Rudy to Pampered Pets Inc. over on Sixty-ninth for a proper grooming and massage or maybe a treatment in the whirlpool. Manhattanites were suckers for their dogs, and she was no different. Viv had mentioned the two of them taking their boys together, but Ellie never had the money. Now that her business was on the rise, she might be able to swing it.

"Is there a particular reason you're smiling?" asked Sam, intruding on her thoughts.

"What? Oh, sorry. No, I was just thinking about my dog."

"You mean your mini-Cujo?"

"He's very sweet, just overprotective where I'm concerned. I don't think he'd bite anyone unless I was threatened."

"Uh-huh," Sam answered, his expression doubtful.

The waiter stopped to take their order, and they asked for the same thing: a burger smothered in blue cheese with fries and cole slaw.

"You never cease to surprise me," he confided.

"Surprise you? In what way?"

"Your lunch. It's not something many women would order."

"I know I'm not a size six but—"

"Hey, as I said before, I like a woman who eats."

"I burn a lot of calories with all the walking I do," she added, not sure he meant what he said.

"And it shows. You have dynamite legs." He grinned. "The rest of you is pretty good, too."

She bit her tongue, positive she was supposed to tell him he was a cretin, but the observation made her warm and fuzzy inside. "Thanks . . . I think."

"You're welcome." He took a drink of beer, then said, "Time to come clean, Engleman. What did you want to tell me at the Marinos'?"

With no more evasive tactics up her sleeve, Ellie explained about the breeders' magazine she'd received from Rita Millcraft and filled him in on the advertisements. But she wasn't about to explain the part about using Randall's key to steal the professor's invoice. It might get Randall in trouble, and she could be thrown in jail for breaking and entering, when she hadn't exactly done either one.

"And you were keeping the information a secret because . . ."

"I wasn't keeping it a secret. I had every intention of telling you, but you wouldn't let me get a word in."

He thinned his lips. "And I apologized, so let it go and tell me about the magazine. Would a canine lover get *Breeder's Digest* through a subscription, or is it available anywhere?"

"Rita had a subscription, but I don't know about Professor Albright. Since I'm not into dog breeding, I've never had to search for the publication."

"Where's the copy Millcraft gave you?"

"At home. If we don't find it at the PetCo, you can have my copy."

"Great. I'll call the magazine and ask for their subscriber bank. The computer guys can run the list through the system and pull out the names of whoever lives in New York."

She gave herself a mental slap in the head. She should have thought of that trick herself. What kind of private eye was she, anyway? "I didn't realize—"

"That the police department can do a number of

things ordinary citizens can't?" he interrupted. "If you watched a few cop shows on TV, you'd know that."

She blew out a breath. "I'm acquainted with databases. I just didn't apply it to police procedure, is all."

"Hang on. Are you admitting I thought of something you didn't? Wait a second while I mark the date on my calendar," he said smugly. "And don't tell me you agree that this city's police department is capable of doing something intelligent."

"Looks like it," she retorted. If the dastardly detective was this chatty all the time, maybe she wouldn't break into a sweat whenever they were together.

The waiter brought their burgers, and they concentrated on their food. Then Ellie caught him gazing at her, and her insides twitched. "So . . . um . . . how do we handle things in the store?"

He leaned back, snagged a French fry, and dragged it through the ketchup pooled on his plate. "Simple. I talk to a couple of clerks and ask if they remember anyone buying the magazine. You can help if you promise to behave." With that, he popped the fry into his mouth and chewed.

"Behave? What are you suggesting?"

"It's not an insult," he said after swallowing. "I'm making a deal. We work together on this lead. I'll quiz the staff while you check out the book rack and see if they carry the magazine. Take a look at whatever else is similar, make sure that's the only ad the professor and Millcraft posted, and see if the Marinos advertised, too. How about it?"

"Are you suggesting a partnership?"

"Don't get excited. It's just for this one project. Think of it as a thank-you for telling me about the magazine."

"Excuse the pun, but throwing me a bone for giving you a lead isn't necessary." When he didn't comment, she grew indignant. "This might be the break we—you—need to blow the case wide-open. If I'd kept the information to myself, you'd still be wondering which end is—"

"Take it easy. I would have gotten to this point on my own, soon enough. And consider this. You're at a dead end unless you have access to a system that can connect you to the publisher, or a court order asking them to release the records." He raised a brow. "Do you?"

There he was, being right again. "No."

"I rest my case." He grinned as if he'd pinned her to the mat. "Do we have a deal?"

"Sure, fine." Ellie finished the last of her burger and pushed away from the table. The bill had already been delivered, and as far as she was con-cerned, the smart-ass could pay the check. "Now if you'll excuse me, I'm going to the restroom."

They reached the pet store fifteen minutes later. Inside, Sam gave her a warning glance.

"Remember what we agreed on. You do your job, and I'll do mine."

He strode toward a checkout counter, while she wandered to the magazine section and scanned the ads in *Dog Fancy*, *Pet Journal*, *Gun Dog*, *Dog and Kennel*, *Canine Review*, and a dozen other periodicals. There were magazines specific to Akitas, Samoyeds, Bezengis, cocker spaniels, and a host of other breeds, but there were none on poodles or bichons. And the magazine she needed, *Breeder's Digest*, was nowhere to be found.

Peeking around an end cap, she spied Sam speaking intently to a female clerk. The man was such a flirt, it was a wonder she'd ever considered . . . what she'd considered. She'd heard of people hooking up at a Borders, but a pet store? Maybe if somebody warned the salesgirl that he didn't like canines, she wouldn't be so eager to please.

Ellie turned a corner and found herself in the pet-food aisle. Recalling that Rudy's supply was running low, she reached for a sack of his favorite kibble, a brand made especially for smaller breeds, and bumped into a man aiming for the same bag.

"Oh, sorry," she said, taking a step of retreat.

"No, no, my fault." The customer passed her a sack. "Here, ladies first."

Glancing at him, Ellie smiled a thank-you. "It's Gil, isn't it?" she said to the Liquid Ice man. "I'm Ellie. We met yesterday."

"At the Davenport, right? You were taking the freight elevator, and I was coming in with a delivery."

"That's correct."

He focused on the kibble. "That for your little guy?"

"It's his favorite. I guess your pal likes it, too."

Gil retrieved another bag from the shelf. "Ah, yeah. It's expensive stuff, but they're worth it."

"You have more than one? What kind are they?"

He squinted, as if thinking. "A bit of everything. Heinz fifty-sevens, I guess. But they're small, like your guy."

"The little ones are the best." Funny, but he hadn't mentioned owning a dog when they'd talked. Of course, he might have, and she'd been too busy fleeing the scene of a crime to remember. It didn't matter, because she had to find Sam. "It was nice talking to you."

"Same here," said Gil, sauntering away.

She meandered to the end of the aisle and spotted the cashier Sam had been speaking to ringing up an order, so she headed for the aisle stacked with canine gear. Raincoats, booties, sweaters with hoods and without, T-shirts with slogans and cartoons, even ball caps, bow ties, and headbands, lined the Peg-Board wall. On the opposite side hung leashes of every size and color, paisley and print, leather, mesh, and cord, along with matching collars and other dog paraphernalia.

After failing to find a collar Twink would accept as a substitute for gold chains, she fingered a red hat, its brim embroidered with the Yankees insignia. Rudy would ignore her for a week if she brought it through the door, and he certainly wouldn't wear it. Ditto a bow tie or T-shirt.

"You're buying your dog a hat?"

She jumped at the sound of Sam's taunting voice. "Yeah, and a tuxedo to go with it." She returned the ball cap to the rack. "Don't be ridiculous. Rudy would give me hell if I brought home anything on this wall."

Sam gave a half smile. "And just how would he do that?"

Oops. "First off, he'd probably run under the bed and hide. And if I did manage to slip whatever it was on him, he'd shake it off, find a place where I couldn't reach him, and tear it to shreds . . . or something."

"Then he's smarter than I thought." Sam nodded toward a group of brightly colored leads printed with tiny flowers. "Leashes for girl dogs, boy dogs, clothes . . . They even sell costumes." He held up a bride's dress and veil. "Who the hell in their right mind would dress a mutt in one of these?"

Not Ellie, but she'd viewed plenty of doggie nuptials on Animal Planet. "It's just for fun. People who love their pets treat them like family."

He crossed his arms over his chest, as if taking a stand. "Dogs aren't human."

"Tell that to the people who love them." When he'd first made his position on canines clear, she'd been angry. Now she simply felt sorry for him. "Everybody needs someone to love. For those who don't have a person in their lives, a dog is a great substitute."

"If you say so." He glanced at the bag of kibble. "I take it you didn't have any luck with the magazines."

"No. How about you?"

"Two of the clerks know the publication exists, but the store doesn't carry it. Said I should try to find them online if I want to subscribe. That means my next stop is your place."

My place? Oh, yeah. She had mentioned the magazine was at her apartment. "Let me pay for this. Then we can go."

Sam grabbed the plastic sack holding the kibble while Ellie paid the clerk; then he followed her out of the store.

"You don't have to carry that for me," she said when they reached the sidewalk.

"It's no big deal."

"I can cart my own stuff," she insisted, trying to snatch the bag.

"I know you can." They arrived at a corner, and he shifted the sack to his other hand, took hold of her elbow, and steered her across the street. "You're place is a couple of blocks from here, right?"

"One up and two over." She fell in step beside him. "I take it you'll be going to the precinct this afternoon?"

"This is supposed to be my day off, but I'm always on call. Some days are better than others."

"Tough job."

"I don't complain." And I don't get involved with anyone who can't understand that, he wanted to say. He glanced over and found her walking with her hands in her pockets, her mouth set in a frown. "Am I interrupting your plans by inviting myself to your place?"

They stopped at a red light and stood amid a throng of restless pedestrians. "Not really. But Rudy's been home alone for a couple of hours. He gets testy if I'm not back when I said I'd be."

"Testy? You talk about him as if he can tell time or understands when you give him a message."

"Not quite, but we do have a mental connection." They crossed the street. "Now he's assisting with my career."

"A career guru? How's that?"

She grinned. "He's a great shill. With Rudy at my feet, no one doubts I love dogs, and he makes friends with all my charges. It helps ease the uncertainty of those first few days, when a dog has to interact with a new group of friends."

"I don't mean to pry, but does walking five or six dogs really give you enough income to live here?" He couldn't afford even a studio apartment in Manhattan. "This is one of the better areas in the most expensive city in the state."

"Not yet, but my business is growing, and I have a mother wealthy enough to support a small country. I owe her, big-time, but I'll pay her back. It's my first priority."

Impressed by her attitude, Sam said, "Sounds like you have a handle on your life. Good for you."

"I'm thirty-one years old. It's about time." She took the steps to her building, and led him into the lobby and up the staircase to her door. "This'll only take a minute."

After opening the door, she headed down the hall while he walked into the kitchen and set the dog-food bag on the counter. Aside from a coffee cup in the sink and two brightly colored dishes sitting empty on the floor, the place was spotless, the exact opposite of his. She hurried in from the living room with her dog on her heels at the same time his phone rang.

"Ryder."

"Hey, partner, it's me." Vince Fugazzo sounded as if he was on cloud nine. "Now that the baby's settled in, we're having some people over tonight. Just family and a few friends. You game?"

"Maybe. What time?"

Ellie placed the magazine, with yellow tabs sticking out the side, on the counter next to him.

"Seven o'clock, and come hungry. Natalie's mother made a couple trays of lasagna, and my mom spent the morning cooking."

"I'll try to make it. It depends on how things go at the precinct."

"What? You still working alone?"

"Budget cuts, so no interim sidekick. I have to manage on my own."

"I won't be back for another four weeks. You sure you're okay?"

"I'm fine, and I'll make time to come by. See you tonight." He snapped the phone closed, and picked up the magazine. Flipping to the tabbed page, he spotted Rita Millcraft's ad, circled in pink highlighter, and began to read. "Thanks," he said when finished. "Guess I'd better be on my way. I have to put in a requisition for that subscriber list."

"It sounds as if you have something special lined up for the evening."

"My partner and his wife had their baby. It's a welcome-home party of sorts."

"Nice. You bringing a gift?"

A gift? "I guess I'd better." She grinned, and he read her mind. "Okay, so I'm a guy, and I have no clue what to get for a new baby. Any suggestions?"

"Lots of them, but only after I ask a few questions. Is it a big family?"

"Italian, so I'd say yes."

"First baby?"

"Yes, but there are a ton of nieces and nephews."

"Then they probably don't need much in the way of clothes or toys."

"How about cash?"

"Cash isn't personal enough."

How the heck was he supposed to know? "Then what?"

"A savings bond is nice. You could add one every year for the baby's birthday or Christmas. The child and parents will thank you when he or she is ready for college."

"It's a she. Angelina."

"Pretty name."

"I talked to the proud daddy a couple of hours after she was born. Apparently she's the most beautiful baby on the planet. Even his mother said so, and Mrs. Fugazzo's a tough nut to crack."

"Okay, then." Ellie glanced at her dog, who'd been staring at Sam with a look of disdain on his fuzzy muzzle. "So . . ."

"I'll call if the computer guys come up with anything."

"I'd appreciate that."

"And you'll phone me if you get more information from your vet friend or hear gossip on the street, right? No more surprise leads?"

"Not if I can help it."

"Then I'm out of here."

She followed him into the foyer, and he stopped to face her. He'd had a good morning, he decided. Thanks to the "bad penny," it had been interesting, relaxed, upbeat. And personal enough to give her another lip lock.

Stepping toward her, he heard a growl and glanced down. Her dog stared at him through narrowed eyes, giving him a nasty scowl that was downright human.

"Stop that," Ellie ordered.

The mutt plopped his butt on the floor, his focus locked on his target.

"Thanks for the magazine and the company," Sam said, his back to the door.

"Thanks for lunch."

When he reached out and touched her cheek, she blushed but didn't pull away. "It was my pleasure."

"Discounting the Marino visit, I had a nice time."

"Me, too, but I'm still going to hunt for Buddy."

"I figured as much. Knock yourself out."

That seemed to put a damper on the moment. "I plan to."

She stepped back, and he walked out the door. Just before he took the stairs, he turned, but she'd already gone inside.

"That was some trick you pulled, bringing home the demonic detective," Rudy groused when they hit the sidewalk a short while later.

"I didn't plan on meeting him, honest. He showed up at the Marinos', and I had to tell him about the magazine." They hit Fifth and headed for Central Park.

"Bet that really ticked him off, huh?"

"Yeah, but he got over it. Mind if I stop at Joe to Go for a hot coffee?"

"Not if I can come inside."

"This Joe's has outside tables. It's the best I can do." Rudy's lack of comment told her he was miffed, so she forged ahead, hoping to mend his wounded feelings. "I know you understand about the health laws."

"I know about 'em, but I don't get it. The public acts as if we canines carry the plague."

"There are hundreds of outside eateries in Manhattan, and you're allowed at all of them. It's just the inside part they don't approve of. Too bad we don't live in France."

Rudy snorted. *"Yeah, those people know how to treat their canines right. I hear some of them even serve special menus for their doggie customers."*

"Maybe sometime we can go there, and check it out," she offered. "Would you like that?"

"Only if you bring me on board in first-class so there's room for a good-sized carryall under the front seat."

"Okay, then," she answered. "It's a deal."

After a minute, they reached the coffee bar, and she tied Rudy to a table leg, then stooped to his level. "Behave, all right. I'll only be gone a few minutes."

"You could sneak me in. Joe wouldn't care."

"I could, but he might not be at this store. The weather's beautiful, and I'll be quick, I promise. And look on the bright side. Maybe Lulu will be at the park. Even better, maybe her owner will hire us to walk her every day."

"I wish."

Ellie slipped inside, checked for Joe, and placed her order for a caramel bliss. While waiting, she kept an eye on her pal, smiling when several passersby stopped to give him a kind word and a pat on the head. Manhattanites really did love their dogs, which was good for her pocketbook.

She carried her drink outside, untied his lead, and fifteen minutes later, reached their destination. Escorting Rudy to the dog run, she took him off lead and settled on a bench while he bounded away to say hello to a few of the dogs he'd met on other play days.

"Hey, Ellie."

She spotted the enormous pair of red high-tops before she made eye contact with the owner of the voice. "Gary, hi. What are you doing here?"

"I told you, I like dogs." He nodded toward her coffee. "You gonna drink all that by yourself?"

She'd planned on it, but couldn't when she spotted his big brown eyes and gaunt expression. "Do you have a cup handy?"

He dug into the pocket of his grimy threadbare overcoat and pulled out a much-used paper cup. "Sure do. I got it this morning. Only had a little soda in it. I rinsed it out at a fountain." He handed her the container. "See."

"Uh, thanks." She poured half her coffee in the cup and passed it back to him.

"Where's Rudy?" he asked as he sat beside her on the bench.

"Over there." She pointed to where her Yorkiepoo and a black cocker spaniel were rough-housing. "He's played with that dog before."

"Ain't you afraid he'll get hurt?"

"Not my boy. He can take care of himself."

Gary heaved a sigh. "I wish I owned a dog that talked to me. That way, I wouldn't be so lonely."

Ellie swallowed her coffee before she choked out, "Talked to you?"

"Yeah, like Rudy does to you."

"Dogs don't talk to people," she told him. "I only pretend with Rudy."

"I wish he'd say something to me sometime. I'd answer him, and we'd be good friends."

"Uh, how do you know Rudy and I talk . . . er . . . do that kind of thing?"

"I can tell. I see the way he looks at you and you look at him. It makes me feel all warm inside."

A nice sentiment, she thought, but not one everybody would share. "How do you know so much about things?"

"I just do. People think I'm invisible, so I see things regular people don't. Sometimes, I wish I didn't."

"What kind of things?" asked Ellie, watching Rudy fetch a ball for a small boy.

"All kinds of stuff. Some of it's bad."

"Bad? How bad?

He shook his head. "You don't wanna know."

"Are you all right?" She could only imagine the hardships he'd suffered that had brought him to this kind of life. "I'd be happy to buy you lunch, if you're hungry."

"Not today. The chef at that restaurant on Broadway met me at the back door and let me have an almost-new turkey sandwich." He scratched his belly. "It was good."

A man and woman walking by gave their bench a wide berth and a disdainful glare, which she ignored. "Gary, has someone tried to hurt you?"

"Me? Nuh-uh. It's just that—" Rudy trotted over and nosed Gary's fingers. "Hey, fella. How you doin' today?"

The dog inched toward Ellie. *"He don't look too good."*

"You sure you're feeling all right, Gary?"

The homeless man's face lighted with a smile. "Is Rudy worried about me? Ask him if he'll say something to me, okay?"

Ellie sighed. It figured the one person who'd key in on her relationship with her dog would be a man most people thought of as a mentally unhinged derelict. And what did that say about her own ability to communicate with canines?

"Is he for real?"

"Be nice." She ruffled Rudy's ears, caught the anticipation in Gary's expression, and said, "Is there anyway you can speak to him, reach him somehow?"

"You're not serious."

"I wouldn't ask if I wasn't."

"What's he sayin'?" asked Gary.

She raised an eyebrow in Rudy's direction.

He yawned, then gave a doggie sigh. *"I don't know, Triple E. You and me, we got a special bond. One I don't want to share with strangers."*

"Just try, okay?"

The dog closed his eyes, and Ellie smiled. The D used to walk a circle around anyone who seemed down on their luck or not of sound mind. The accepting attitude of her canine companion gave her reason to be proud.

"Hey, Gary, can we go see where you live today?"

Gary's eyes widened. Grinning like a clown, he rose to his feet. "I heard him, Ellie. Rudy wants to visit my house. Tell him yes." He started to walk away, then turned and hurried back, his huge sneakers slapping merrily on the sidewalk. "Come on, come on. I got new curtains. You gotta see 'em. Come on."

She gazed at Rudy. "I'm sorry I asked you to do that. We may never find our way out of the park."

"Sure we will," he answered, dancing in place. *"I got the nose, remember?"*

She stood and dropped her coffee cup in the trash. "I sure hope so."

"Come on, Ellie, hurry up."

She shrugged as she hooked Rudy to his lead. Maybe Viv was right. She really did need a hobby . . . or a life. If her mother or her best friend found out what she was about to do, they'd have her committed.

Chapter 16

"You did what?" Vivian leaned back in the kitchen chair, her disapproval clear. "Are you insane?"

Ellie winced. "I've already asked myself that question a couple dozen times." She'd told Viv about her stop at Gary's hole-in-the-woods residence, and now realized the visit might not have been the most prudent thing to do. "Nothing happened, so stop yelling. You're giving me a headache."

Gary's home, a soggy grouping of cardboard boxes hidden in the bowels of Central Park, had been an eye-opener. The secondhand curtains he was so proud of hung in the square sections he'd cut for windows. He'd lined the damp floor with more cardboard and added stained and mismatched sections of carpet, while wooden crates and shoe boxes filled with who knew what doubled as chairs and shelves. A set of battered TV trays mimicked tables, and, situated in a back corner, a mattress swathed in mildew-covered drapes substituted for a bed.

"The man probably has fleas or lice or both. Anything could have happened to you out there, alone with him. You know the park is a drug dealer's vacation spot. You're lucky you weren't mugged, stabbed . . . killed. People go in, but they don't come out."

"Stop exaggerating." Ellie held her fingers to her temples and stared at the shriveled peas, dry turkey, rock-hard stuffing, and cementlike cranberry surprise she'd nuked for dinner. Why hadn't she listened to her stomach and stopped at her favorite Chinese restaurant for takeout on her trip home? "I know my way around."

"Hah! You're the easiest mark in this city. I've seen you give bums your entire lunch. Come Christmas, you pass out dollar bills like candy canes."

"I gave away the D's cash, not mine, and now that things are tight, I've stopped being so generous."

"Wait. Let me guess. Instead of money, you invited this Gary person here for a meal."

Ellie walked to the trash can and dumped her dinner. Her heart ached at the memory of the meager rations that made up Gary's food supply.

His cooking apparatus—a dented pot, a couple of chipped ceramic mugs, and a can of sterno under a homemade metal tripod—looked as if they hadn't been used in weeks. But when she'd invited him back to her place for real nourishment, he'd declined, and no amount of coaxing, by either her or Rudy, had convinced him to change his mind.

"The man's harmless, just down and out. You gave me a helping hand when I ran short of funds after the divorce. I simply want to do what they suggested in that movie—the one with Kevin Spacey and the kid from the *Sixth Sense*—pay it forward."

"Nice idea, but the film was a flop, and you know why?" Viv inhaled, not waiting for an answer. "Because it's a dumb idea. People have to take control of their own lives. Gary's an adult. I agree a handout now and then is okay, but an open-door invitation is not."

"I have more than I need, so why can't I share?"

Viv rolled her eyes. "For God's sake, Ellie, think about what you've been doing. You're treating this homeless guy the same way you've been handling that missing dog: taking on a crusade it's impossible to win. If Gary doesn't want help, you can't make him take it. If the police can't find Buddy, he won't be found. And it's not your job to catch the professor's killer. You cannot save the world."

The day's exploits had worn Ellie out. She wanted nothing more than a warm bed, as did the canine dozing at her feet. Unfortunately, she'd opened her door to Vivian, in the throes of a melt-down, ranting about the man who'd stood her up. When Viv heard how Ellie had spent most of her afternoon, she'd re-directed the tirade to Gary and added a host of opinions on the rest of Ellie's life.

"Good Lord, you're grumpy. Don't take it out on me because your date didn't show."

Viv propped an elbow on the table and rested her chin in her hand. "I know, and I apologize. Men. Just when I think maybe a couple are worth the effort, one comes along and slaps me upside the head for no good reason."

"Where's Jason this weekend?"

"Beats me." She began shredding a paper napkin, a sure sign things were not going well with that relationship, either. "To tell you the truth, I think it's over."

"Oh, no. He seemed like an okay guy. What happened?"

She shrugged. "Remember the open-door policy I said we had? Well, someone else walked through the door and locked me out. And get this: She's his secretary."

"You mean you know her?"

"We've met, but I never thought he'd be attracted to a mousy little thing like Ashley. The woman wears polyester, for God's sake." Viv

307

smoothed her violet cashmere sweater. "Tacky and tasteless at the same time."

"Maybe she has a great personality?" Ellie flinched internally at her words, the standard designation for a second-rate date. "She could be sweet or a good listener."

"Who are you, Little Mary Sunshine?" Viv shoved the pile of tattered napkin to the middle of the table. "You're supposed to take my side, not make excuses for the woman."

"Sorry. But I've heard some men are drawn to mousy. Having a woman to take care of makes them feel important. You're strong and independent. You need someone who admires your pluses."

"You think so?"

"Sure. Although nice works, too."

"I've tried being nice, and all it's ever gotten me is a kick in the head. Now I'm a bitch, and trust me, it's a lot more fun. Or at least it was."

Ellie went to the freezer and pulled out her own generic prescription for depression, a container of Häagen-Dazs Caramel Cone. Opening Viv's leftover ice cream, she set it and a spoon on the table. "Here, drown your sorrows." She took a seat. "It's the only thing I have for consolation."

"So," said Viv, after sucking down a couple of spoonfuls, "besides tromping into the park and putting your life on the line, what else did you do today?"

A vision of Ryder's sexy smile and smoldering eyes appeared in her mind. "Promise not to get upset, and I'll tell you."

"I promise. Now spill."

"I went on a fishing expedition. I'm getting closer to locating Buddy. I can feel it in my bones."

"Didn't that detective tell you to stay out of his investigation?" Viv asked, her tone even and calm.

"He did, but I ran into him today, and he actually let me tag along while he looked into a lead." She filled Viv in on her trip to the Marinos' and the pet store, but left out the part about lunch and the time Sam spent in her apartment. "He's running a check on the subscription holders. There's a chance one of them might be the killer."

Viv arched a brow. "Did anything else happen I should know about?"

"Hardly. I'm certain once this case is solved I'll never see him again."

"Too bad. He's a good-looking guy. Just what you need to jump-start your return to the dating pool."

Sam was a jump start, all right. He'd shocked her by showing up at the Marinos', bossed her like a drill sergeant, then followed her around as if he cared. But of course he cared, she reminded herself. It was his business to care. She had a lead on the professor's killer. The fact that he'd bought her lunch, let her accompany him to the PetCo, and allowed her to do a little supervised snooping didn't mean much.

"I can find my own men, thank you," Ellie intoned.

"I still have a rain check working with the lawyer and his stockbroker buddy. All I have to do is call."

"Maybe next week." *Or next year.* "Did I tell you about Georgette? She accepted Stanley's proposal."

"Good for the exterminator. When's the big day?"

"She's talking about a June wedding. Can you believe she's been married five times and never been a June bride?"

"Maybe that's her goal. She'll take a walk down the aisle once in every month, then make her own wedding calendar. She can call it 'a year of alimony in review.'"

Ellie frowned. If Georgette knew what some people thought of her husband history, she'd have a hissy fit. "I don't think the money is what she's after, really."

"I know. She's looking for someone like your father, but what are the chances she'll find another handsome, burly man with a heart of gold and a weakness for debutantes, especially the aging ones who refuse to admit it?" Viv capped her container and pushed from the table. "I'm ready for bed. How about you and Rudy take one last walk with me and Twink?"

There was no point in defending her mother, when Viv's comments were so close to the mark. "Fine. I'll get my sneakers and meet you downstairs."

Ellie returned the ice cream to the freezer, then sat and slipped into her shoes. After tugging on her denim jacket, she put a hand in her pocket and found the business card she'd given Mrs. Steinman. Turning it over, she read the woman's address. At least one good thing happened today. She'd met Mrs. Steinman walking Lulu on her way home from Gary's, and Mrs. Steinman told her the Best family was thrilled with the way she handled Bruiser. Based on that, and Natter's recommendation, she wanted Ellie to begin walking her baby on Monday morning.

While Rudy and the Havanese romped, they came to an agreement on price and Mrs. Steinman wrote her a check. That officially brought her canine count to six. Tomorrow, she'd stop in the same building to see the women who'd moved into the penthouse. If that worked out, she'd be firmly ensconced in the high-rise. Natter would receive more cards on Monday morning, along with a thank-you coffee for his kind words and referrals.

"Come on," she said to a still-dozing Rudy. "Last walk of the day."

He stood and stretched. *"So I heard. Viv made some racket. Poor T's gonna suffer tonight."*

She snapped on his lead, and he followed her to the door. "What does that mean?"

"Viv's a crier, especially when things don't work out with men. She waits until she's ready for bed. Then she climbs in, turns out the light, and sobs like a baby. It drives T crazy, especially when she pulls him close and uses him for a pillow."

"Vivian cries? Like a baby?" Her tough-talking, no-nonsense, high-fashion friend was a closet crier? The idea was impossible to comprehend. "Are you sure he said that?"

"Sure as the sun rises in the east. Underneath all that bravado, Viv's a tender soul."

Viv? Tender soul? The words didn't compute. Ellie walked to the landing and down the steps, where Viv and Mr. T stood ready and waiting.

"You okay?" Ellie asked her.

"I'll live," Viv replied. "But I can't wait to get to sleep. It's been a long day."

The next morning, Ellie and Rudy popped in to Natter's high-rise to see her potential new clients. Dodging moving men, who carted paintings and furniture from the service elevator to the door of the sprawling penthouse, she waited for a break in the stream before sticking her head around the doorway.

"Hello, Ms. Fallgrave? It's Ellie Engleman. I'm here about your dogs."

She stepped back as another man, this one dressed in a navy Armani suit and pristine white shirt with a red-and-yellow-striped tie, hurried into the foyer. "Which Ms. Fallgrave are you looking for?" he asked, spinning in place as he bustled by.

"Either one. I'm their—I hope to be their dog walker."

The man, a Cuba Gooding Jr. look-alike, rolled his eyes. "Thank God you're here. Helping take care of those oversized rats is driving me to drink. I'm Jackson Hall, Janice Fallgrave's manager." He held out his hand. "And I'm not a dog lover, so beware."

Ellie accepted his greeting and they dodged sideways as a trio of movers charged out of the apartment and down the hall. When the coast was clear, he said, "Wait here, and I'll try to rustle up one of them."

"I don't like that guy," Rudy said with a snort. *"He reminds me of your mother."*

"Georgette? I hate to break it to you, pal, but my mother isn't a man, nor is she African-American."

"But he isn't a dog lover, and that puts them in the same boat, as far as I'm concerned."

She heard voices a few moments before two women and Jackson ambled into view. Each of the women wore a designer warm-up suit that cost, she guessed, more than her entire wardrobe, and each carried a Chihuahua.

"Ellie Engleman," said Jackson, "this is Patti Fallgrave and her sister, Janice." He air-kissed Janice and waggled his fingers at Patti. "Be good, both of you. Don't scare the nice dog walker away, because as of this minute, I'm no longer on babysitting duty."

The women smiled in unison. If not for the difference in their heights, they could have passed for twins. Both had identical wide-set green eyes, curling dark hair, and a classically beautiful face.

Ellie extended her hand. "Hi. It's nice to meet you. Natter tells me you're looking for a dog walker"—she focused on the dogs they carried—"for those two cuties."

"He's right. Come on in, but mind the mess," Patti, the taller of the two, stated. "The kitchen is sort of organized, so we can talk in there."

Ellie followed, sidling around boxes, furniture, and rolling racks filled with clothes and stacks of shoes. The enormous apartment, covered from end to end in "stuff," was bigger than her mother's, with more windows and a great view of the park. In the kitchen, Janice pointed to a chair. "Have a seat. I'll make coffee."

"Thanks." Ellie nudged Rudy with her toe, and he lay at her feet. "This is Rudy, my own companion. He'll be with us on every walk."

"Oh, isn't he adorable?" Patti dropped to her

knees and scratched Rudy's head. "Look, Cheech, a new friend." She made kissy noises as she brought her dog close. Unfortunately, Cheech wasn't as charming as his mistress, and growled low in his throat. "Hey, hey, no grumping." She stood and took a chair across from Ellie. "Sorry. He hasn't been around other dogs very much. Just his brother, Chong."

Cheech and Chong? Ellie smiled. "How old are they?"

"A year last week. We got them when I did my first cover for *Vogue*."

"You're a model?"

"You bet she is," said Janice, crossing the room.

Patti stood, passed Chong off to her sister, and twirled in place. "All six feet of me. I was the ugly duckling of my high school graduating class in Union, New Jersey."

"Wow, I'm impressed," Ellie said. "You're beautiful."

"Hah! It's all smoke and mirrors. Expertly applied makeup, a fifteen-thousand-dollar dental bill, four-hundred-dollar haircuts, and ta-daa." She twirled again. "A girl-next-door look every woman thinks she can achieve."

"Maybe so, but the basics have to be there to begin with. For starters, you're thin as a pencil." Ellie remembered how difficult it had been to keep her size-eight figure. "That can't come naturally."

"Well, no," Patti agreed. "I mean, I do splurge—"

"Yeah, sometimes she has *two* crackers with her bouillon," her sister said, grinning. "I'm on her all the time to eat like a real person."

"What do you do?" Ellie asked the shorter sister.

"I'm a singer. Right now, I have a gig at Club Fifty-two, but I'll be cutting my first album in a couple of months. With any luck, I'll have a successful singing career."

Ellie opened and closed her mouth. "Are you telling me I'll be a dog walker to the stars?"

The girls giggled. Janice passed her sister both dogs and left to finish the coffee while Patti took her seat. "We might be stars, but we promised each other a long time ago that we wouldn't let fame go to our heads. Didn't we, babies?" She snuggled the dogs against her chest, then set them on the floor. "Here, make nice with your new friend."

Sniffing daintily, the Chihuahuas circled Rudy while he gave them a full-body inspection of his own. After a few unsuccessful attempts at humping him for dominance, the tiny canines backed off and returned to Patti, who scooped them up and set them on her lap.

"What do you expect in the way of walks?" Ellie asked.

"I don't know. What do you think, Jan? Two a day?"

"Sure," Janice answered, carrying a tray with

coffee cups and a plate of cookies to the table. Sitting down, she passed a cookie to her sister. "Eat," she commanded. "That sounds good. Do you dog-sit, too?"

"You mean stay here with them when you're away? I suppose I could . . . unless you want me to bring them home."

"Whichever is good for you. Patti sometimes travels for fashion shoots, and I'll be going to LA in the next few months to sign a recording contract, God willing."

"It won't be a problem. At the moment, I don't have a lot of customers, so I can do whatever you want."

Ellie sipped her coffee while Patti wrote a check for the rest of the month.

"Where's that extra key?" Patti then asked her sister.

Janice dug in her Mark Cross bag, pulled out a full key ring, unhooked one, and passed it to Ellie. "We like to sleep late, so let yourself in and call the boys. If they don't come, yell until one of us gets up. I'm sure things will work into a schedule after a week or so."

Ellie finished her coffee and set a few of her cards on the table. "It was great meeting you. Please hand these to anyone you think might need a dog walker. I'd like to stay within a ten-block spread so . . ."

"We won't send you to the West Side," Patti finished. "And we'll tell Natter you're on the list, so you'll have access tomorrow morning."

"Great." After a few more minutes of small talk, Ellie pushed from the table. "See you in the morning, and thanks again for the business." She headed to the foyer, impressed by the quality and quantity of furniture she passed. Georgette would die for a place like this, and she was well-to-do. The Fallgrave sisters had to be loaded.

"So what did you think of Cheech and Chong?" she asked Rudy as they rode the elevator to the lobby.

"I don't think they speak English."

"Of course they speak English."

"Maybe, but it was hard telling. I'd ask to see their green cards, if I were you. Or mention INS."

Ellie *tsk*ed. "You're terrible. How about we make another pass at the shelter in case Buddy's turned up?"

"Do you really think we'll ever see him again?"

"I hope so. But the chances of finding him alive are getting slimmer with each passing day. I keep thinking that Randall or Kronk will have good news tomorrow. Keep your paws crossed."

"How about a trip to the park?"

"If you're a good boy."

"Jeesh, what a nag."

Monday morning was business as usual for Ellie and Rudy. They walked Mr. T, then set out for the

318

Beaumont and picked up a coffee for Natter along the way. After introducing Bruiser to Lulu, Cheech, and Chong, Ellie gave the dogs plenty of time to sniff, play, and posture before leading them across the street to the park.

Rudy, entranced with Lulu, dominated the group, standing guard around the Havanese as if she was a burger and he a starving man.

"Back off, bub," he groused to Bruiser when the Pom wandered too close.

The usually subdued Pomeranian growled, while Lulu preened. *"One at a time, gentlemen, please. There's plenty of me to go around."*

Ellie sighed. "Don't lead them on, Lulu. It's not nice."

"It's not my fault I'm a looker," the Havanese replied, shaking her fluffy brown-and-white coat. *"It's only natural they're enthralled."*

Great, thought Ellie. A dog with an overinflated ego. "No fair disturbing the balance of the group—is that clear? And don't try to con me. I'm not as gullible as Mrs. Steinman."

"She's a bore. Mr. Steinman was more my cup of kibble, but he passed on. He was such a dear."

Ellie kept her opinion to herself until she'd returned the four dogs to their homes. Then she said to Rudy, "You really know how to pick 'em. Lulu is a tease."

"Maybe so, but what a doll. Too bad I've been . . . fixed."

319

"Trust me, sometimes abstinence is the best way to live."

"You oughta know."

"Stop being such a wiseass," Ellie said as they entered the Davenport. "Hey, Randall, how was your weekend?"

"Quiet. How about you? Any news on Buddy?"

"Nothing. I even went to the ASPCA yesterday to check. Have you heard anything?"

"Detective Ryder was by this morning. Told me most of the test results were in on the professor."

And he didn't call me? "Did he drop any hints about what killed him?"

"Not really, but he did say they were now positive it was murder. He examined my log again, too. It appeared as if he was looking for someone specific."

"You sometimes see the mail a tenant gets. Did he happen to ask if you knew of anyone receiving *Breeder's Digest*?"

"Heavens, no. Is there really such a publication?"

"You bet." She raised a brow. "You've never heard or seen the magazine?"

"No."

Ellie began her rounds in a snit. How dared the dastardly detective not tell her about the ME's conclusion? He knew how much all this meant to her—how much Buddy meant to her. He was such a liar, pretending to let her in on the investigation, then keeping important information to himself. She'd be damned if she'd share anything with him again.

"Come on, Stinker," she prodded, hurrying the beagle down the hall. "At this rate it'll take an hour to get everyone walked and back home."

She collected Jett, Buckley, and Sweetie Pie, ignoring their grumbles and complaints as they headed down in the elevator. On the sidewalk, she continued to fume instead of focusing on her destination. The inattention caused her to steer her horde into another walker's group of larger dogs, which led to chaos.

No voices echoed in her mind. Instead, growls, snarls, and yowls sounded as the dogs fought for dominance. Leashes tangled as she and the other walker strove for control. The stranger's canines were larger, heavier, and a lot more boisterous than her charges. Pedestrians and delivery people plowed past without a care for the disturbance, which made regaining order difficult.

When Ellie got a good look at the man handling the second group, she groaned. Eugene, his expression mutinous, shouted at the top of his lungs while tugging his canines into line.

"Call off your dogs, Engleman," he ordered. His cigarette flew from his mouth and landed on an Old English sheepdog. "Kee-rist!" Eugene slapped madly at the dog's smoking fur. "Look what you made me do. I'm calling the cops, you bitch."

Passersby finally gave them a wide berth. Ellie scooped up Jett and Buckley, and dragged Sweetie Pie, Rudy, and Stinker away from the fray by their leashes. A doorman she didn't know ran from the nearest building, and she handed him the leads, then charged back into the mass of animals to give Eugene a hand.

Not bonded with any of his canines, she had no idea if her mental manipulation would work, but she gave it her best shot. "Sit! I said sit!" she ordered, grasping three of the leashes. "Calm down or you'll all go to the pound." The dalmatian, German shepherd, and standard poodle dropped to their haunches, which allowed Eugene to bring the remaining five dogs to heel.

Heaving a breath, she said aloud, "Good dogs. Very good dogs. Thank you so much for behaving."

His eyes narrowed to slits, Eugene sneered. "Stop talkin' to my dogs and get the hell out of here. You are a boil on my ass—you know that? Gimme those leads." He snatched the leashes from her hand. "Why the hell didn't you watch where you were going?" He gave the Old English's back another pat, cringed at the singed fur, and muttered a curse.

Ellie retrieved her own dogs and thanked the doorman. Then she took a few calming breaths. "I'm sorry, Eugene. It was entirely my fault. I'm just glad no one was hurt." She stepped toward the sheepdog and smiled. "You're okay, aren't you, fella?"

"Get out of my way," Eugene said through gritted teeth. After swiping a hand over his face, he rearranged the leads and steered his gang down the street.

Ellie hung her head. Great. She'd almost caused an innocent animal to go up like a torch. Of course, if Eugene didn't smoke it wouldn't have happened, and he was handling too many dogs. But it was still her fault they'd collided. She glanced at her crew. "Is everyone all right?"

"Fine," grumped Buckley.

"Okeydokey," chirped Sweetie Pie.

"I'm good," Stinker moaned.

"Nothing a little Scotch wouldn't cure," said Jett.

"Rudy, what about you?"

"I'm okay, too, but, um, Ellie, I think there's something you should know."

Just then her phone rang. "Hang on a second," she told him, searching her bag. "Hello."

"Ellie, it's Sam."

She led the dogs across Fifth toward the park as she talked. "Is there something I can do for you?" *Like kick you around the block a couple of times?*

"I have news. First off, the professor was definitely murdered. His pacemaker was scrambled by some type of electrical device. We don't know how it was done, but we agree it was no accident.

And I looked into that magazine. The subscriber list shows about a hundred names in Manhattan. It's going to take a while to sort through them all. I have three men working on it."

Okay, so he'd just filled her in. Still, he could have called her before he'd told Randall. "I see. What do you plan to do next?"

"The publisher also gave me the names of a couple of pet stores that carry the magazine, so I'm off to check them out. There're two in Queens, two in Brooklyn, and one in Manhattan."

"Manhattan? Where in Manhattan?"

"Never mind where," he said after a long silence. "I already told you, I'm handling things from now on."

When she didn't comment, he said, "Ellie, you still there?"

"Yeah, I'm here."

"I was wondering, what are you doing tonight?"

"Tonight?" She blew out a breath. "I have a date tonight. And right now I'm walking the group from the Davenport, so I have to go. See ya." She closed her phone and dropped it in her bag. The big jerk. Did he really think she'd agree to go out with him, when he didn't trust her enough to give her the latest information?

"So what did the hot-to-trot dick have to say?"

"Nothing of any importance."

"Atta girl. The guy's up to no good. Don't give him another thought."

She sighed as they entered the park, wishing she could take Rudy's advice. Instead of stewing, she decided to give her charges an extra-long walk to make up for the morning's excitement. "Come on, gang. Let's go see what's happening in the play area."

Chapter 17

Sam disconnected the call and tossed the phone on top of his desk. Okay, so maybe he should have called Ellie when he received the ME's report. And maybe he should have told her which store in Manhattan carried *Breeder's Digest*. Either way, she was pissed. But that didn't give her the right to get her nose out of joint or stick it into his investigation.

And he should have his head examined for asking her what she was doing tonight. Still, dinner and a couple of laughs—and maybe another round against her apartment wall—might have been interesting. Being told she had a date was the last thing he had wanted to hear.

He drummed his fingers on the desk. She was probably seeing that preppy veterinarian, the one who'd given her those leads. David Crane was more her type anyway—respectable job, moneyed background—and a dog lover. Ellie's own upscale apartment and the comments she'd made about her mother told him she came from an upper-class family, just like the vet. Dr. Crane was tailor-made for her, since she probably wanted the same thing Carolanne and every other woman wanted: a guy with money to burn and the time to spend it on them.

Screw women and screw the ditzy dog walker, too.

His gaze landed on the magazine in question, and he refocused, searching for the connection in this case. What did the publication have to do with Albright's death and the other missing canines? And what the hell had scrambled the professor's pacemaker? Dr. Bridges thought the killer had used an electrical device, but had no idea what it was.

Frustrated, he thumbed the pages, sizing up the photos of dogs available for stud and the bitches looking for service. Most of the ads instructed interested parties to call for pricing and details, but there were a few that posted their rates. As Ellie had explained, the more championships a dog had behind them, the more their value as a breed specimen. Depending on the animal's ranking and number of awards they'd won, the fees ran anywhere from a couple of hundred to thousands of dollars.

He flipped through the articles until he found one on breeding and showing dogs in other countries. After reading it carefully, an idea began to gel. Pushing from his desk, he stuck the magazine in his coat pocket, strode through the precinct, and headed for the Manhattan bookstore that carried the dog magazine. If he didn't have luck there, he'd strike out for Brooklyn.

Ellie made a point of having another talk with her street pals, Marvin and Pops, about Buddy. She then spoke to a few of the friendlier dog walkers, and even asked Sean Turner, a guard who worked at the Metropolitan Museum of Art, if they'd seen the bichon or knew of anyone who had.

In return, she'd gotten nothing. Nada. Zip. Zilch.

Dejected, she shared her usual hot dog lunch with Rudy, then leaned back in the bench and let the spring sunshine warm her face. Taxis flew past while tourists on the way to the museum walked by, gazing at the huge high-rises on Fifth Avenue. Most of the visitors were so entranced with this part of the city they didn't notice her or her little pal, but a few smiled when they saw her feeding Rudy, as if they, too, knew how great it was to have a dog.

Clouds gathering in the east signaled an upcoming thunderstorm, a change from the mild weather that had blanketed the area for the last week. She didn't usually wear a rain slicker, but she always kept one in her bag, just in case. Summer would soon arrive, which saddened her because it meant time was passing at an alarming rate. The longer it took to locate Buddy, the less likely it was they'd find him alive . . . or not.

She heaved a sigh. So what if Sam hadn't thought to call her immediately with the ME's report? He had a lot on his plate. He'd warned her that he didn't want her meddling. But would it have killed him to try to reach her?

He and Vivian were probably right. It wasn't her responsibility to locate Buddy, and it definitely wasn't her job to find the professor's killer. Still, Professor Albright had been her first official client after Viv. It didn't matter that the man's bichon was a champion; she would have fallen for him, anyway. Dogs like Buddy, Rudy, and Twink were special. They only came into a person's life once in a great while, which was doubly important to her now, because she'd just started enjoying her new career and her freedom.

Aside from this mess with the professor, her world couldn't get much better. Being a dog walker allowed her to make her own hours while she interacted with animals she loved. Her circle of friends, once dictated by the D, was now her own, and included only those with whom she had a bond. She had a mother she cared about . . . most of the time. And her standard of living would rise as she expanded her customer base. Someday she might actually welcome another man in her life, if he could accept her feelings for Rudy.

She smiled at the dog dozing at her feet. To top

it all, she had a unique best friend, who understood her, who listened when she talked and offered his own quirky guidance, who cheered her up when she was down.

Who loved her no matter what she thought or said or did.

"I hear the wheels turning." Rudy's voice echoed in her mind. *"It's frightening, what sometimes goes on in that brain of yours."*

"I have a lot to think about. It's nothing you need to focus on."

"This thing with Buddy's really got you down, huh?"

"I'm annoyed more than despondent. I'm an intelligent woman, so what have I missed? There has to be something I've failed to recognize where Buddy is concerned. Even the big, bad detective can't figure it out."

"The big, bad butthead is a jerk. You said so yourself."

"I might have been too quick to judge him. Sam's not such a terrible guy. He's just like most men used to being in charge. You know, brash, bossy—"

"Bullheaded, belligerent—"

She tapped his rear with the tip of her shoe. "Stop. You haven't seen his other side. He can be funny—and kind when he remembers. He has a crappy job, nothing like what people see on television."

"How would you know? You don't watch those shows."

"I can imagine. Just one look at the professor lying dead in his hallway told me I never want to see that kind of thing again. How would you act if you had to deal with violence and death on a daily basis? From what I can tell, murder isn't exciting or mysterious, or anything it's cracked up to be in books or on TV."

"Maybe we should watch a few episodes of CSI and check out what really goes on in the police business."

"No, thanks. I'll pass."

"So do you want to know what I saw today, while we were rumbling with that dope Rudegene?"

"Ugh! Don't remind me. What a horrific experience. How could I let myself bump into him like that, then allow all of you to get tangled with his dogs? I'm lucky none of you got bit. And that poor sheep-dog. He could have gone up in flames."

"But he didn't. And it's stupid of that idiot to smoke around canines, anyway."

"Next time I see him, I'll tell him what you think."

Rudy rose on his hind legs and put his paws on her knee. *"I'm trying to clue you in on something, Triple E. I don't know if it'll help find Buddy but—"*

She scratched his ears. "But what? I'm listening. You know you can tell me anything."

"It's about that water guy—Gil."

"You mean the man who delivers Liquid Ice?"

"Yeah, him."

"What about him?"

"This morning, in the middle of the fracas, he walked by pushing one of his carts."

"He was probably making a delivery to the building. It was so crazy, I doubt I'd have noticed Georgette if she'd walked past wheeling the judge."

"Probably not. But guess what he had sticking out of his back pocket."

"I haven't the faintest idea."

"A copy of that magazine."

"Breeder's Digest?"

"One and the same."

"Are you sure?"

"I can read, can't I?"

"You can? Since when?"

"Since forever. There's a lot of things I can do."

"Such as?"

"Never mind. What do you think it means?"

"It means I have a very intelligent dog. Maybe we could make some money from those skills you say you have."

Rudy stuck his nose between her knees and moaned. *"Forget about my talents. Why would the water man have that magazine? Does he have a champion dog?"*

"When I ran into him at the PetCo, he told me he

has one or two, but they're mixed breeds. Heinz Fifty-sevens he called them."

"You ran into him at the PetCo? Doing what?"

"Buying food for his dog . . . er . . . dogs."

"What kind of food?"

"The same brand I buy for you. Why?"

"Don't you think it's funny that he never mentioned owning a dog when we met in the freight elevator?"

"He did tell me, at the PetCo."

"So why did he wait until then?"

"I saw him buying the kibble and I asked, you goose."

"What kind of dog food did Buddy eat?"

"The same kind you do," she told him. "I started using it because the professor recommended it. He said it was the only chow Buddy would—"

"I rest my case."

Three hours later, Sam ground his back molars in frustration. So far, not a single clerk remembered which customers, if any, had bought a copy of *Breeder's Digest*. They sold a flotilla of pet periodicals to hundreds of people, and the staff worked in shifts. Any one of them could have sold the magazine. He'd have to return to each store and speak to every cashier individually, and even then chances were slim that anyone would remember ringing up the publication.

First thing tomorrow, he was going to Kennedy

and LaGuardia. With any luck, the airlines would give him access to their flight manifests for animal shipments. Never in a million years would he have believed foreigners paid big bucks for AKC-registered champions until he'd read that article while flipping through *Breeder's Digest*, but according to the magazine, wealthy Japanese and Brazilians ranked owning a Westminster winner right up there with owning a horse that had won the Kentucky Derby.

When his phone rang he checked the caller ID, sighed, and pulled the phone from the dashboard stand. No point in putting it off. He might as well speak to her now instead of later.

"Ryder."

"Sammy? It's me."

"Hey, Ma. What's up?"

"They buried Frank Jeffers a few mornings ago, and Tricia stopped by today."

Crap. He'd forgotten about the funeral. "Did you go?"

"Of course. Someone from the family had to be there. Your sisters barely remember the man, and I knew better than to ask you, though Carolanne seemed to think you'd show up."

He'd kept his promise to his ex and made the wake. What more did she expect? "I suppose the two of you talked."

"Carolanne is a wreck, and so is her mother."

"Of course, they lost a family member."

"Unfortunately, over coffee, Tricia told me more than I wanted to know. It seems Carolanne and her mother were listed jointly on Frank's life insurance policies, so your ex is already spending her share of the money. Can you imagine?"

He could. "I wouldn't put it past her."

"She told Tricia to ask me to ask you if she was still the beneficiary on your policy. Can you believe it?"

"Don't worry, Ma. I changed them over before the divorce was final. You, Sherry, and—"

"I don't want to know! Nothing's going to happen to you, and if something did, we wouldn't want your money. Besides, when you marry again, you'll leave everything to the new Mrs. Ryder."

"I told you that won't happen, Ma. I don't plan on making another woman worry the way you do." And Carolanne didn't. "It's not fair."

Lydia made a rude noise. "Someday you'll find a girl who deserves you, and you'll think differently. Mark my words."

"I gotta go, Ma."

"All right." Her sigh echoed over the line. "Did you need something else?"

"A visit from my boy might be nice."

"We had dinner a couple of nights ago. Remember?"

"I do, but all this talk of death makes me miss your father. I could use some cheering up. Are you coming to dinner this Thursday?"

"I can't commit so early in the week."

"I'll take that as a no."

He glanced at the magazine on the seat next to him, a reminder that he had yet to stop at the stores in Queens. "I might be able to drop by later."

"Really? What time?"

He checked his watch. Traffic was a bitch this late in the afternoon. "Give me a couple of hours."

"We'll have dinner. It'll be just the two of us." Her voice quavered with anticipation. "I'll make stuffed pork chops and glazed carrots. Your favorites."

"Don't go to any trouble. I might not be able to stay."

"Of course, you will. And I'm saying good-bye. I have to start the stuffing."

"Ma." He heard the dial tone and stuck the phone back in the holder. Nobody made stuffed pork chops like his mother, but if he hit a home run at one of the stores carrying that magazine, it would ruin her plans.

He headed into traffic, torn between eating a good meal and finding someone in Queens who knew about the damn magazine.

"This is the pits."

Ellie peeked around a corner at the back of the Liquid Ice distribution center. From the front, the building appeared modern and the parking lot

335

neat, but the rear was a different story. Empty containers stacked a mile high abutted the walls, while pallets with refuse and overflowing Dumpsters abounded. A chilly rain drizzled, adding to the misery.

"I know," she said. "But what was I supposed to do—call the delivery station and ask for Gil's address? I don't even remember the man's last name."

"We could go home."

"I'm not leaving until I find out where he lives."

"You're not going to do that back here. The employee cars are in the side lot."

"Then I guess I'd better get another taxi and have the driver wait until we spot him leaving, huh?"

"That would be my advice," Rudy answered, lifting his leg on a pile of soggy cartons.

She waited until he finished his business, then hoisted her tote over her shoulder, tugged up the hood on her rain gear, and returned to the front of the building. At the curb she raised a hand, shivering when a trickle of freezing water dribbled down her wrist and inside the slicker sleeve. After fifteen minutes of frantic waving, a taxi pulled over. Rudy scrambled inside, and Ellie climbed in after him.

"Where to?" asked the female cabbie as she peered into her rearview mirror.

"I'm not sure. We need to hang out here until the

person I'm waiting for leaves the Liquid Ice building."

The driver, an attractive middle-aged woman, grinned. "You a stalker?"

"A stalker?"

"You know, one of them women who follows people around, spyin' and stuff."

"Why would anybody stalk someone who works at Liquid Ice?"

The driver raised a shoulder. "People got their reasons. A spurned lover, maybe, or a cheating husband? I had me one of those once, and I made him pay, the bastard."

The D rose to mind, and Ellie nodded. "I know exactly what you mean. Cheating husbands deserve to be strung up."

"By their balls," the cabbie added. "So you just tell me when you see the bastard, and I'll stay on him. Won't even charge you for the wait time." She turned in the seat, snapped her gum, and held out her hand. "Names Marta, by the way. Marta Cruz."

"I'm Ellie, and thanks for the freebie."

"Hey, us girls, we gotta stick together." She gave Rudy a once-over. "Cute dog."

"Thanks. Without him, I wouldn't have gotten through the last couple of weeks."

A few minutes passed; then people began leaving the building. "So what's this creep of yours look like?"

Ellie could barely remember Gil's face, let alone give a description. "Um . . . he's tall and on the thin side, and he has brown hair."

Marta scanned the crowd of mostly men. "That covers about half the guys out there. What's he driving?"

Driving? Ellie gazed at Rudy.

"Tell her you don't know. He sold the family car and got the money."

"I'm not sure. He took the car when he left, and a . . . a friend told me he sold it and kept the money for himself."

"Bastard. You got kids?"

"Three," Rudy answered.

"Three," Ellie parroted. "Two girls and a boy."

Another group trundled from the building, and she spotted her target. Ducking down, she said, "There he is, the guy coming this way in the plaid jacket . . . wearing the baseball cap."

"Got him." Marta started the engine. "Looks like he ain't found a replacement vehicle yet. He's heading for the bus stop. Hang on while I go to the next street and find a spot to wait."

A moment later she steered into traffic. "Okay, he's on. It's an express, so it probably won't make too many stops."

Now what? Ellie mouthed to Rudy.

"Let Marta do her thing. She can handle it."

Ellie peered over the front seat. "Where are we going?"

Marta stayed a car length behind the bus. "Looks like we're on our way to Queens. You good with that?"

Ellie had been to Queens maybe twice in her life, with the D, who had a big-shot client in the borough. "A time or two. Is it nice?"

"Depends on what part you're goin' to. Sunnyside's good." Up ahead hung a green sign directing them to the Queensborough Bridge. "I got the toll. Pay me when we settle, and sit upright. The bus won't be stoppin' for a while."

"Thanks," Ellie mumbled. Climbing on the bench, she gave Rudy a pat.

"Why'd you bring the dog?"

"He doesn't like my ex much, so I thought he could help with . . . protection."

"Smart. Who's watchin' your kids?"

"Ah . . . my mother," Ellie answered with a roll of her eyes. Yeah, like that would ever happen. "Little Gil is two. Janie is three, and Vivian is five."

"Now you're catching on," said Rudy.

"Nice. Me, I got two. Carlos is in eighth grade and Chulo's in sixth. Lucky you got your mom. I got family, too, but my bum, he's always late with the child support, so it's really tough."

"Oh, that's terrible," Ellie commiserated.

"How about yours?"

"Mine? Oh, mine. He doesn't pay when he's supposed to, either. The bastard."

"You can say that again."

Marta laid on the horn and just avoided being cut off. Gunning the engine, she stuck on the bus's tail until Ellie thought she'd pass out from the fumes. The rain now beat against the windshield in a steady slanting rhythm. The expressway, five lanes of bumper-to-bumper traffic in both directions, made her dizzy. After what felt like miles, the bus finally pulled off the clogged road and headed for a more residential area.

"He's still on board," the cabbie said after the first stop. Six blocks later, they hit pay dirt. "Looks like this is his neighborhood. You owe me thirty-two and change with the tolls. You don't got it, I'll give you a card, and you mail it to me."

"I have it," said Ellie, amazed at Marta's kindness. Most taxi drivers would never trust a fare they'd just met. "But I'd still like your contact information. You've been very nice." She passed two twenties across the seat back, grabbed Marta's card, and dropped it in her bag. Gil headed up the street, and she slipped from the cab. "Thanks."

"Be careful and good luck," Marta called, speeding away.

Ellie ducked behind a parked car, dug an umbrella from her bag, and stuck her head around the bumper. Her quarry was about a block away, power-walking to his destination.

She glanced at the uneven smattering of overhead lights, some out completely, and read a street sign, noting they were on Thirty-ninth Avenue. "Do you think he'll notice us?"

"It's not like he's taking a stroll. This rain is coming down in buckets."

"It's dark. Pick up the pace, or we'll lose him."

Gil turned on a side street, and they followed. From Ellie's perspective, every house was identical to the next, all built of brick and aligned like soldiers guarding an encampment. Some were detached, but many were connected side by side. Some had gated front yards, while others were lined in shrubbery or had enclosed porches with balconies built under bay windows. And it seemed as if every street had a row of stately trees, which, she imagined, looked nice in the day, but were forbidding in a storm.

A minute later, Gil stopped at a gate. Tugging Rudy toward her, she dropped behind a set of garbage cans, watching as her target opened the gate and scuttled up the walk.

"Now what?" asked Rudy when the lights inside the house flickered to life.

Ellie bit her lower lip. "We need to get closer, and find out if he has Buddy."

"It's creepy out here. I don't like the rain."

Before she could answer, a gust of wind turned her umbrella inside out. She shoved the worthless mass of metal and fabric into the nearest trash can and reseated the hood on her slicker. Rudy shook himself, sending water flying in all directions. Bending to soothe him with a pat on the head, she found him shivering like Jell-O on a plate.

"You're freezing. And I didn't bring your coat."

"N-n-never mind about m-m-me. Get m-m-moving."

Great. Her pal was going to contract pneumonia, just because she had a bee in her bonnet about a dog that wasn't even hers. Now at Gil's gate, she opened it, slipped inside, and closed the latch. Striding across the walkway, she aimed for the side of the house and what she guessed was a kitchen window. Rising up, she peered inside and saw Gil, still in his jacket and hat, go through a door and disappear down a set of stairs.

"He's in the basement." She dropped to a squat and almost landed on Rudy. "Oops, sorry. I didn't mean to—Oh my God."

"What? What?"

She scooched over so he could see through a lower window. "Look, it's Buddy. And Jimmy. That black poodle must be Gemma."

"I can't make out a thing. What's the bozo doing?"

"He's getting leashes, probably so the dogs can go out and do their business." Still squatting, she said, "I've got to think a minute."

"How about we jump him when he gets to the sidewalk?"

"I'm calling Sam first. I don't want to get reamed for doing something stupid."

"Like following the guy here wasn't stupid enough? Come on, you don't need that detective. We can take the water boy down together."

She plastered herself against the side of the house when she heard the front door open and close. "Get back," she whispered. "He'll see us." After watching Gil and the three dogs head across the street, she pulled the phone from her bag. Between the darkness, the driving rain, and fumbling for Sam's number, it took three tries to make the connection.

"Ryder here."

"Sam, it's Ellie."

"Speak up. I can't hear you."

"It's me," she hissed, wiping water from her mouth. "Ellie Engleman."

"Ellie? What's up?"

"I've found Buddy."

"You what?"

"Don't shout. I've found Buddy and the other missing dogs, too."

"Where the hell are you?"

"I'm in Queens."

"Queens! Where in Queens?"

"I'm not sure. I just passed a main street with a sign that said Thirty-ninth Avenue."

"Is it a house? An apartment? And who has the dogs?"

"It's a row house. And it's the guy who delivers water to the professor's building." She heard pages rustling. "Gil somebody or other—the Liquid Ice man."

"Gil Mitchell. He's new to the job. My men questioned him, but he didn't raise any suspicion. Read like a normal guy making deliveries." He muttered something to a voice in the background, then asked, "Can you see him? What's he doing?"

"He left to walk the dogs, but I've lost sight of him." She peeked around a bush. "I don't know where they are, but they'll be back soon. What should I do?" Rudy growled, and she grabbed his muzzle. "Quiet. I have to hear Sam."

"Stay where you are. Do not attempt to apprehend. Once he goes in the house, you stand on the corner nearest Thirty-ninth, and I'll find you. I'm on my way."

Ellie heaved a breath and snapped her phone closed, then let go of Rudy's muzzle. "What's wrong? Why are you looking at me like that?"

Rudy darted around her legs, and she shrieked as she stood. A booted foot kicked out, and Rudy yelped in pain, flying through the air into the darkness. Before she could run to him, a hand clawed at her shoulder and spun her in place.

Then icy fingers gripped her throat.

Chapter 18

"I knew you'd be trouble the minute I caught you sneakin' onto the freight elevator." Gil squeezed his hand around her neck, plucked the cell phone from her fingers with his other hand, and heaved it into the street. "Come on. We're going inside."

"You hurt my dog." Pulling back, Ellie slammed the toe of her boot into his shin and turned to run. "Rudy!"

"Yeow! Bitch!"

Gil grabbed at her shoulder. She jerked free, but he caught the hood of her slicker and hauled her back. The soft snick of metal sounded; then she saw the knife.

"You're coming with me," he hissed.

She slumped against him, furious but not stupid. "You kicked my dog, you creep. I have to find him."

"Forget the mutt." He held the blade to her throat, wrenched her arm behind her back, and jerked her ahead of him as he walked to the rear of the house. "If I'm lucky he'll get hit by a car, and that'll be the end of him."

She stumbled along, but dug in her heels at the rear stairs. "You stole Buddy—and those other dogs." She swiped the water from her eyes. "And you killed Professor Albright."

"Move," he commanded, pushing her up the steps.

She fell forward, and he righted her with a painful tug. "Thought you were smart, following me from the bus stop. But I saw you right away, brought the dogs out, circled around to the alley, and dropped 'em back here. Now get inside before you make me do something I don't want to do . . . at least, not yet."

Stiffening in his arms, she trudged up the porch. Damn if she'd make this easy for him. Inside, he continued shoving her toward the basement stairs. "Walk like a lady, or I'll give you a push. Who knows? You might break your neck in the fall and save me the trouble of killing you."

He released her at the bottom, and she peered into the darkness. Buddy, Jimmy, and Gemma, each imprisoned in a tiny crate, were situated in a far corner of the room.

"Ellie! Hey, Ellie!" Buddy's eager voice cut through the anger in her brain. *"I told these guys someone would save us."*

"I see you, little guy, and don't worry. I'll get you out of here."

Gil laughed, a nasty chuckle that echoed in the dank dirt-floored cavern. "You and what army? Jeez, you are nuts." He pointed the knife toward a wall. "Sit down over there and shut the fuck up."

Eyeing the low-hanging pipes, drooping electrical wires, and cobweb-covered windows, she walked to a battered vinyl chair. "Nice layout. Who decorated this place? Dr. Frankenstein?"

"Not that it's any of your business, but this is a rental." He threw her a length of rope. "Tie your ankles to the legs of your throne."

She crossed her arms and leaned back, letting the rope slide to the floor. "You've got to be kidding."

Still waving the knife, he took a step closer. "Do it, bitch."

She sighed, muttering as she worked. "Don't worry, Buddy, I'll take care of everything. Just hang tight."

"I said shut up!"

She tied the rope in loose loops, then glared at Gil. "Now what, big shot?"

He pulled a pair of handcuffs from his pocket and skulked toward her. "Hold out your hands."

"Make me."

Stabbing the air, he lunged at her, and she lurched back. "I'm serious. It'd be a shame cuttin' that pretty face of yours. Now do like I said."

Arms rigid, she obeyed. He snapped a cuff on one wrist, then jumped behind her and pulled the other arm in position, weaving the handcuffs around the chair back and locking her firmly in place. Squatting, he set down the knife and anchored her legs to the chair.

"That oughta hold you."

Buddy's fear reached out to her, his whimper echoing in her mind. The pups were terrified, especially Gemma, and she didn't blame them one bit. And what had happened to Rudy? "What do you plan to do with me? With them?" She nodded toward the dogs. "Kill us?"

He snapped the knife closed and stuck it in his coat pocket. "Don't be stupid. Why would I kill them, when I went to all the trouble of stealing them?" Shuffling to the crates, he set his foot on top of the one holding Jimmy. "These dogs are gonna make me a wealthy man . . . at least wealthy enough to get out of here and start fresh."

"Wealthy? You're crazy. You can't sell those animals. Their owners have reported them missing. The authorities are watching for them."

"Oh, really?" He gave another chortle. "I doubt that. They're just dumb dogs. The cops don't care. Not like foreigners do."

"Foreigners? What are you talking about?"

Gil shook his head. "The Japanese, for one. These mutts are leaving tomorrow on a flight to Osaka, with my girlfriend and me. After the buyer claims them, we'll spend a few days celebrating. Then we'll move on."

Ellie looked at Buddy, who'd stuck his nose against the cage's metal grid. *"He sold each of us. He's getting twenty-five thousand for me, not so much for Gemma and Jimmy, 'cause they don't have the Westminster win behind them."*

"Have you've done this before?"

He raised a brow. "I've hit LA, Chicago,

348

Atlanta, and a couple of other metro areas. The Big Apple is my last haul."

Ellie didn't know which part of his confession to tackle first—the idea of a female accomplice or that he'd been stealing champion canines for several years. "I don't get it. How can you sell them? What about tracking chips? Papers? Those tattoos used to register show dogs?"

"You'd be surprised how many people don't bother with chips or ID numbers, but even if they did, everything can be removed."

"Won't the Japanese realize they're accepting stolen goods?"

"Shows what you know. All you need is a decent printer and the smarts to hack into a database, and any idiot can forge AKC papers. Hell, it's as simple as printing money . . . at least it was until the government cracked down on us. Now I use my top-of-the line system to dummy up all kinds of official stuff. Plenty of people pay big bucks for fake IDs and passports. It's a snap, even after nine-eleven."

So dognapping wasn't Gil's only crime, but who was his girlfriend? And how many other people had they killed? "You murdered the professor."

"Oh, yeah. Thanks for reminding me."

"But why? How?"

"You want to know how, huh?" He scratched his jaw. "Okay, since you'll probably die down here, I'll tell you." He stomped to a workbench and lifted a small metal case. "See this? It's a portable battery jumper—you know, for a car."

Ellie gave him a blank stare. She rarely drove, so she had no idea what it would do.

"You don't get it, do you?"

"Afraid not, but I'm sure you're going to tell me."

He thrust out his chest, as if proud of the idea. "It works like a stun gun. I clipped the charger grips to the apartment doorknob and turn it on, then give the door a rap. When the person on the other side grabs the knob, the metal conducts enough volts to knock them on their ass."

"And you go in and take their dog."

"Bingo. Only I didn't know the professor wore one of them pacemaker things. He was only supposed to be out for a couple minutes, then wake up and find the dog gone. How the hell did I know he was hooked to a contraption that kept his heart beating?"

It sounded so simple, she was at a loss for words. Why hadn't anyone figured it out? Then again, how many people jump-started automobiles for a living? And what normal person would figure a way to use the device in a robbery?

"You're impressed," Gil continued when she didn't speak. "You should be."

"And your girlfriend? How much did she have to do with all this? Was she there when the professor died?"

"She'll be here any minute. If she feels like coming down, you can ask her yourself. No more questions." He headed for the stairs. "I got things to do."

"Wait. What do you plan to do with me?" And where was Rudy? She peered up at the nearest basement window, but the rain was coming down so hard she couldn't see a thing. Thunder crashed and she jumped, while Gil laughed.

"This storm's gonna last all night, so no one'll hear if you yell. We'll leave for the airport in the morning, and you'll stay here. The rent's paid until the end of the month, same for the utilities. It might take you a while to get free, or you could stay shackled to that chair until you die. Either way, it's no skin off my nose."

Sam drove slowly up Thirty-ninth Avenue, his heater running at full blast, but he still had to hunch over the steering wheel to get a clear view through his fogged-up windshield. Pounding rain, booming thunder, and lightning this severe always made traveling difficult. Luckily, he'd been at his mother's, just a couple of blocks away, when Ellie called, because a trip here from Manhattan would have been a nightmare.

So where the heck was she? He squinted past the slapping wipers, but all he saw were bits of leaves and branches mingled with the slashing rain. There'd been a huge pileup about a half mile back, fender benders at every corner, and a few of the side streets were flooded. If not for the roads blocked with traffic cones and signs warning of high water, he would have gotten here a lot sooner.

With that in mind, he knew it might take a while for the boys from Queens to arrive, which meant he'd have to start this bust alone. He was about to park and begin a house-to-house search when a small, sopping-wet animal limped into the street and stared as if it had been waiting for him.

Blinking, Sam slammed on the brakes and did a double take. It was a dog, and it looked just like Ellie's little guy . . . Tooty . . . Scoobie? No, Rudy. That was it. Her dog's name was Rudy.

He pulled the car over as sirens sounded in the distance. They could be coming to his assistance, or heading for the accident—there was no way of telling. He dug a flashlight from under the front seat and scuttled out of the car and into the driving rain. Dropping to a squat, he held out his hand. "Hey, Rudy. Remember me? It's Sam, your friendly neighborhood detective."

The dog peered through matted hair and shook itself. Instead of coming closer, it trotted crookedly toward the curb, then glanced over its shoulder, as if to say, *Come on, doofus, follow me.*

Sam stood and swiped a hand over his dripping face. The animal lifted its snout and continued limping to the sidewalk. Damn, he thought, squishing in the hound's wake. The scraggly mutt wasn't Lassie or one of those genius TV canines. And it sure as shit wasn't a search-and-rescue dog or a trained companion. Hell, from what he could remember, the animal wasn't even obedient . . . just like his mistress.

Only a fool would follow a dumb mutt, no matter how dangerous a situation they might be in.

The dog took a few more feeble steps, and Sam caught him in the glow of his flashlight. Rudy's eyes glimmered with awareness. After a second, he disappeared around a car bumper, and Sam shrugged. He'd come this far without seeing Ellie, and she and the terrier were inseparable. The dog had to know something.

He followed the animal for about a block, before it stopped in front of a house and nosed the gate. Still not believing that she would have been so scatterbrained as to expect her dog to find him and lead him here, he had to ask, "Is Ellie in there waiting for me?"

The dog nosed the gate again, then glanced back at him.

Sam scanned the street, took note of the exact address, and hit SPEED DIAL for the local precinct. When the desk officer answered, he gave his location and asked about the status of his emergency call. Told there were accidents and roadblocks up and down the borough, he snarled out the severity of his situation and disconnected.

Standing on hind legs, Rudy pushed at the gate and whined. Sam heaved a sigh, slipped the latch, and walked after the dog, down the sidewalk, and around to the rear of the house. After giving the cluttered lawn a once-over, he sized up the dwelling. Except for its poor condition, the row house looked a lot like his mother's, which helped him envision the interior. Three bedrooms and a bath up, a large kitchen, living room, and dining room down, and a basement, probably good for nothing better than storage or growing mush-rooms.

The dog waited until he again made eye contact, then sidled near to the house and ducked between the bushes. Sam cursed silently, annoyed at being led on a wild-goose chase. Still, when he arrived at Rudy's side, he saw a pale glow of light through the basement window.

Sinking silently to his knees, he peered inside.

Someone was sitting on a chair, but there was little more he could discern through the grime-encrusted pane of glass. Between the howls of wind and claps of thunder, he heard the mumble of a man's voice, but couldn't make out the speaker. Then a woman shouted, "You'll never get away with this. And if anything happens to Rudy, I'll hunt you down and kill you myself."

He shook his head. It was his "bad penny," all right. And she sounded pissed. Shifting his weight, he realigned his view of the basement and spotted a man, probably Gil Mitchell, striding up the stairs.

Sam fumbled with the edges of the window and found it locked. Breaking glass would give away his position, so that was no good. If the guy had a gun, a likely scenario, he couldn't just barge in and strong-arm him, because Ellie might get hurt.

Standing, Sam gazed at Rudy and muttered, "Now what?" Then he cursed. Christ, he was as loopy as all those idiot dog lovers. He had to get in that house and down the stairs to free Ellie. Then he'd concentrate on the takedown.

When a car door slammed, he peeked around a corner and spotted a taxi pulling away. A figure carrying a suitcase barged through the gate. Fingers crossed, he raced to the rear of the house and onto the porch, where he tried the back door. Finding it open, he slipped inside while Mitchell welcomed his visitor at the front. Then he crept to the basement door while the pair talked.

Halfway down the steps, he stopped and softly called, "Ellie, it's Sam," before continuing his descent. When he spotted her, tied to the chair with her eyes wide and staring, he grinned. Walking to her, he whispered, "You're nothing but trouble—you know that?"

Stowing the flashlight in his pocket, he bent and untied her ankles. She gazed at him with tears in her eyes, and he held a finger to his lips. Then he stood and walked behind the chair, saw the hand-cuffs, and found his key ring. After a bit of jig-gling, the key for his own pair clicked, and the first cuff opened, then the second. When he helped her to stand, she fell into his arms.

"How did you find me?" she asked on a hiss of breath.

"Your dog. I followed him here."

"Rudy? You found Rudy? Where is he?"

They gazed around the cavern and saw him sit-ting at their feet. When she dropped to her knees and hugged him, he gave a muffled yelp. Ellie continued to whisper words of comfort, running her fingers over the dog while he whimpered.

After a moment, Sam pulled her to her feet and pointed to the ceiling, then sat her back in the chair, tucked her arms behind her, and crossed to the steps. Ducking under the staircase, he drew his gun and nodded.

Without asking, Ellie knew immediately what Sam wanted her to do, though she doubted he expected her to do it the way she planned. Locking her arms in place, she threw Buddy a look of command. "Buddy. Play dead. Now."

All three dogs fell on their sides, and she smiled. "Hey! Hey, Gil, get down here!" she shouted. "I think there's something wrong with the dogs."

Footsteps rattled the ceiling. "Quit your belly-achin'," a voice called from overhead.

"No, I mean it. Buddy's on his side, breathing

funny, and the others look sick, too. They're not moving."

"This better not be a trick," Gil grumbled, stomping down the stairs.

Gil got to the bottom, headed for the cages, and squatted. When he saw all three dogs lying still as death, he cursed and opened each door, then reached inside to wake them.

Sam crept behind him and held the gun to his head. "Stand up real slow, Mitchell. And keep quiet."

Gil froze and followed orders, and the detective slapped him in his own handcuffs, then said, "Call down your friend, and no funny business," in a harsh whisper.

Gil glared at Ellie. "She's such a smart mouth, tell her to do it."

"I'd just as soon knock you out as play games, shit head. So call your pal."

He hesitated, and Sam jabbed the gun in his back.

"Hey, Bibi. Come on down here!"

Ellie gasped. Bibi Stormstein? Had to be. The name was so unusual, there couldn't be many women out there with the identical name.

"What's the problem?" Goth girl asked from the top of the stairs.

Sam nodded at Ellie, and she sat back in the chair and assumed the position. Then he shoved the gun to Gil's ear.

357

"It's the dogs. I need a hand."

After angling him toward the steps, Sam ducked into the shadows.

"Jeez, can't you do anything? They're little suckers. Just give 'em a drink or something." Bibi plodded down the stairs, stopped on the bottom step, and sneered at Ellie. "Hey, Engleman, long time no see. Told you I'd take care of things, didn't I?" She continued walking to the crates and dropped down. "Come on, you little turds. Get up."

"Hold it right there." Bibi turned to stone as Sam glided into view. "Now stand up nice and slow. Ellie"—he tossed her the other set of hand-cuffs—"do the honors, please."

Ellie stood, caught the cuffs, and started across the dirt floor. Goth girl spun and crouched low, diving at Ellie and tackling her legs. Ellie screamed and fell in a heap. Gil rammed his shoulder in Sam's stomach, jolting him backward. Then all hell broke loose.

The three dogs scrabbled from their crates, snarling and yapping like rabid wolves. Rudy dashed from beneath the stairs. Buddy and Gemma each grabbed one of Gil's ankles while Buddy and Jimmy latched on to Bibi's.

"Get 'em off me! They're killin' me!" Gil screamed like a girl. Sam slammed a foot in his back and held him prisoner.

Bibi kicked her legs to dislodge the dogs and fell on her hands and knees, cursing and shouting.

Ellie jumped onto Bibi's back and pinned her to the floor.

"Enough! Ellie, call off the dogs," Sam yelled, dragging Gil to his feet.

Ellie wrenched Bibi's arm behind her. "Rudy, Buddy. Off! Gemma, Jimmy, you, too!" The dogs, continued to growl and pant, but did as they were told. Heaving a breath, Ellie glanced up at Sam. "Told you little dogs were scrappers." She gasped for air. "Anything else you need done?"

His mouth twitched almost into a grin, but Sam shook his head. "Find those cuffs and put her out of commission."

Still perched on Bibi, Ellie squinted into the dirt. Within seconds, Rudy approached, the handcuffs hanging from his mouth.

She blew a damp curl off her forehead and grinned as she took hold of the cuffs. "Thanks, pal, for everything."

Ellie sat on her living room sofa with Buddy, Gemma, and Jimmy gathered on her lap and Rudy lying across her feet. They'd left the row house after hours of answering questions, giving explanations, and trying to connect the dots. It was three o'clock in the morning, and though the storm had let up a bit, rain continued to saturate the area.

"Ellie, Ellie, Ellie." Buddy licked her face. *"You got any treats?"*

"I have food, if you're hungry."

"Starving," he said.

The three dogs jumped off her lap and followed fast on her heels as she walked into the kitchen. Sam, still on his cell phone, watched with interest as she brought out bowls, filled them with Rudy's kibble, and set them on the floor.

While the dogs ate, she leaned back against the counter, and he put his arm over her shoulder, drawing her near. "Yeah, that's right. . . . Call the owners first thing in the morning. . . . I'll bring the dogs in about eight. . . . Right. See you tomorrow."

"Who was that?" she asked when he disconnected the call.

"Desk officer. He'll contact the Marinos and Ms. Millcraft with the good news and tell them to come to the station. They'll need to make a positive ID and fill out paperwork before they can bring their property home."

"Can the dogs stay here tonight?"

He sighed. "I'll probably get in trouble for saying yes, but by the time I rouse the city pound and have them open up, it'll be time to bring the dogs to the station." He swiped a hand over his eyes. "Sure, go ahead. Just don't lose one of them, or there'll be hell to pay."

"Thanks. I'll make sure they sleep, or at least rest while I catch a couple of winks."

"Can you meet me outside your building at seven tomorrow? I'll drive you all in."

"Of course." Finished with their meal, the dogs circled her feet. They were tired, Ellie knew, just as she was. "Guess it's time for bed."

Sam stepped away from her. "Sorry. I should have gone home a while ago." He grinned. "Do you want me to admit you were right now or later?"

She shrugged. "There's no need. If you hadn't found me, who knows when I would have gotten out of that house?"

"I never thought I'd say this, but something tells me Rudy would have found a way to take care of you. Guess I really underestimated the little guy."

"Rudy is special." Ellie walked Sam to the front door. "So, see you in the morning?"

He raised a hand and brushed her cheek with his fingers. "Sure. We can talk then."

Ellie locked the door and led the dogs to her bedroom. "Okay, I don't mind having everyone on the bed, but only if you lie still." She stripped out of her damp, grimy clothes and let them fall to a heap on the floor. "And no snoring."

Rudy yawned as he settled alongside her pillow. *"They got it, Triple E, but there's one little problem."*

"I gotta get back to the professor," said Buddy before Ellie could ask Rudy what the problem was. *"I know he's been worried about me. I can't wait to see him."*

Ellie ignored the ache in her heart and sat on the

edge of the bed, running her hand over the bichon's fur. "Not right away. The police have to finish their paperwork and . . . stuff."

"But that detective just said the others could pick up their dogs in the morning. Can't you call my human and tell him to do the same?"

She pulled Buddy close and kissed the top of his head. "In the morning, okay. We'll take care of it then."

She settled under the covers and closed her eyes. Now what? Gemma and Jimmy had been strangely quiet for the entire evening, and she wondered if there was a connection between them or if they were so shell-shocked from their horrifying experience they simply couldn't communicate. Either way, they would be returned to their families, while Buddy was an orphan. Someone had to tell him about Professor Albright, and she accepted that it should be her.

She recalled Victoria Pernell, the professor's greedy niece, and the tag sale scheduled for later in the week. The woman had already told Sam she didn't care about Buddy, didn't even want him if he were found. She'd sell him for certain now that he'd been recovered. But that didn't mean the bichon would go to a good home or to a family who loved him.

And what about the other dogs Gil had stolen, sold, and shipped out of the country? Those poor canines would never see their owners again.

Sam had told her there were a dozen details to iron out before the police would fully understand the extent of Gil's crimes. Besides being a forger and a scam artist, the man was a thief and a murderer. But what about Bibi? How long had she been working with Gil? How much did she know about what her boyfriend had done?

Saddened over the entire affair, Ellie drifted off to sleep, but her last thought was of Buddy, curled up at her feet and pining for the professor.

What would the little guy do when she told him he was now alone in the world? How was she supposed to explain that he'd lost his best friend?

Chapter 19

"You mean the professor is gone, and I'll never see him again? But we didn't get to say good-bye . . . or anything."

Ellie swiped at her tear-filled eyes and hoisted Buddy on her lap. She, Rudy, and the bichon were in a conference room at the police station, where Gemma and Jimmy had just been retrieved by their owners. After the happy reunion, she could no longer put Buddy off or lie to him about Professor Albright, so she'd told him the truth.

"You might see the professor later in your life, maybe recognize a little of him in a new caretaker. Who knows? You could even find him again, like Rudy and I found each other after he'd been lost."

"Ellie and I are proof that miracles happen, pal." Rudy put his paw on her knee. *"Some things are meant to be. If you and a certain human are supposed to be together, you will be."*

She gazed at Rudy, read the love in his eyes, and wanted to sob all over again. She'd only gotten a couple of hours' sleep last night, and she'd spent most of the morning watching Gemma, Jimmy, the Marinos, and Rita Millcraft interact. It broke her heart to know Buddy would never experience the same joy.

"I wish I could say something more positive, but I do believe in karma. Things will work out." She gave Buddy another hug. "You'll see."

Sam took that moment to walk through the door with a sheaf of papers in his hand. "We've been able to unravel some of Gil's past. His real name is Gregory Forentsky, by the way, and he's got a rap sheet from way back all around the country: petty crimes, some forgery and falsification of documents. The dognappings took place over the past two years. Bibi wasn't in on any of those. She only met him when he started delivering Liquid Ice and took part in this one job.

"Whenever he arrived in a new city, he found a way to enter the homes of the elite in the dog world. Here in Manhattan, delivering water was the easiest, along with cozying up to a dog walker. According to Stormstein, she had no idea he had a shady past until she heard it from us."

"And Eugene? Did he have anything to do with the thefts?"

"He's been in interrogation all morning, but we're not getting anywhere. Stormstein refuses to incriminate him, says she knew exactly where Buddy lived and had a good idea of his pedigree from their friendly conversations. She walked Jimmy, so nabbing him was easy, and she mentioned Buddy to Forentsky."

"Is there any way the other owners can recover their lost pets?" asked Ellie, still dejected over the fact that so many canines and their families had been separated.

Sam pulled up a chair and sat across from her. "It's possible. Depends on which country they went to, how softhearted the buyers are, and our ability to locate their money and return it. Fortensky claims he didn't keep detailed records, so it'll take a while to untangle the transactions."

"And the professor's death was an accident?"

"That's the way our guy tells it. Insists he only meant to knock the professor out and take the dog, as he did to the other victims. I tend to believe him, since there's no more than a slim chance he knew Albright wore a pacemaker."

"Then he won't be charged with murder? They'll do one of those plea-bargain things?"

"My guess is he'll go to prison for a while, and your friend Bibi will get probation. That's not the way I'd handle it, but it isn't my decision.

Depends on the judge, the DA, and the attorneys."

Ellie blew into a tissue. "It seems so unfair. The professor is gone, families and beloved pets have been torn apart, and Buddy is alone." Intuiting his unhappiness, she rested her chin on the top of the bichon's head. He'd grown contemplative and quiet, as if grieving. "What's going to happen to . . ." Her eyes drifted downward. "You know?"

"I've been in contact with Ms. Pernell—"

"I don't like her," Buddy whispered. *"And she doesn't care for me. She always complained about how much money the professor spent on me."*

"I know. She's not a nice person. You don't have to live with her if you don't want to," Ellie assured him, then realized what she'd done. Raising her gaze to meet Sam's, she read his questioning expression. "He doesn't, does he?"

"You're telling him Pernell isn't a nice person?" Sam asked, narrowing his eyes.

"I'm sure he already knows. I didn't form that opinion until *after* you repeated the conversation you had with Ms. Pernell to me, remember? As for talking to Buddy, I believe he takes comfort in the sound of my voice, so why not?"

"You trying to tell me the dog is worried about his fate? That he's aware of what's going on?"

"Of course, he's aware. He knows Professor Albright is no longer with us or he'd have been here by now. And besides being in mourning, he's frightened."

"Even so, maybe the niece will want to keep him after she hears he's been found."

"I doubt it."

Sam narrowed his eyes. "And you think this because . . . ?"

"Because I do." She huffed out a breath. "How many times do I have to tell you? Dogs have feelings. They experience a lot more than people realize."

"Okay, okay." Sam raised a hand. "Don't get your panties in a wad."

Ellie ignored the comment. Sam had been amazingly considerate throughout this entire ordeal; she'd allow him one crass remark. "I still can't believe that a battery charger could be used in such a deadly manner."

"Yeah, well neither did we," Sam acknowledged. "Once word gets out about how easy it was, we'll probably have to handle a rash of identical B & Es, or a bunch of idiot college kids stunning their dorm mates for the hell of it." He shuffled through the paperwork. "Anything else you need to know?"

She shook her head. "I'm still trying to process it all. Right now, Buddy is my only concern. What's going to happen to him? Who's going to take care of him?"

He clasped her hand. "I know this ordeal has been difficult for you. It's hard for me to commiserate, because I'm not a dog lover, but it's apparent you're having a problem dealing with . . . things."

"You don't know the half of it," she answered, dabbing her eyes with her free hand. "Buddy is desolate."

"Are you sure you're not projecting your emotions onto the dog?" he asked, though it was apparent he didn't believe his own words. "Sort of a transferal of feelings?"

"I'm not." She sighed. "Buddy is a wreck."

Standing, he headed for the door. "Let me see what I can do about Ms. Pernell. Hang tight for a minute."

Rudy snorted as the door closed. *"He just doesn't get it, does he?"*

"I don't want to go with Victoria or stay in a shelter," Buddy said, his tone a plaintive whine. *"Please, Ellie, take me home with you."*

"I think that's going to depend on the professor's niece." She sniffed back more tears. She'd just started to pull into the black financially. She could only imagine the amount of money the professor's niece would demand for Buddy, so there was no way she could afford to buy him outright. Still, she might be able to take out a loan or borrow what she needed from the judge. Sitting back in the molded plastic chair, she hugged the bichon to her chest. "Detective Ryder said he'd talk to Ms. Pernell. Maybe he'll come up with something."

Five minutes later there was a knock on the

door; then a man strode into the room, followed by Sam. The man held out a hand as big as a dinner plate. "I'm Michael Carmody, Ms. Engleman. Ryder's just filled me in on a potential problem."

Ellie set Buddy on the conference table, and the captain engulfed her hand is his. "I know. I shouldn't have stuck my nose into the investigation or gotten involved with the arrest." She stiffened her spine. "But I'd follow Mitchell—I mean Forentsky—to his house again if need be. Buddy was in danger and I had to—"

"I take it this is Buddy?" The captain's gray eyes focused on the bichon.

"This is Buddy. He's a Westminster—"

"Champion. I know." Carmody held out his fingers for the bichon to sniff, which Buddy did; then the captain ran his hand across the dog's back in a slow and gentle manner. "I watched his big win on television a couple of years back. He's quite a competitor."

Ellie opened and closed her mouth. "He's a wonderful dog."

"How old is he again?"

"He's eight, but bichons can live a good fifteen years, even longer if they're cared for properly." She gazed at Sam, noting his smug look and knowing smile. "He belongs in a home with owners who will love him as he deserves to be loved."

The captain nodded, then cleared his throat. "Sam, get Ms. Pernell on the phone for me, will you? Tell her there's someone at the precinct who needs to talk with her."

"I can't believe it. You're going on a date. A real, honest-to-god, man-to-woman, I-might-get-laid date." Vivian beamed as she watched Ellie dress. "No, not that sweater, it's too baggy. Try on the red one. And wear those Ferragamos with the sling backs. Lucky thing your feet didn't expand like the rest of you did after the divorce, and you can still wear all those yummy shoes."

"Size nine since I was eleven," Ellie observed, reaching for a pair of flats.

Viv shook her head when she spotted the plain black shoes. "Ugh. Those are so boring."

"Boring but comfortable. Heels are killers, and I don't enjoy wearing them."

"Okay, but try on that cute little skirt, the one with the slit up the side. You're legs are one of your best features."

"I'm going to dinner, not a job interview at a strip club." Ellie tugged the sweater Viv suggested over her head, stepped into a pair of black slacks, then slid on the flats. "And I don't plan on getting laid."

"Don't bet on it," her friend said, grinning. "Ryder's had the hots for you from day one. I'll bet he's planning on it."

"I rest my case," said Rudy, observing the proceedings from the queen-sized bed. *"Viv has a lot on the ball, especially where humping is concerned."*

Ellie frowned in his direction. "You are so bad."

"Not bad, just practical," Viv responded, unaware there was a second conversation taking place in the room. "And always prepared." She opened her Chanel handbag, brought out a box of prophylactics, and tossed them on the coverlet. "I bought these this afternoon. Ribbed for a woman's pleasure. Say thank you, and tuck a few in your purse."

"Maybe you'd better do what she says, Triple E. Remember Ryder's pheromones."

Plopping on the mattress, Ellie eyed the Trojans. "I'm not even going to pick the box up, so you might as well take it home. I'm sure you'll need them soon."

"I certainly hope so, and smart-assed insults will not make me change my mind on the subject." Viv crossed her arms. "And don't tell me you have condoms stashed in your nightstand or your medicine cabinet, because I'd have to see them before I'd believe it."

Ellie warmed from her head to her toes. Between her dog and her best friend, she was mortified. "You're right. I don't have any, nor will I need them. This is just a friendly dinner at Ryder's expense. A payback for helping him with the case."

"Keep telling yourself that, girlfriend, but I know better." Viv followed her into the kitchen. "I still can't believe the bit about the Liquid Ice guy, by the way. I hope they toss him in the slammer and throw away the key."

"Sam warned me he'd go the way of all smart crooks and cop a plea or some such nonsense. If he does, he'll be eligible for parole in no time. And he said they dropped the old forgery charges when he magically recalled the owners' names and addresses of all the dogs he'd stolen." She shook her head. "I really want to testify so I can tell them about the emotional damage the creep caused."

"And what's going to happen to Goth girl?"

"Sam says one year, at the most. Which means she'll be back on the street in less than three months. It just doesn't seem fair."

"But she'll never walk dogs again. That's got to be some consolation." Viv set her elbows on the table and propped her chin. "And the good thing is, you got most of her clients."

"Some, not all. Rita Millcraft is moving out of the city, and a few of Bibi's customers live below Fifty-ninth. That was my cutoff point, if you'll recall."

"Still, things worked out great for Buddy. That police captain is the perfect new owner."

It had taken a hefty chunk of Captain Carmody's change and some cajoling to convince the professor's niece not to put Buddy up for auction, but he'd charmed the woman to his side by telling her he was buying the dog as a gift for his wife on their fortieth wedding anniversary. According to Sam, the captain had practically made Ms. Pernell cry when he mentioned the first bichon they'd owned.

"I think so, too. As I've always said, things happen for a reason. Not that the professor had to die so Mr. and Mrs. Carmody could get a new bichon, but because they're definitely the right mom and dad for him. And the little guy seemed to like them—"

"How could you tell?" Viv asked. "Wait. Let me guess—the dog told you so."

Ellie rested her backside against the counter. "I know you don't believe me, but he did."

"I bet the big, bad detective was thrilled to hear that."

Sam had simply rolled his eyes, though the captain and his wife seemed to immediately sense her connection with Buddy and her worry over finding the proper adoptive parents. They'd even invited her to drop by their home whenever to make certain the bichon was happy.

"Ryder didn't say much, but then he never does unless he has a serious opinion."

"The strong, silent type. Mmm . . . delicious."

The buzzer rang, and Ellie's heart skipped a beat as she walked into the foyer. "He's right on time."

"Anal, like I said," Rudy chimed.

"A man who knows how to properly gauge time, especially in the bedroom, is worth his weight in gold," Viv decreed.

"You're wrong," Ellie said to Rudy, though her gaze rested on her best friend. "I mean, it doesn't matter, because we won't be spending any *time* in that room."

The buzzer rang again.

"Well, answer it. Unless you want me to go downstairs and let him in?" Viv offered. "And don't forget, I'm taking Rudy for a walk when I give Twink his last out. That way, when you come home, the road to the bedroom will be clear."

Ellie pressed the button, then put her hand on Viv's lower back and ushered her from the apartment. "Thanks for that. Now good night."

A minute later there was a knock on the door.

"I can't believe you're going out with the creep. I think I'm gonna hurl," said Rudy, planting himself at her feet.

"Don't you dare," she warned. "Go to the bedroom if you can't face Sam in a refined canine manner."

"With pleasure." Muttering, the Yorkiepoo sauntered down the hall with his tail held high.

Ellie licked her lips and fluffed her hair, pasted a smile on her face, and opened the door. Dressed in formfitting faded jeans, a chocolate brown sweater, and a camel-colored blazer, Sam looked better than any man had a right to. Heat suffused her cheeks as his honey gold gaze swept over her.

He smiled and thrust out a bouquet of bright yellow tulips. "I got them at the florist over on Eighty-third. Thought they'd add a festive touch to tonight's celebration."

Accepting the flowers, she stepped back so he could enter. "They're lovely. Let me put them in a vase, and we can take off." She searched a kitchen cabinet, found a cut-glass container, and filled it with water. Arranging the tulips, she set the vase on the table. "Thanks again. It was a very thoughtful gesture."

"You might not believe this, but I do try." He took her arm. "Does your dog have to go out before we leave?"

The question surprised her. Was he actually concerned about Rudy's welfare? Was he starting to understand how much the little guy meant to her?

"He's good for the night." Thanks to Vivian. "All set?"

"Ready to go."

After she locked her door, he led her downstairs and to the curb, then hailed a taxi, and helped her inside.

"Where's your car?"

"In a nice, safe, *legal* parking space. I'm trying to turn over a new leaf and cut down on the citations." He gave an address to the driver and leaned back in the seat.

"Where are we going?"

"Remember that buddy I told you about? The one in Traffic Violations?"

"The officer who fixes your—"

"The very one," he interrupted. "His uncle owns Bella Luna, so he put in a good word and got us a table, but I had to promise to go easy on future paperwork."

Impressed that he'd gone to some trouble to make the evening perfect, she smiled. He really wasn't such a bad guy. Maybe they did have a chance at forging a relationship. "It's been a couple of weeks since the arrest. I appreciate the phone calls updating me on the case."

"I only wish I'd had better news. As far as I'm concerned, both Fortensky and Stormstein are getting off easy. The captain thought so, too, if that's any consolation."

"Speaking of the captain, has he said how Buddy's doing?"

"Carmody asked me to tell you things are great. Said his wife is thrilled, and Buddy seems to be settling in fine."

"Did he mention my coming to visit?"

"Told me you should call him and work out a date. He suggested I come with you, if that's okay with you."

Could the captain be a matchmaker, as well as a dog lover? "I'd like that."

He clasped her hand, and she smiled. "You know something? So would I."

• • •

After a memorable meal at a restaurant with inviting decor, old-world elegance, and delicious food, Ellie and Sam cabbed back to her apartment. The evening had been fun. They'd made small talk and discussed things that had little to do with the case and everything to do with them personally. Their light, flirtatious banter made it an intimate yet enjoyable evening.

Now, at her apartment door, it was obvious from the way Sam dismissed the taxi that he intended to come inside. She handed him her keys, and he undid the locks. "I have beer and wine, or I could make coffee."

With his amber eyes smoldering, he focused on her mouth. "I don't need alcohol. I'm high just being with you."

Her stomach hitched, but it was too late to answer. When he pressed into her, she closed her eyes and raised her lips, and he melted her resolve with a gentle kiss that grew so demanding it made her blood race and her legs tremble.

Then he led her inside and slammed the door with a kick. Stepping near, he raised a brow. "I'm reaching here, Ellie, trying to figure out what happens next. I feel like a sixteen-year-old on his first date."

"But you're not sixteen, and neither am I," she whispered.

"Thank God for that." He placed his hands on

her shoulders and brushed his nose against hers.

She tilted her head, and he kissed her again, and this time Ellie thought she'd died and gone to heaven. What had she been so worried about? Sam was here, and he wanted her. She wanted him. What else was there to say?

He continued kissing her as they edged down the hall. "Which way to the bedroom?" he muttered into her mouth.

"The room on the right. Hurry." She slid the blazer from his shoulders and let it drop to the floor, where it was quickly joined by her jacket. He kept them walking as her sweater, shoes, and slacks slid from her quivering body.

By the time they arrived at their desired destination, she stood in her bra and panties, gazing at him in the pale light of the hallway. "One of us is wearing too many clothes."

He slipped off his shoes and stepped out of his slacks, then tugged the sweater and T-shirt up his shoulders and over his head. "Better?"

"Much."

Stalking her with a sexy grin, he pushed her onto the bed. She groaned when his lips grazed her neck, glided to the swell of her breasts, tongued her nipple through the silk of her bra.

Rudy growled his displeasure, jumped off the bed, and padded from the room, but his departure barely registered. It had been too long since she'd been touched by a man, and Sam was starving.

His searching hands caressed her skin while his hungry mouth suckled her breasts, tongued her navel, licked her knees, and tasted every point in between.

The bed became a comforting haven, a joyous playground, a dangerous war zone. They rolled together, shifting positions, and she marveled at the feel of his fingers skimming her body, teasing her nipples, learning her curves. He groaned when she captured him in her hands and gauged his length, palmed his butt, delved intimately between his legs.

Her insides hummed with pent-up frustration when he left her to find his wallet, but she smiled at the sound of tearing foil. Maybe she'd need Vivian's jumbo box of Trojans after all.

He kneeled between her thighs, and his teeth flashed white in the darkness. "I want to make this good for you, Ellie. The best you've ever had."

"It's been pretty darn wonderful so far," she told him. "But I'm greedy. I want more."

He lay on top of her, nestled between her thighs, and rose onto his hands, pushing inside of her, thrusting his hips slowly, steadily, until she writhed beneath him.

"Oh, God, Sam. Please finish this before I scream."

Mindful of her request, he took her in long, deliberate strokes, building the tension between them until Ellie thought she'd fly from the bed.

She pounded his back with her fists, clawed his shoulders, shouted her pleasure until, finally, he shuddered and collapsed on her chest with a groan.

Ellie fought the urge to open her eyes. She had to pee, but the bed was warm, and her muscles ached . . . in a very good way.

A muffled snore made her smile. Last night had been amazing. Sam had been the lover of her dreams for two stupendous bouts of sex—intuitive, caring, and thoughtful during both couplings. As the first man she'd allowed into her bed since her divorce, he was everything she'd hoped for.

The snores continued, and she furrowed her forehead. When they turned to a whimper, she blinked with recognition. Rolling to her side, she locked eyes with Rudy, his fuzzy head resting on the pillow where she'd hoped to find Sam.

His doggie lips curved into a grin. *"Was it as good for you as it was for me?"*

She blew out a breath. "Where's Sam?"

Yawning, he stretched. *"Who?"*

"Sam Ryder." She listened for sounds from the bathroom or kitchen. "The man I shared this bed with last night."

Rudy stood and gave a full-body shake. *"Sorry. Don't know the guy."*

She frowned. "Never mind. I'll look for myself."

Throwing off the covers, she slipped on her robe and tied the belt. In the hall, she strained to hear the shower, then sniffed, hoping for the scent of coffee. No such luck.

Padding toward the front of the apartment, she saw no sign of their clothes until she reached the living room, where she found her sweater, slacks, and underthings folded in a neat pile on the sofa. Still unsure of the situation, she walked into the kitchen, where Rudy was already sitting by his food dish waiting for his morning nibble.

"See. Nobody here but us chickens," he all but shouted. *"I told you it would be like this."*

She spotted a note on the table and took it in hand.

Ellie,
  Got called out on a case at five a.m. Didn't want to wake you. I'll phone you later.
  Sam

She plopped into a chair. The detective was a busy man—of that, she was well aware. After seeing all he'd done to investigate and solve the professor's murder, she knew how hard he worked, how many hours he had to put in to do a decent job. She also realized his work was important to him and the public he served, while she'd just come into his life.

He didn't owe her anything, nor did she expect

hearts and flowers or undying gratitude for a single great night in the sack. But a thank-you might have been nice.

Rudy sidled over, stood on his hind legs, and rested both front paws on her knee. *I heard his cell phone ring and followed him when he took the call.*

"Thanks for not biting him or doing something rude."

"Who says I didn't?"

She ran her fingers over his ears and scratched his favorite spot, the underside of his jaw and neck. "I can tell by the way you're talking to me, all nice and sweet, you don't want to hurt my feelings."

He nosed her hand, licked her fingers. *"I'd never hurt you, Triple E. Just don't count on seeing the dastardly dick anytime soon. Okay?"*

"Oh, and why do you say that?"

"Just an impression. After he talked to someone, he wrote that note, then raced out of here without a backward glance."

"Duty called. He's an honorable guy."

"Maybe, but I still don't trust him." Rudy dropped to all fours. *"I got an idea. How about you shower and we go for a morning walk? Bread and Bones is open for breakfast. Then we can hit Joe to Go for a cup of java and a bowl of water."*

Ellie stood and did as Rudy suggested. Sam said he'd call. There wasn't a doubt in her mind that he would.

JUDI McCOY lives with her husband and three pocket pooches—Rudy, Buckley, and Belle—on Virginia's beautiful shore. In her spare time, she's a women's national-level gymnastics judge and an avid orchid grower. She plans to take Ellie, Rudy, and the rest of the Paws in Motion gang through a dozen more escapades, so please come along for the ride. Visit her Web site at www.judimccoy.com, or e-mail her at judi1022@earthlink.net. She promises to answer every e-mail personally, and she's always willing to talk about dogs and Best Friends Animal Society.

Center Point Publishing
600 Brooks Road ● PO Box 1
Thorndike ME 04986-0001 USA

(207) 568-3717

US & Canada:
1 800 929-9108
www.centerpointlargeprint.com